DEEP HEAT

A KENZIE GILMORE THRILLER
BOOK 5

BIBA PEARCE

LIQUID MIND PUBLISHING

Liquid Mind Publishing

KENZIE GILMORE CRIME THRILLER SERIES

<u>The Kenzie Gilmore Crime Thriller Series</u>

Afterburn

Dead Heat

Heatwave

Burnout

Deep Heat

Fever Pitch

Storm Surge (Coming Soon)

Do you like Audiobooks? Find the Kenzie Gilmore Crime Thriller series on Audible here:

1

It was the height of the summer solstice, the longest day of the year. But here, in the makeshift temple in the backroom of a dingy store in Little Haiti, Miami, it was dark as night. The only light came from aromatic candles positioned around the room, casting flickering shadows on the skulls, potions, and other paraphernalia in the shop.

The Voodoo priest, a man named Samuel Utanga, danced around the room, seemingly in a trance. The rhythmic drumming, at first low and pulsing then building to a pounding crescendo, filled the air. A female voice—a recording as there was no woman present—joined in, rising above the music, her angelic tones conjuring the spirits.

The priest's chanting got louder and louder until it became a mournful cry. He rubbed his hands on his white tunic, smearing crimson across the front. A headless chicken lay on the altar in front of him. A sacrifice to the ancestors. They were here; he could feel them. They were listening.

The priest evoked their power and told them what he wanted. A curse. A non-believer had disobeyed the spirits and must be punished. The ancestors answered.

The priest's eyes rolled back and he grasped the air, clawing at an invisible entity. His shoulders shook and he quivered from head to toe like a puppet on a string. Just when it couldn't get any more frenetic, he collapsed forward onto the altar, breathing heavily.

The music ceased. A pungent fragrance enveloped the shack, making it hard to breathe. Incense, perhaps. The priest lay still, only his back rising and falling as he gulped in the cloying air. Slowly, he rose, pale eyes gleaming with an unearthly quality. He lifted his face to the spirits and muttered something in a different language. Haitian, most likely.

His voice was different. Deeper, creepier. Unlike his normal voice. Was he possessed? Were the spirits talking through him?

The chanting continued for some time, then he closed his eyes. Nothing happened. For a brief moment, time seemed to stand still. Wooden faces stared down from the shelves above, their blank expressions holding no judgment. They'd seen it all before. The heavy beaded curtain hanging from the door frame tremored, even though there was no breeze.

The customer waited.

Eventually, the Voodoo priest opened his eyes and straightened up. His breathing returned to normal. The spirits had left him.

His smile was chilling. "It is done."

Reid Garrett turned his face to the sun. Christ, it was warm. The air felt hot and heavy, the humidity pushing down on him like a damp cloak. The barometer had been rising throughout the day. They'd be in for one hell of a storm later.

Sweat glistened on his bare torso as he lifted planks of timber from the truck and placed them on the ground next to what remained of his cabin, which wasn't much. The wildfire earlier in the year had wiped out half of the Everglades National Park and along with it, his two-roomed wooden cabin, his pickup truck, and all his worldly belongings. He didn't even have a damn coffee cup left.

Thank goodness the insurance company had finally come around to his way of thinking. Act of God, seriously? The perpetrator was now serving multiple life sentences at the Jefferson Correctional Institution, and even that was too good for the lowlife human-trafficking scumbag.

The rebuild was underway, but in the meantime, Reid was living at the Gator Inn, a two-bit motel deep in the South Florida glades. At least he could drown his sorrows at Smiley's, the next-door dive bar, which was within stumbling distance of the motel.

Reid bent down and picked up a twisted plastic object that may have been part of his stereo system, but he couldn't be sure. The cleanup job had taken months before the construction could begin. His wasn't the only residence to have been leveled by the inferno. Several glade communities had lost their houses and were in the long process of rebuilding, relocating, or moving out of the area altogether.

He'd considered that. Moving out. But after two years in the glades, he'd realized with some surprise that he didn't want to leave. Despite moving out here as a way of escaping his life, of running away from his problems, the murky waters of the swamp had seeped into his soul and healed it. Now he felt restless without it. To be honest, the thought of living in an urban area turned him cold.

There was nothing like looking out over the sea of sawgrass, feeling the warm breeze on his skin, and smelling the pungent odor of the swamp. The chirping cicadas sent him to sleep at night, and he awoke to the fluttering of birds squawking overhead. And he sure as hell did not miss the constant hum of traffic, blaring sirens, and noisy neighbors. Out here, the only neighbors he had were the four-legged kind.

"Over here," called the foreman of the construction crew that was building his new property. The foundations were in place and the stilts had been secured into the swampy ground. Reid picked up the planks and moved them, the sun burning his back and shoulders.

Weeks pouring over plans with an architect had not only cost a bundle but had filled him with a desperate need to see the structure come to life. Gone were the two dilapidated adjacent buildings, remnants of the failed airboat company, and instead, they were building one long wooden structure on chunky stilts with a deck that extended over the water. They were also reconstructing the wide launch jetty for his airboat and building a garage at the back of the property for his new pickup.

It would be incredible once it was finished. A phoenix rising from the ashes. To save costs, he was helping out on weekends. The manual labor took his mind off his cases and prevented him from thinking (too much) about Kenzie. Self-analysis had never been his thing – it was easier to block things out, store them in boxes in his mind. Reid had a lot of unopened boxes in his past, and he doubted if he'd ever properly sift through them. Kenzie was just another one.

His phone buzzed in his pocket. Detective Willie Vargas, his colleague, was calling from the station landline.

"Vargas." Reid straightened up, stretching out the kink in his back. "What's up?"

The young detective rarely called him on the weekend unless it was an emergency. Reid steeled himself for what he suspected was coming.

"Hey boss, sorry to interrupt you." Everyone knew he was working on the building site. "I thought you'd want to be informed. We've got a male DB near an alligator farm down Homestead way, not too far from your place. He was found by a bird watcher this afternoon."

"Yeah? Was he attacked?"

"No, that's the strange thing. The officer on the scene says he can't figure out how the guy died."

"It could be natural causes." Reid relaxed. There was no point driving to Homestead for a heart attack. The ME could handle it. "How old is the vic?"

"Mid-thirties. Unlikely to be a heart attack or anything like that," Vargas said, contradicting what he'd been thinking. "There are no obvious signs of an attack, no contusions, no stab wounds, no bullet holes. I'm going to go down and check it out."

"Okay, keep me posted." There must be something. People didn't just drop dead for no reason.

"Will do. Oh, the other thing is the expression on his face. The officer at the scene said it looks like the victim had seen a ghost."

"The death grimace," Reid pointed out. "We often see that post-mortem."

"I know about the death grimace. It's worse than that." Vargas wasn't one for hyperbole.

Reid frowned. "Got a pic?"

"Yeah, sending it through now."

Reid's phone vibrated a second time. Holding it away from his ear, he checked the photograph that had just come through. The man did indeed look terrified. Open mouth, body rigid with shock, not helped by the rigor that had set in and the eyes that bulged out of their sockets.

Something stirred in Reid's gut. This didn't feel right. He couldn't explain it, but the man's expression was disturbing. Not like anything he'd seen before.

"If I didn't know better," Vargas was saying. "I'd say he died of fright."

Reid wiped the sweat from his forehead. Fright, nah. But something had happened before he'd taken his last breath to put that expression on his face. He ran a hand through his hair. It came away wet. It was time for a break anyway.

"Send me the location," he said. "I'll meet you there."

2

Kenzie was about to sit down with a much-needed coffee when the doorbell rang. She sighed. Darn, who was that? Tucking a damp tendril behind her ear, thanks to the rain shower she'd been caught in dashing from her car to the front door, she stood up.

"Nick, hi." Her cheeks burned as she shot him a sheepish grin. Last time they'd talked, she'd stood him up. Not something she was proud of, especially since Nick was such a nice guy. He had a great job, he loved animals, he drove a Porsche. On paper, he was perfect.

But he wasn't Reid.

That realization had pole-axed her on the way to the restaurant. So much so, it had taken her breath away. She was over Reid. It had been she who'd called it off, after all. Not him. She'd looked him straight in the eye and said, let's be friends.

Then, mere weeks after that, she'd invited him to stay over. Kenzie squeezed her eyes shut at the cringy memory. To be fair, his house had just burned down leaving him homeless. Not that he was a charity case or anything, but she'd thought he might need a place to stay. Except they both knew where that would lead.

He'd said no, of course. But not after staring at her with those unfathomable eyes. The kind that either burned with an intensity that shook her to the core or were so guarded she had no idea what he was thinking.

"Hi, Kenzie," Nick said.

Halfway to the restaurant where they were having their date, she'd pulled over, unable to go any further. Taking out her phone, she'd made some dumb excuse like she'd been held up at work. It didn't really matter what she'd said, Nick had been sitting at the restaurant waiting for her.

Of course, he'd been chivalrous about it. Don't worry. It doesn't matter. They'd take a raincheck. But they both knew it was a lie.

Now here he was, standing outside her door in the pouring rain. A crack of lightning exploded overhead, making her jump. "You'd better come inside."

The handsome veterinarian traipsed in, leaving a puddle on the floor. "I'm sorry to surprise you like this," he began, smoothing his hair back. "But I need to talk to you."

Great. Her heart sank. The last thing she felt like discussing right now was their relationship, or more accurately, the lack thereof. To be honest, she didn't know why she'd pulled out of their date at the last minute. It wasn't as if she had any future with Reid. He'd made that clear after their last case together. That was it. She couldn't have it both ways. He'd practically shoved her out the door.

Kenzie cleared her throat. "Look, now isn't a good time, Nick. I'm sorry. I've just got in and it's been a long day."

"This isn't about us." He waved a hand dismissively in the air.

"It isn't?" Now she just felt stupid. What was he doing here then?

"No. I need your help."

She shook her head. "I don't understand."

"It's my brother-in-law. He's gone missing. He hasn't been home in three days."

Kenzie stared at him. That was not what she'd been expecting. "O–Okay, why don't you come and sit down. Can I get you some coffee?"

The guy was soaked through. The storm had broken late afternoon, as was the pattern in Miami. The humidity built throughout the day, only to dissipate in a sticky, drenching washout just before sunset. Most locals knew to expect it. The pressure built and built until the sky was charged with static, and then bam! ... The lightning would erupt, accompanied by a deep rumble and the heavens would open. Kenzie could almost sense the moment it was going to happen, but even so, she'd been caught running from her car.

The same must have happened to Nick. He nodded distractedly as she led him to the living room and gestured for him to take a seat. A moment later, she was back with another cup of coffee.

"Have you reported his disappearance to the police?" she asked, handing it to him.

"No, my sister thought he'd come back, but—" He shook his head.

Kenzie sat down opposite him. She'd never seen Nick look so dejected. He was usually such a positive, upbeat person. "What happened? Did they have a fight?"

"No, nothing like that. As far as I know, they're happily married. Jacob left one morning last week and hasn't been seen since. Gail called me at the practice when she couldn't get a hold of him, but I don't know what else to do. I've been driving around all day looking for him. He's not at any of his usual haunts."

That would explain Nick's disheveled state.

"My advice is to go to the police," she said. "They'll file a missing person report and get officers out looking for him."

Nick nodded. "Yeah, I know you're right. My sister still thinks he's holed up somewhere. Apparently, he was acting weird."

Kenzie frowned. "Weird? In what way?"

"Erratic. Nervous. Like he was scared of something, or someone."

"Did he say what, or who?"

"Not that she told me. Kenzie, I need your help to find him. You've got contacts, you're good at finding people."

Kenzie scratched her head. "I'm a reporter, Nick. My contacts are for work purposes, besides, I have no way of tracing a missing person. You really need to go to the cops for that. They might be able to track his phone or check when he last used a cash machine."

"His phone is off," Nick replied. "Gail has tried repeatedly to call him, as have I. It goes straight to voicemail." He paused, gnawing on his lower lip. Finally, he sighed, "What if Jacob's got himself into some sort of trouble and is in hiding? I don't want to waste the police's time. Please, can't you see what you can do? If we can't locate him in a day or two, I'll go to Miami PD and file a missing persons claim. I promise."

Kenzie pursed her lips. "Okay, I'll see what I can do, but only for a few days. After that, you must let the police know. Your brother-in-law may be in danger."

Or worse.

But she didn't say that. If the guy had been acting scared, he'd probably gone into hiding like Nick had said, or was laying low at a friend's house or an out-of-the-way motel somewhere.

"Did he owe money?" That was usually the cause of this type of behavior.

"I don't know. Gail didn't say."

"Okay, well the first thing we have to do is talk with your sister."

Nick gave a weary nod. When she raised her eyebrows, he straightened up. "Oh, you mean now?"

"Yeah, now. No time like the present, right?" Besides, she had work to do. This little investigation was going to mess up her schedule. Keith, her dictatorial editor, was expecting five hundred words on Congressman Leonard's new proposals for greener energy in the city by 8 a.m. tomorrow morning. To be fair, it wasn't something she was looking forward to writing. Everything seemed to be an anticlimax after cartel boss Maria Lopez's death and the subsequent media frenzy.

Reporters all over Florida had dined off her dramatic demise for months, rehashing her life story, her secret takeover of the Morales cartel, and her rise to fame – but the momentum had finally stalled, and Maria had become old news.

Kenzie got to her feet. Nick downed his coffee and did the same. "We can take my car." He fished in his pocket for his keys. "Gail lives on the other side of the bay."

"Okay, let's go. You can tell me all about your sister and her husband on the way."

He hesitated. "Thanks, Kenzie. I mean it." There was an awkward moment where he gazed at her. Unlike Reid, she could guess what he was thinking.

She shrugged. "I haven't done anything yet."

"Still, I know it's an imposition."

"Don't worry about it. Come on, let's go before it gets any later." She grabbed her purse and walked out of the house.

3

Gail Peters lived in a two-bedroom townhouse in the Pinewood area of Miami. It was nothing special, but it had a lived-in feel that Kenzie appreciated. The couple had been here for some time. She could tell by the chipped ornaments on the mantelpiece, the well-worn Persian rug on the terracotta tiled floor, and the jumble of family photographs in mismatching frames arranged on every available surface. It was a happy home, or it had been until Jacob had disappeared.

Now it was unkempt, crumbs gathering on the floor next to the sofa, mug stains on the coffee table, and a vase of blackened roses on the sideboard, their color having long since deserted them.

Gail herself was a surprise. A tall, elegant woman in her forties, she moved with a grace that made Kenzie think she may have been a dancer or gymnast in her youth. Long, slender fingers intertwined with each other, and she had to wrench them apart to shake Kenzie's hand. Uptight, nervous, and worried. That was obvious.

"When last did you see your husband, Gail?" Kenzie asked, even though Nick had filled her in on the way there.

She ran a trembling hand through her prematurely silver hair.

"Three days ago. He said he wasn't feeling well and didn't go into work. Then he paced up and down for about an hour, his phone in his hand. It was almost like he was trying to make up his mind about something. I was very concerned. He's usually so calm, you see."

Kenzie gave an encouraging nod. "Did he say anything?"

"No. When I asked if he was okay, he ignored me. I didn't want to push, so I left him to it. Then the doorbell rang."

Kenzie raised her eyebrows. "Yes?"

"It was so strange, because there was nobody there."

"Nobody?"

She shook her head. "Jacob peered through the peephole. They must have run off. Anyway, he opened it a crack, but kept the chain on." She was back to wringing her hands again. "We've never had security problems in the past. I don't know what he was afraid of."

It certainly sounded like Jacob was scared of something. "What happened next?"

"He went straight to his study and shut the door. I could hear him rummaging around, then he rushed out of the house without saying a word." Her eyes were huge, wounded saucers in her pale face. "That was the last time I saw him."

"When was this?" she asked.

"Wednesday afternoon."

Kenzie frowned. Something had spooked him. But what? Had there actually been someone at the door, but Gail just hadn't known? Had Jacob kept that from her? Was there a note left there? A threatening message of some kind? A horse's head?

She scoffed at the direction her thoughts had taken.

"What did Jacob do for a living?" she asked.

"He was an accountant." Gail spread her arms. "Absolutely harmless. Who would want to hurt Jacob?"

"How do you know he's been hurt?"

She bit her lip. "I don't. It's just that this is so unlike him. I feel like he'd have come back if he was able to. I can't help but think that something's happened to him." Her eyes filled with tears. Nick put his arm around her.

"I'm sure he's fine, Gail. Try not to worry."

"I'm trying, but why is his phone off? Why won't he answer my calls?"

It didn't look good, Kenzie had to admit. Still, there was a chance he'd gone on the run.

"You said he'd been acting strangely in the days leading up to his disappearance," she began, thinking out loud. "How exactly was he acting?"

"Oh, I don't know." She took a shaky breath. "He seemed agitated and anxious. When I asked if there was something wrong, he said he was just busy. But he couldn't sit still. He wasn't sleeping, he spent all night in his study."

Hmm... There was definitely something bothering Jacob.

"Who did he work for?" she asked.

"A man named Felix Hammond. He's in shipping. Jacob does the bookkeeping for him."

Kenzie frowned. "Hammond Holdings?"

"Yes, that's his company."

She arched an eyebrow. Hammond Holdings was a huge shipping company with interests in logistics and even industrial property. She knew this because she'd been researching them in relation to Congressman Leonard's modernization plan. Hammond Holdings had funded a vast portion of his campaign. The two were thick as thieves.

She turned to Nick. "What's he like?"

"I've never met him," Nick confessed, glancing at his sister.

"He seemed nice. Charming, you know, like all those wealthy men are." It was clear she didn't include herself in that category. While their house wasn't big, it was stylishly decorated. The focal point was a large gold-framed painting of a ballerina on the wall.

"Do you dance?" she asked, gesturing to the artwork.

Nick gave a little cough.

She smiled, the first time since they'd arrived. "I used to."

"Gail was a prima ballerina," he informed Kenzie. "She trained at the Royal Ballet School in London, didn't you Gail?" Kenzie smiled at the brotherly pride.

"Once upon a time." Gail's smile turned sad. "A long time ago."

Nick's eyes clouded over. Kenzie detected a weird undercurrent, but she didn't comment on it. Something had happened to stop Gail's dancing career. Had it been Jacob? Kids? Something else? She made a mental note to ask him about it later.

"I give dance lessons now," she said, filling the sudden silence. "I have a small studio out back."

"That's wonderful," Kenzie said, warming to the woman. "I've always wanted to dance, but I'm afraid I'm all arms and legs. No coordination."

Nick grinned. "Maybe Gail can give you a few lessons."

She shot him a look. "I wouldn't put her through that."

Gail gave a wobbly smile, but it didn't reach her eyes.

Kenzie looked around the room. "I'm sorry to have to ask, but what was your financial situation like? Is it possible your husband borrowed money from someone?"

"You mean like a loan shark?" Nick cut in.

Kenzie nodded, her eyes on Gail.

"Our finances were fine," she said. "Jacob's job pays well, and I supplement our income. We don't need money. I mean, we're not like Felix Hammond, but we do okay."

"And he didn't gamble or anything like that?"

"No, certainly not."

"Sorry, but I have to ask. If he owed money that he couldn't repay, it would explain his erratic behavior."

"I can check his bank statements, but he would have told me." She frowned. "We talk about everything. Jacob is my best friend, not just my husband. We're a team, always have been."

Nick nodded, while Kenzie gazed wistfully at her. That sounded perfect. A team. Married, lovers, friends. Was that too much to ask for?

Reid's face appeared in her mind's eye, and she could almost feel his hurt.

Goodbye Kenzie.

Those were the last words he'd said to her, and she still got a pang in her gut when she thought about it.

"Do you have his bank statements?" She dragged her thoughts away from Reid. "Do you mind if we have a look?"

"Oh, um, yeah. Sure. They'll be in his study."

Kenzie and Nick followed Gail down the hallway and into a messy, but very male study. Large windows overlooked the alleyway beside the house, beyond which was a lush hedge, its sad yellow flowers drooping in the rain.

Jacob's large wooden desk was cluttered with paperwork. A coffee cup sat on the top, half empty, a milky film floating on the surface. The wastepaper bin was overflowing, and the two-seater leather couch had a discarded blanket on it. Jacob had been spending far too much time in his study.

"He was sleeping here." She nodded to the blanket, her cheeks flushed with embarrassment. "He said he didn't want to keep me awake."

Understandable.

"Does he have a computer or laptop?" Kenzie asked.

"Yes, it's probably under there." She nodded at his desk.

Kenzie glanced at the plug socket and followed the laptop cord upward to where it disappeared under the mound of paper on the desk. Sure enough, a slim laptop was hidden underneath all the documents.

What kind of man went on the run without a laptop? He must have been in a panicked state when he left. Not thinking clearly. His only instinct had been to get away.

"Do you mind if I take this with me? There might be something on it to indicate where he's gone."

Gail shrugged. "It's only his work stuff on there."

"Still, I'd like to try."

"You'll need his password." She wrote it down on a yellow notepad and tore off the page.

Kenzie pocketed it. "Thanks."

The papers on the desk appeared to be various invoices, waybills, and shipping delivery notices. She picked them up one by one and put them in a neat pile, glancing at each as she did so. Nothing struck her as out of the ordinary. Some of the sums were quite large, but in line with what you'd expect at a shipping company.

A small rectangular note caught her eye, and she picked it up. It was wrinkled with age or frequent use. The blue scrawl faded.

Marcy 7:30 p.m. Underneath was a phone number.

"Who's Marcy?" she asked.

Gail, who was reaching for a file on the bookshelf, tottered for a moment. "Marcy? No idea." She didn't turn around.

Surreptitiously, Kenzie slid the note into her pocket.

Gail pulled down the file and flicked through it. "Here, this is the most recent one."

It was dated last month. Kenzie took a look at the bottom line. Healthy. She scanned upwards. No untoward withdrawals, no scattered spending patterns, no indication of gambling or betting of any kind. His salary was good, but then Hammond Holdings was a wealthy organization.

"Okay, thanks."

It seemed Gail was telling the truth. Then what the hell was Jacob Peters running from? And who was Marcy?

4

Reid pulled over when he saw the flashing lights. A tent had been erected over the body to protect it from the elements. Big splodges of rain pelted down, splatting against the windshield, making it hard to see. Blurry white blobs in raincoats hurried around, gathering what evidence they could and carting forensic equipment to and from the waiting vehicles.

There was a knock on his window. Vargas stood there, rain dripping off his eyelashes. Reid lowered it. "How's it going?"

"They're preparing to take the body away," his colleague said, shading his eyes. "The medical examiner is with him now."

"I'm coming."

Reid climbed out of the pickup truck and squinted against the rain. It wouldn't last long. These tropical squalls never did. Soon the deluge would stop, the sun would come out and the humidity would creep up again, and so the cycle would repeat itself.

Walking to the tent, Reid glanced out over the swampy green expanse of water, pockmarked by the rain. It was still beautiful, stretching for miles in all directions. A splash a couple of yards to his left made him jerk his head in that direction. A gator farm, Vargas had said.

"Do we have a lookout?" he asked, ducking under the tent flap.

"Hamilton's on it," Vargas replied with a grin. "He's not too happy about it."

Reid gave a curt nod. The last thing they needed was a surprise attack while they were working.

"Hello, Doc." Reid greeted the medical examiner who he recognized from previous cases. The diminutive doctor with his thinning hair and sharp, beady eyes was one of the best in the business, in Reid's opinion. Certainly, the best he'd ever worked with. Careful hands inspected the victim, gliding over the pallid skin, inspecting the wrists and ankles, studying the neck and throat, and finally closing the bulging eyes.

He grunted, then glanced up at Reid. "It's not often I'm stumped, but I admit, this one has got me, Garrett."

"Really?" Reid gave the victim a careful once-over. He couldn't see any immediate signs of trauma either. There was no bruising on the body, no restraint marks on the wrists or ankles, no defensive wounds, grazed knuckles, or facial discoloration. "You don't know how he died?"

"Nope. Not yet anyway. I'll take a more detailed look when I get him back to the lab. But at first glance—" He shrugged. "Nothing."

Reid frowned. "There must be a reason."

The ME got to his feet. "There always is. Finding it is the tricky part."

Reid patted him on the shoulder. "That's why we have you."

The ME grimaced. "I can tell you one thing, he was frightened half to death when he died. Excuse the pun." He gave a watery smile.

Reid didn't return it. "His expression, you mean?"

A crime scene photographer had captured the body in situ, so they had a record of where and how he was found. Those pictures would find their way into his inbox in due course.

"Yeah, creepy stuff. Never seen anything like it. We do get the occasional contorted expression postmortem, as you know, but this guy looked like he'd seen a ghost."

"Something scared the bejesus out of him before he died," Reid summed up.

The ME nodded.

"Could it be a heart attack? Natural causes?"

"It's possible, although he's not showing the usual signs of cardiac arrest. Of course, I can't tell if he suffered from ventricular hypertrophy or myocardial fibrosis or inflammation until I open him up. This man appears to be in good shape too."

"What about a brain aneurysm or something like that."

The doctor looked doubtful. "Maybe, but again, there are no outward signs. If anything, I'd say he asphyxiated – there is slight dilation of the blood vessels and some hemorrhaging – but I can't tell you why. There is no obvious cause of death."

Reid frowned. "Can you give me a time of death?"

"That I can do. He's been dead for at least three or four days."

"What's that?" Reid pointed to a leather thong around the victim's neck.

The ME opened the collar for a closer look. At the bottom was a crude sort of amulet. It looked like something a hippy or surfer might wear, not a suited and booted office type.

"What is it?" Reid stared at the small leather pouch.

"It looks to be a container of some kind," said the ME. He bent in closer, inspecting it. "There's something inside."

Using his tweezers, he pulled out a soiled note about a square inch in size. It had tiny writing scribbled on it. "Not English," the ME said.

"Is it a message?" Reid wondered.

"A love note, perhaps?" The ME shrugged. "Never seen that before." He removed the necklace and dropped it into an evidence bag.

"I'll take that," said Reid, signing for it. It was important the chain of custody wasn't broken in case it had a relevancy to the case.

A shot rang out, echoing through the wilderness.

The ME glanced up as Reid spun around. "What the—?"

"That's Hamilton." Vargas poked his head into the tent. "We have a couple of unwanted visitors."

"Okay, let's bag him up and get him to the morgue," Reid instructed, nodding at the ME. "Let me know when you do the autopsy. I wanna be there for this one."

"Will do."

Reid emerged to find Hamilton, a graduate police officer, standing with a rifle in his hand, scowling at the murky surface of the water. At least it had stopped raining.

"You okay?" Reid joined him. It was twilight, hunting time.

"Yeah, just a warning shot." Hamilton didn't take his eyes off the water.

"Where's the owner of this farm?" Reid asked.

Hamilton pointed up the dirt track. "Back at the house. It's a couple of miles in that direction. He was down here earlier, then left us to it."

"Got his details?"

"Yeah, but he didn't see anything. He arrived after the bird watcher discovered the body."

"Where's the bird watcher?"

"In the back of the ambulance having a hot drink. He's kinda shook up."

Reid marched over there. The first thing he saw was a giant Stetson, followed by the tangy smell of sunscreen and an unwelcome sight of hairy legs sticking out of cargo shorts.

Tourist.

"You the one who found the body?"

"Yes, sir. I ain't never seen anything like it before. Hell, I ain't never seen a dead body before." The man had a southern drawl, a worried frown, and long hair tied back in a ponytail. He didn't look like a bird watcher.

"Where are you from?" Although it wasn't hard to guess.

"Austin. My wife and I are on vacation. Thought I'd do some bird watching."

"Not the best season for birdwatching," Reid remarked. That was more popular in the dry season.

The man shrugged.

Reid read the writing on his T-shirt. *I do things Texas style.* Underneath was a picture of a cowboy on a horse swinging a lasso. "See anything interesting?"

"Yeah, I spotted a roseate spoonbill earlier today and a swallow-tailed kite, such majestic creatures." Okay, so maybe he was the real deal.

"Where are you staying?" Reid asked the Texan.

"The Hyatt. We're here till Friday, then we're going down to the Keys."

Reid nodded to Vargas. "Make sure we've got his details before he goes."

"Sure thing, boss."

"Hey, man. That guy looked terrified." The Texan shuddered. "What you got out here to make him look like that?"

"Don't know." Reid shrugged. "A couple of big gators, most likely. Maybe a python."

"No one told me the glades were so dangerous."

What tourist guide had he been reading?

"They can be, yeah. You should take care."

"I think I'll stick to the beach from now on." He nodded toward the body, which was being wheeled to a waiting ambulance. "No way I wanna end up like that fella."

5

"Is this Marcy?"

"Yes." Kenzie could hear the questioning tone in her voice. "Who is this?"

"You don't know me, but my name is Kenzie Gilmore. I'd like to speak with you about Jacob Peters."

"Why? Has something happened to Jake?" Her response was hurried, concerned. There were voices in the background and music. Faint, but upbeat, like in a shopping mall.

"Can we meet?" Kenzie asked. "I'll tell you everything then."

There was a pause. "Why can't you tell me over the phone?"

"Please, I'm just after some information. It won't take long."

"I'm sorry, but I don't know you."

"I'm a reporter; I work at the *Miami Herald*. I'm on their website if you want to check me out, although this has nothing to do with the newspaper." She hesitated. Marcy obviously needed more persuading before she would meet. "I'm helping a friend look for him."

"Why? Where's he gone?" Definitely worried. Kenzie wondered at the relationship between them.

"He hasn't been seen since Wednesday. I thought you might be able to help."

There was another long pause, then Marcy said, "Where do you wanna meet?"

Kenzie suggested a coffee shop downtown. The meeting spot was in a convenient, busy area with plenty of people around.

"Sure. I can meet you after work. How's six o'clock?"

"That's great." Kenzie smiled into the phone. "I'll see you there."

Kenzie got there early, choosing a spot by the window where she could see the door. She was checking out the front-page feature in a rival newspaper when a woman with glossy dark hair in a figure-hugging dress and heels that weren't designed for running dashed in. The new arrival scanned the coffee shop.

Kenzie raised a hand. "Marcy?"

With a hurried nod, she sashayed over. "Kenzie?"

"Yes, thank you for coming." Kenzie smiled and gestured for Marcy to sit down.

The woman eased herself into the seat opposite. She was shorter than Kenzie, but more voluptuous, with an enviable hourglass figure and a natural sexiness that made men turn their heads to stare. "What's happened to Jake?"

Kenzie could tell she was worried about the missing accountant. "He's gone missing. Nobody has seen him since last Wednesday."

"Oh no..." She shook her head, clearly perturbed. "I knew it."

"Knew what?" Kenzie asked.

"He's dead. I know he's dead." She ran a hand through her hair. "Oh, God."

Kenzie stared at her. "What do you mean, he's dead?"

"As soon as I saw it, I knew."

"Saw what?" Kenzie asked, exasperated. "Marcy, slow down."

"Sorry, it's just that I knew this would happen."

"How could you possibly know he'd go missing? What are you talking about?"

"The voodoo doll." Her liquid brown eyes were wide. "He found it on his doorstep and brought it to show me." She shuddered. "I knew it was bad luck as soon as I saw it. There was no way he was bringing that into my house."

Kenzie was struggling to keep up. "Are you saying someone left a voodoo doll outside Jacob's house?"

She remembered what Gail Peters had said.

The doorbell. Nobody was there.

What if they'd left a package? A package Gail hadn't seen because Jacob had taken it straight to his study. That would explain the agitation.

"Yes, haven't you been listening to me? That's exactly what I'm saying. Someone put a curse on Jacob, and not just any curse either. A death curse."

Kenzie frowned. "How do you know?"

"The voodoo doll had a pin sticking out of its heart."

It didn't get much clearer than that, Kenzie supposed.

"How did Jacob react when he got the doll?" She watched Marcy clench and unclench her hands on the table.

"He was freaking out. I don't think I helped much, but I know things... from back in..." She paused. "Cuba. You gotta take Voodoo seriously. I told him to get rid of it and go to an oungan or manbo for protection."

Kenzie ran a hand through her hair. "What's an oungan and a manbo?"

"You know? A high priest or priestess. Someone who can cancel the curse, ask the spirits for protection." It was clear Marcy believed in this stuff.

"Did he? Did he see someone?"

The Hispanic woman leaned back in her chair. "I don't know. Maybe not, if he hasn't come home."

Kenzie let this filter in. A voodoo doll? A death curse? Eventually, she said to Marcy, "Why would someone put a curse on Jacob Peters?"

"I don't know. I asked myself the same question. He's such a sweet guy."

There was something Kenzie had to ask. "Marcy, are you having an affair with Jacob?"

There was a pause, then Marcy said, "Yes, I thought you knew."

"No, I didn't."

"But how did you get my number?"

"I found it on Jacob's desk in his study." She put the yellow note on the table. Marcy touched it with her finger.

"I gave that to him when we first met. I can't believe he kept it all this time."

"How long have you two been together?"

"Ten months, give or take."

So not a fling, then.

"Do you mind if I ask how you met?"

Marcy gave a knowing snort. "Why? Because you can't figure out why I would be interested in a man like Jake?"

"No, I'm sure he's very nice," Kenzie stammered. "It's just he's quite a bit older than you."

Marcy looked around her. "I need coffee for this conversation."

Kenzie got to her feet. "Sure, what are you having? I'll get it."

Marcy gave her preference and Kenzie went to the counter. She ordered and once the coffees were ready, returned to the table. Once she'd sat down, Marcy continued, "We met when he came into the store to buy a birthday present for his wife. A scarf, in arctic blue."

Kenzie imagined that would go well with Gail's silver hair and pale skin.

"I helped him select one – you know what men are like – and we got talking. He asked where I was from. I said Cuba, and he told me he'd been there on vacation a couple of years back. He was nice, so when he asked me out for a drink, I said yes." Simple as that.

"Didn't it bother you that he was married?" Kenzie asked.

A shrug. "No, not after he explained that his wife doesn't like sex."

Kenzie blinked. "Excuse me?"

"She's frigid." Marcy tossed her hair over her shoulder with the confidence of someone who wasn't plagued by the same affliction. "Something happened to her long ago. He wouldn't tell me what. I didn't need to know. They love each other, but their relationship isn't sexual."

"Does she know about you?" Kenzie wondered at Gail's reaction to her question back in the study. She'd faltered, but only slightly. It could be nothing.

"I don't think so," Marcy said. "Jake didn't want to upset her, although he's had lovers before and she didn't mind."

"He told you that?" Kenzie asked.

Marcy nodded. "She understands he has needs."

"I see." Gail must be a very open-minded person, which was not the impression Kenzie had gotten. In fact, the prima ballerina had seemed fairly highly strung. The two women were polar opposites. Maybe that's what Jacob liked about Marcy. She was all hot-blooded Latino passion, while his wife was cool and reserved. Fire and ice.

"Why did Jake think she'd be upset if he told her about you?"

"I don't know. Maybe because with us it's not just sex, you know? We have fun together. It's different."

Could Gail have found out about Marcy and been jealous? Was she afraid their marriage was in trouble? That Jacob might leave her for the Cuban?

That was motive.

Did Nick know about Marcy? She'd have to find a way of asking him without upsetting him. The veterinarian thought his sister and her husband were happily married, and perhaps they were, in a way. It was not Kenzie's place to judge other people's relationships. But in her humble opinion, happily married men did not seek out lovers, with or without their wife's permission.

"Marcy, when did you last see Jake?"

"It was Wednesday," she said without needing to think about it. "We see each other every Wednesday and Friday. Those are our days." Her tone was mildly possessive, like those days were sacred. "I waited for him on Friday, but he didn't show up. I was worried, so I sent him a couple of messages, but he didn't respond. I wanted to call him, but he told me not to, so I didn't." Her face dropped into a sulky pout.

Wednesday was the last day anyone had seen Jacob.

"When you saw him on Wednesday, did he tell you who had sent him the voodoo doll?"

"No, I'm sorry. I don't think he knew. He kept saying it was a warning."

"A warning? What kind of warning?"

She shook her head. "He didn't tell me."

"Did he say anything else? Anything that could help me find him."

"No, I don't think so."

Kenzie hid her frustration. "What mood was he in when he left? Did he say he was going home?"

"He was far too freaked out for... well, you know. So we talked, and then he left."

Kenzie nodded. "What time was this?"

"Not late. Around ten."

"If he didn't go home, do you know anywhere he might have stayed?"

She shrugged. "Usually, we go to my place." A moment passed, and Marcy asked, "Does this mean the party's off?"

Kenzie glanced up. "What party?"

"The one Jake promised to take me to. A work thing. Fancy, you know? I was gonna dress up." The wistful look on her face made Kenzie think she wasn't used to dressing up. Not fancy, anyway.

"When is this party?" Kenzie asked.

"It's supposed to be this Tuesday. At the yacht club. We don't usually see each other on a Tuesday, but it was a special occasion."

Kenzie's mind was racing. There were hundreds of yacht clubs in Miami. "Did he say which one?"

"Um, I can't remember. Mimosa... Azalea... something like that?" She shook her head.

"Acacia?"

"Yes, that's the one."

Acacia Yacht Club was an upmarket marina near where she lived in Bay Harbor. Only the very wealthy could afford the exorbitant mooring charges.

Marcy's face fell. "It's not going to happen, is it?"

"It's unlikely," Kenzie admitted. "Not unless we can find Jacob before then."

Her eyes clouded over. "I hope he's okay."

"He means a lot to you, doesn't he?" Kenzie asked.

She gave a little nod. "Jake makes me feel safe. I didn't always feel safe back in my country."

Kenzie studied her across the table. "Cuba, you said?"

"Yeah." Marcy held her gaze.

"How long have you been here?" Kenzie broke eye contact and reached for her coffee.

Marcy's shoulders stiffened. "You checking up on me now?"

"Of course not. I'm just trying to figure out what happened to Jacob."

"Then you don't need to know how long I've been here, or what my story is. It's got nothing to do with Jake, or anyone." She raised her eyebrows and shot Kenzie a pointed look.

"Okay, fair enough." Kenzie held up her hands, not wanting to rile the woman. It was strange, though, that she wouldn't talk about her past, or how long she'd been in the country. Almost like she had something to hide. "I didn't mean to pry. Thanks for talking to me, Marcy. If you think of anything else, please let me know." She handed the woman her business card. "That's my cell on the back."

Marcy gave a stiff nod, and Kenzie felt the woman's gaze burning into her back as she left the coffee shop.

They love each other.

That's what Marcy had said about Jacob and Gail's relationship. Sure, Gail Peters had a motive, but so did Marcy. What if the mistress had wanted more than Jacob was prepared to give? Maybe they'd argued because Jacob had refused to leave his wife, and one thing had led to another. Was the fiery Marcy capable of murder?

Kenzie got into her car and leaned back against the seat. The Cuban woman had seemed genuinely concerned about Jacob, or Jake as she'd called him. If she did have anything to do with his disappearance, she was doing a good job of hiding it.

She started the car. A love triangle, but which of the two women had the most to lose? Fire or ice?

6

Reid called a briefing first thing on Monday morning. He hadn't seen any point in bringing in the team last night, since they had no idea who the victim was or how he had died. It would be days before the autopsy could be performed, thanks to a backlog at the morgue, so there was very little they could do that couldn't wait until the morning.

"As most of you know, we have a new case." Reid glanced around at his young team. Vargas, always active, fidgeted beside him, while Detective Diaz sat in the front, her legs crossed, shoulders back, eagerly awaiting the briefing. Next to her sat Hamilton, the rookie who'd recently graduated from the academy, along with veteran street cop, Dwayne Griffith, who'd transferred from Miami PD a couple of months back. Monroe, the eldest detective in the department at nearly sixty, stood at the back, his hands thrust into his pockets.

"A man was found dead on an alligator farm near Homestead yesterday. Detective Vargas and I attended the scene. Here's what we know so far." Reid gestured to the whiteboard that had been set up at the end of the squad room. Sweetwater PD wasn't a big station, and they didn't have a proper incident room, only some offices off the main open-plan area that were too hot and stuffy for anyone to use. He'd considered taking one as an office, but in the end, had opted to work out here with the rest of the team. Those rooms were used as filing cabinets now.

"The victim is a Caucasian male in his mid-forties. No ID on the body. His fingerprints aren't in the system either." They'd used an AFIS machine at the scene, but it had turned out to be useless.

"I'll look into missing persons," Diaz volunteered.

Reid held up a finger. He wasn't done. "In addition to that, we don't know how he died."

There were a few puzzled looks.

"The victim didn't have any marks or bruises on his body," Reid explained. "He hadn't been shot or stabbed, and there was no indication of an altercation of any kind."

"Natural causes?" suggested Monroe from his perch at the back.

"Maybe; we're waiting for the ME to confirm. So far, all we've got is possible asphyxiation, but no known cause."

Vargas had pinned some color photographs of the crime scene to the whiteboard. "One thing to note was that the victim was wearing an unusual amulet." He pointed to the relevant photograph on the board. "It's a leather pouch with a note in it."

"That looks like a gris-gris," said a female police officer who worked with Hamilton. She was fairly new to the department, like most of the team.

He frowned. "What's that, Officer.... Martinez, is it?"

She nodded. "It's a talisman. It's supposed to protect the wearer from evil."

There was a short silence, then Reid cleared his throat. "Okay, so what are we saying? This guy was superstitious?"

"Or he had a curse on him," Martinez murmured, just loud enough for Reid to hear.

"A curse?" He blinked several times. "You mean like a voodoo curse?"

"Yes, sir. If someone had cast him, he might wear something like that to protect himself." Martinez nodded to the board.

"It doesn't look like it did much good," Monroe remarked from the back of the room.

Martinez turned to him. "Curses can be powerful."

Beside him, Vargas shivered. Reid shot him a look as if to say, not you too.

"Well, this gris-gris is the only thing we have to go on." Reid looked at Martinez. "Where would one go about getting one of these?" He pointed behind him.

"You'd have to consult an oungan or manbo," she replied. At his blank look, she elaborated. "That's a Voodoo practitioner, a priest or priestess."

"Do you know where to find these practitioners?" Reid asked.

Martinez gave a half-nod. She knew, but she wasn't keen to get involved. Too bad. She was best placed to find out where he'd bought the amulet. Reid glanced at Diaz.

"I'll go with Officer Martinez to see if anyone recognizes our victim," she said. "There are several Voodoo practitioners in Little Haiti."

He shot her a grateful grin. "Great, thanks. Monroe, you get on to missing persons. Let's see if anyone has reported our guy missing."

The veteran detective gave a grunt and turned to go back to his desk. Vargas held up his hand. "Actually, there's something I'd like to say, if you can all spare a moment."

Reid turned in surprise. Diaz was smiling. It must be good news.

Monroe stopped walking, and everyone turned towards him expectantly.

Reid gestured for him to go ahead.

"I've got some exciting news," he said, grinning from ear to ear. "You all know Shannon, who I've been dating for the last year or so." There were nods of approval, and some jeering. "Well, I've asked her to marry me, and I'm happy to report, she's accepted."

There was a stunned silence, and then the squad room broke into raucous applause. Officers came up to shake his hand and thump him on the back. From the look on Diaz's face, Reid could tell this wasn't exactly news to her.

"You knew about this?" he hissed, under his breath.

She grinned. "Yeah, he told me this morning."

Vargas was his right-hand man, and he'd had no idea things had progressed so fast. To be fair, he'd had a lot on his plate recently. With the fire and the rebuild, the persecution of the human traffickers and the breakdown of his relationship with Kenzie, he hadn't had much time to come up for air. Or maybe he'd just had his head up his own ass.

"Congratulations, Vargas. I hope you'll be very happy together." He pumped his colleague's hand.

"Thanks, boss." Vargas couldn't stop smiling. "We're having celebratory drinks at the Tavern tonight after work, and we'd love you all to join us."

There was more cheering.

"Drinks on you?" someone shouted.

"Right, that's enough of that," Reid said, when the noise finally quietened down. "We have work to do." Everybody filtered back to their desks.

Reid turned to his beaming colleague. "You kept that under wraps."

Vargas grinned. "I was waiting for the right time to spring it on the department. You coming tonight?"

Reid didn't meet his eye. "Wouldn't miss it for the world."

"Great. Thanks, boss. That means a lot."

The Blue Water Tavern was a sports bar with cold beer on tap and a great burger menu a few blocks from the Sweetwater Police Department. It had been there for as long as Reid could remember, and was such a popular cop hangout, that the owner, Joe, knew most of them personally.

"Evening, Garrett," he said as Reid walked in. For some reason, Joe liked to call cops by their last names.

"Evening, Joe. How's it going?"

"Busy, as always." The tough, ex-baseball player grinned. "I hear you're celebrating tonight."

"That's right. Vargas got engaged."

"Shannon." He nodded. "Great lass. Lively too. Always up for a good time."

"That she is." Reid moved off to find the others.

Shannon, Vargas' glowing fiancé, spotted him and came rushing over. "Reid, we're so glad you could make it." She threw her arms around him, and he was enveloped in a cloud of exotic perfume.

"Congratulations," he said, extricating himself.

Shannon was definitely the touchy-feely type. Her red hair bounced around her shoulders, while her green eyes flashed with joy. "Thank you. I'm over the moon." She showed him the diamond on her finger. It wasn't as big as he'd expected, but then Vargas was on a cop's salary. Somehow, he'd imagined Shannon would have gone for something more elaborate.

"Beautiful," he said, sincerely.

She turned and beckoned to Vargas. "Honey, Reid is here."

Vargas never called him by his first name. He was either boss, or LT. Rarely Garrett, but never Reid.

"Hey, boss." Vargas, still grinning, came over. Reid was pleased to see him so elated. "Can I get you a drink?"

"Thanks, but it's on me." He moved off to the bar.

"Hello, Reid," came a soft voice over his shoulder.

He turned, his heart skipping a beat. "Kenzie, I didn't know you were coming."

Worry flickered across her face. "Is that a problem?"

"No, of course not." He forced a laugh. "Not at all. In fact, I'm glad you're here."

"You are?" Her face broke into a smile, showing her dimple. Damn, he'd missed that smile.

"Yeah, how've you been?"

"Good. How about you?"

"Good." They stared at each other. Reid didn't know what to say, even though there was so much to say. At least Kenzie was having the same problem.

"What can I get you?" asked the barman, coming to the rescue.

Reid cleared his throat. "Oh, two Coronas and a glass of white wine. Thanks." He turned back to Kenzie. "Do you want something?"

She held up a glass. "I'm good, thanks."

There was another pause, then she asked, "How did the prosecution go?"

She was talking about the human trafficking case they'd solved together a couple of months back. "Fine." He studied her. It had been a while since they'd seen each other. Two months, maybe more. Her blonde hair was longer than he remembered, past her shoulders. Makeup wasn't really her thing, but tonight her eyes were rimmed with smokey black eyeliner, and her lips shone with a rosy gloss. She looked great. More than great. "We got him. The bastard got life."

"Good. That's nothing short of what he deserved."

"How's Seb?" Sebastian was Kenzie's ward. She'd agreed to foster him after he'd been trafficked from Cuba and his mother had been killed by the man who'd brought them here.

She grinned. "He's doing well, actually. He's having guitar lessons, and doing martial arts, as well as trying to finish school."

"That's great." It was thanks to Kenzie that he was able to flourish. Reid recalled finding him in that deserted warehouse, starving, dehydrated, and reeling from his mother's murder. He was a different boy now.

"I see you won some sort of prize," Reid said, not that he was following her career or anything.

She looked surprised. "Yes, for my feature on Maria Lopez. That was a shock, but a good one."

"You deserved it," he said. "After what that woman put you through."

Kenzie shrugged, modest as ever. "I was just doing my job." She gave an enigmatic smile. "Not as exciting as catching bad guys, but it'll do."

He chuckled. She'd once told him how desperately she'd wanted to become a cop, but an accident right after graduation had killed her dream. The scar on her knee was a stark reminder of the day she nearly lost her life, and the injuries that meant she could never qualify as a police officer.

"Hey, party's over here," came a loud voice. Monroe, who always perked up after he'd had a few, beckoned them over.

Kenzie grinned. "We'd better join them."

"Yeah." Reid took Vargas and Shannon's drinks back to them, and they got absorbed in the general conversation. Everyone wanted to know how Kenzie was, including Shannon who'd adopted her as her new best friend. He could tell Kenzie wasn't too comfortable with this, but then Shannon could be a little over the top sometimes.

Despite his best efforts, Reid didn't get a chance to talk to Kenzie alone again. He watched her say her goodbyes and leave around ten, stating she had an early start. The evening seemed to sag after she left, even though Shannon was making everybody laugh with some really dirty Irish jokes, the adoring Vargas at her side.

That was a strange coupling, Reid mused, but then what did he know? His longest relationship had lasted a couple of months and it had been with an undercover agent who'd been killed in the line of duty. Whatever had been happening between him and Kenzie hadn't even gotten off the ground. He gave a snort and downed the rest of his beer. Time to call it a day.

Reid left without saying goodbye. Given the amount of alcohol being consumed, he didn't think anyone would notice he was gone.

"See ya," called Joe, as he left the Tavern.

Reid raised a hand in response and made his way back to his truck.

7

KENZIE MET Nick during her lunch hour at the Mug and Bean, a coffee shop near the *Herald*'s offices. She didn't have long; Congressman Leonard was unveiling a new smart freeway which had been under construction for a year, messing up the downtown traffic, and she needed to be there. Unbeknownst to her editor, Keith, she'd gotten her research assistant, Raoul, to look into the source of the freeway's funding. Everyone had their skeletons, and the Congressman was pissing her off with his new squeaky-clean image, when she knew for a fact he was anything but.

"Tread lightly," Keith had warned her. Last time she'd written an expose on Leonard, the newspaper had been sued for libel and she'd nearly lost her job. This time she'd be more careful.

"Kenzie, what's up?" Nick slid into the vacant chair opposite her. Freshly shaven, wearing blue jeans and a white shirt, he looked incredibly suave, unlike Reid who was always a little rough around the edges. Outside, his Porsche gleamed in the midday sun. She must be crazy to spurn his advances. Still, after seeing Reid last night, she'd been left with a longing that she couldn't explain, but she knew it couldn't be filled by another man. Not Nick, not anyone. That was the problem.

Thrusting her feelings for Reid firmly out of her mind, she turned to Nick. "Thanks for meeting me. I wanted to run something by you."

He leaned forward. "Yeah? Is this about Jacob? Have you got a lead?"

Kenzie held up a hand. "Not really."

He slumped back in his chair. "Damn. I was really hoping you had something."

"Sorry," Kenzie paused. How best to say this? "I met with a woman named Marcy yesterday. Have you heard Jacob mention her before?"

His forehead crinkled. "No. Who is she?"

Kenzie took a deep breath. "His mistress."

There was a pause. Nick stared at her for several minutes, apparently stunned.

"I take it you didn't know he was having an affair?" Her voice was gentle, sympathetic.

"N–No. Are you sure?"

"I'm afraid so. Marcy and Jacob have been seeing each other for nearly ten months now. He met up with her the night he disappeared. She's worried about him too."

Nick was shaking his head. "I don't understand. An affair? Surely Gail would have told me."

"Maybe she was embarrassed," Kenzie suggested. "Nobody likes to admit their husband is having an affair."

He nodded abstractly. "Yes, but still..."

"There weren't any cracks in their marriage?"

"No, not at all. They seemed happy."

"Appearances can be deceiving," she murmured, remembering what Marcy had told her about the couple's sex life.

Nick sat upright in his chair. "This Marcy, who is she, and how did you find her?"

"Her telephone number was on Jacob's desk," she said. "I found it that day we were in his study."

Nick fell silent.

"I asked Gail who Marcy was, if you remember? She said she didn't know."

"Then she didn't. He must have kept it from her."

Kenzie nodded.

Nick shook his head, as if trying to wake himself up. "You said Jacob was with her the night he vanished. Do you think she had anything to do with his disappearance?" Nick's scrutinizing gaze probed her. "Maybe they were planning on running away together."

"That's not the impression I got," Kenzie told him. "She was as worried about him as you and Gail are."

He grunted, as if that couldn't possibly be true. That some other woman couldn't feel for Jacob the way his sister did.

"There is something else," Kenzie said, watching his hesitant gaze turn toward her.

"What?"

"Marcy seemed to think he'd had a curse put on him."

"A curse?" Nick spluttered. "Is she crazy?"

Kenzie paused to smile. "I don't think so, no. Jacob received a doll, a voodoo doll, the day he disappeared. Apparently, he found it on his front porch."

"Gail didn't mention it."

"Maybe she didn't know about it. Gail said the doorbell rang, remember? There was nobody there. The package could have been left then."

Nick folded his arms across his chest. "I guess so," he admitted.

"He showed it to Marcy, though." Kenzie didn't mention the pin sticking out of the doll's heart.

"Who would put a curse on him?" Nick asked.

"That is what we need to find out." Kenzie leaned forward. "Jacob was afraid of someone, that much is obvious. It supports your theory that he may have gone into hiding."

Even though Marcy thought he was dead, Kenzie was trying to be optimistic – if only for Nick and Gail's sake. Until they knew different, there was no point in assuming the worst.

Nick sighed. "Okay, so he's on the run. Someone's after him. This curse... Do you think it was done to scare him?"

"That would be the obvious conclusion."

Nick gave a stiff nod. "I need to speak to Gail. If what you say is true, if Jacob was having an affair, there might be things she hasn't told us."

"I agree," Kenzie said. "I'll leave that to you. She's much more likely to open up if I'm not there."

He nodded, a forlorn expression on his face. "I'll go and see her after work."

She was about to reach out and pat his hand, then thought better of it. "I'm sorry it's not better news, Nick."

He got slowly to his feet, as if a weight was pressing down on him. "That's okay. I know you're just doing what I asked you to. I don't know what I expected, but it wasn't this."

"Call me later," she said.

"Will do."

Kenzie sat and watched him through the tall glass window as he walked back to his Porsche.

Detective Diaz, with Officer Martinez in the passenger seat beside her, pulled over outside a store called Degi Botanica. It was the fifth voodoo shop they'd visited that morning and the last one in Little Haiti.

"It's tiny," Martinez remarked, climbing out of the police car and staring at the little pink building. An old-fashioned lamp post was attached to the front of the store from which hung weathered bamboo chimes. A bright mural on the side wall depicted a woman in a blue gown wearing a crown. She was holding a baby, who had a golden halo around his head. Diaz was Catholic, so she recognized the iconology. Next to the familiar figures, however, was another woman, this time with wild gray hair and huge eyes. She wore a pale green robe and had flowers in her hair. Diaz had no idea who that was.

Diaz glanced up and down the street. There was nothing there. The store stood alone on a five-hundred-yard stretch of vacant road. The property to the right was a residence, set back from the road, while on the left was a precast concrete wall, beyond which was a playground. Also deserted.

"Creepy," Martinez said. On cue, the breeze picked up and the wind chimes outside the store tinkled ominously.

"Come on. This is the last one." Diaz headed towards the front door. They'd been at it for hours, driving around, enquiring whether the store owners recognized the victim, or the charm he wore. So far, none of them had.

"Why would they talk to us anyway?" Martinez asked. "We're the police. Nobody talks to the police anymore."

It was true. Witnesses were more likely to turn a blind eye or run the other way when they saw them coming. That was the problem with modern policing. There was no trust. "I know, but we have to try."

Focusing on the little pink store, she said, "Come on, let's go talk to the owner."

There was no buzzer, so Diaz rattled the chimes. "Hello?"

"It looks empty," said Martinez, peering through the window. Inside, they could see a display of statues and religious figurines, but the light wasn't on, and the interior was in darkness.

Diaz called out again, then giving up, walked around the side of the building. It didn't take long, the place was so small.

"Hey there!" A humped back woman sat on an upturned bucket, sliding beads onto a length of thread. The woman sat at an angle, so all they could see was her silver hair, her gnarled hands as she worked with the beads, and her stooped back. Perhaps she was the lady in the wall mural.

"Excuse me." Diaz tried again. Still no reaction.

She walked around so she was in the woman's line of sight. "Hello there."

The woman jolted as if she'd been hit by lightning. The bowl toppled over, and beads scattered over the ground like tiny marbles.

"Oh my God." She fell to her knees to rescue the beads, then looked up. "You scared me half to death."

"I'm sorry. We did call to you." Diaz bent down to help the woman collect the beads. Officer Martinez did the same.

"What is it you want?" the woman asked, nodding gratefully as they scooped up handfuls of beads and dropped them back into the bowl. She had a slow, articulate way of speaking, over pronouncing every word. "You want to find a lover?"

Officer Martinez giggled. Diaz did not.

"No, thank you." She didn't ask how the woman knew she was single. "We need your help to locate someone."

The woman was staring at her mouth. "Speak slower, girl. Can't you see I'm deaf."

Diaz realized the woman was lip reading. "Oh, I'm sorry. I didn't realize. I'm looking for this man." She stopped picking up beads and showed the woman a photograph of the victim.

The woman froze, her eyes fixed on the picture. "He's dead, isn't he?"

"Yes." It was one of the photos taken at the crime scene. They didn't have any others. "I'm sorry about how he looks." The pallor, the bulging eyes, and terrified expression were not easy to see.

"Not an easy death," she whispered.

"No. He was murdered." Diaz watched the woman for a reaction, but she shook her head.

"It was forecast."

"Excuse me?" Diaz frowned, but Officer Martinez scuttled back.

The woman glanced up. "You know Voodoo?"

Officer Martinez gave a scared nod. "My auntie practiced."

Diaz pointed to the photograph. "Do you recognize the amulet around his neck?"

The old woman glanced at it but didn't reply.

"Did you give him the gris-gris?" asked Officer Martinez.

The woman rocked back and forth on her knees, as if trying to decide. Eventually, she gave a stiff nod. "This man came to me. He asked for protection against the spirits. I told him Voodoo is very powerful for those who believe."

"Did he believe?" asked Martinez.

The old woman stroked the photograph. "Not enough."

"When was he here?" Diaz got back to the particulars of the investigation.

The woman thought for a moment. "Last week... Thursday," she said after crinkling up her forehead. "That's it. I remember because he was waiting for me when I opened shop. Begged for my help. I've never seen anyone so desperate."

"Did he say why he needed this gris-gris?" Diaz asked.

The woman tutted. "A curse, of course. He said there was a curse cast on him."

"What kind of curse?" Diaz asked.

The woman stared at her with rheumy eyes. "The worst kind. The death curse."

8

KENZIE SAT in her car outside the entrance to the yacht club and checked her reflection in the rearview mirror. Heavily made-up eyes stared back at her. Guileless, wide, and very blue. A flush of coral accentuated her cheekbones, while strawberry gloss shimmered on her lips. She smiled to herself. It was perfect.

As a journalist, Kenzie often went undercover to get a story. Pretending to be someone else came easily to her. Too easily. Tonight, she was Marcy Guerrier. Sales assistant and Jacob Peters' mistress. After all, he'd invited her to this event, hadn't he? She was to meet him here. That's what she'd tell anyone who asked, anyway.

Jacob had told Marcy this was a work event. A fancy one. So Kenzie wore a floor-length sapphire blue designer gown that glittered as she walked. It would be impossible not to attract attention. Her only jewelry was a pair of diamante studs that glittered in her ears. No one needed to know they weren't the real deal.

This wasn't the first time she'd visited the Acacia Yacht Club. Elitist, expensive and filled with egotistical boat owners, but tonight she was here to suck up to them. To befriend Jacob's boss, Felix Hammond. "He's tall, silver-haired and always impeccably dressed,"

Gail had told Nick, who'd passed the information on to Kenzie. That didn't narrow it down much. Not in a place like this.

She'd done some research on the Florida businessman before she'd come out tonight. Turned out he owned several companies, mostly in shipping and logistics, but there was also an impressive industrial property portfolio. Hammond Holdings, the umbrella company, was a monster.

Kenzie draped a pale blue pashmina over her shoulders and got out of the car. She walked the remaining distance to the front door where a liveried doorman gave her the once over. "I'm meeting my partner inside," she told him, flashing a dimpled smile.

He nodded, his gaze going straight to her cleavage, before waving her in.

"Thanks." Sometimes having breasts had its advantages.

After calling the yacht club, Kenzie had discovered the event started at seven-thirty, and it was now nearly eight. Most of the guests were already inside, judging by the laughter and the clinking of glasses emanating from the large bar area off the hall.

Last time she'd been here it was with Don Ingleman, the infamous loan shark. That hadn't ended too well for either of them. She shivered when she thought how close she'd come to... Well, she didn't want to go there.

Shrugging off the thought, she glided through the well-heeled crowd toward the bar. A waiter intercepted her. "Champagne?"

She took a glass but didn't sip from it. Instead, she scanned the partygoers, none of whom she recognized. Breathing a sigh of relief, she relaxed. Her cover was intact.

"She's a forty-footer. A real little beauty." A deep voice rose over the noise. Kenzie turned toward it and saw a group of four men, beers in hand, listening avidly to what one silver haired gentleman was saying. Tall, distinguished, and wearing a signet ring on his left little finger.

Felix Hammond.

She brushed past, making sure they noticed her, then went to stand alone by the window. One sip of champagne later and the youngest of the four men had approached her. "I don't believe I know you?"

He had a smooth, tanned face, with hard eyes and designer stubble to conceal a weak chin. She smiled and held out her hand. "Marcy Guerrier. And you are?"

"Milo Hammond. It's a pleasure to meet you, Marcy. Do you work for one of our companies?"

She laughed. "Oh no. I'm meeting my partner, Jacob Peters. You haven't seen him, have you? It's not like him to be this late." Kenzie thought she saw the man start, but he covered it well.

"Jacob? Well, well." He smiled softly to himself. "No, I don't think he's here yet. Allow me to keep you company while you wait."

"Thank you." There was a pause as Kenzie sipped from her glass.

"How long have you known Jacob?" Milo's appreciative gaze roamed over her body.

"Ten months or so," she said casually. "I'm sure you know he's married."

Milo grinned. "I had heard, yes."

She shrugged. "His wife doesn't like to go out."

"Lucky for you," Milo drawled. "So what do you do, Miss Guerrier?"

"Marcy, please." Another smile, this time she allowed it to reach her eyes. "I'm a sales assistant. I work at a luxury clothing store."

"I'd have thought you were a model with a figure like that."

A chuckle. "You're sweet." They locked eyes. Kenzie glanced away first, giving him the victory. "I wonder where Jacob's got to."

"Perhaps he's stood you up?" Milo asked, hopefully.

"Oh no. Not Jacob. He's a man of his word, as I'm sure you know."

"Yes, yes of course."

"Do you work closely together?" Kenzie asked.

Milo cleared his throat. "You could say that. I'm his boss."

"Oh, gosh. I'm so sorry. You must think me very rude. I thought Mr. Hammond, your father, was his boss."

"My father is everybody's boss," he said dryly.

"Including yours?" Her eyes sparkled as she took another sip of champagne.

"I'm afraid so." Milo watched her, his gaze on her mouth now. "I wonder why Jacob never mentioned you?"

"Oh, come on," she gushed. "I'm sure you can guess the answer to that one."

He smiled slyly. "I suppose. Even so, I wouldn't want to keep you a secret."

Kenzie gave an enigmatic smile. "Not all secrets are bad."

Milo put a hand on the small of her back. "Indeed."

A band started playing at the other end of the bar. Soon, the entire place would become a dance floor. Alcohol was flowing and everyone around them was having a good time.

At half past eight, Kenzie sighed. "You were right. It looks like he's not coming."

"I'm sorry."

"Perhaps I'll call him." She glanced at Milo from under her eyelashes. "He doesn't like it, but I really am getting a little concerned."

"By all means." Milo extended a hand, then moved away to rejoin his father. Kenzie didn't want to stop quizzing him, but she couldn't appear too clingy. Besides, it was an obvious thing to do if your date didn't arrive.

Going out into the hallway, she rang Jacob's number. As expected, there was no answer. Frustrated – in case anyone was watching – she hung up and returned to the bar. "I'd like a vodka sour," she told the barman. He mixed the drink, then poured it into a glass over some ice.

"No luck?" Milo was behind her, his breath warm on her neck.

"No. I just got his voicemail." Her tone made it clear she was annoyed. "I can't understand it. He said to meet him here. He knows I don't know anybody."

"That's not true," drawled Milo, his dark eyes flashing. "You know me."

She met his gaze. It was time to start reeling him in. "Not really, but I'd like to. Why don't you tell me about yourself?" With one look, the atmosphere changed.

Milo drew closer. "What would you like to know?"

"What part of the business do you run?" She swirled the cocktail around in her glass.

"Shipping. I'm in charge of imports and exports," he told her, reaching into his pocket for a business card. "This is me."

She glanced at it with an arched eyebrow. "Director. I'm impressed."

"Not hard. It is a family run business."

She laughed. "True. I guess Jacob reports directly to you?"

"Yes, Jacob handles the accounts for my part of the business. We have a team of accountants, of course, but he's in charge of our shipping accounts."

"Lucky Jacob." Her voice was huskier than it had been.

He chuckled, and she allowed herself a small grin.

"You know why I like you, Kenzie?" Keith, her editor, had asked her once. "You know how to play the game." And playing she was.

"Would you care to dance?" Milo asked, taking the drink out of her hand and placing it on the bar. Clearly, he wasn't taking no for an answer.

"Sure." She felt his hand press into the small of her back. "Why not?"

They were halfway to the dance floor when the tall silver fox intercepted them. "I don't believe we've met," said the fox, extending a hand. "Felix Hammond."

"This is Marcy Guerrier," Milo said with a flash of annoyance. Relations with his father were strained, then.

"Marcy Guerrier?" His forehead scrunched. "Why is that name familiar?"

Why indeed, Kenzie thought.

"She's Jacob Peters' date," Milo replied, his dark eyes fixed on his father.

"Jacob. Is he here?" He glanced around expectantly. Very good, thought Kenzie. The old man hadn't missed a beat. Of course, he might have nothing to do with Jacob's disappearance, but it was her job to suspect everyone. That's what made her a good reporter. She never took anything, or anyone, at face value.

"He's not." She shook his hand. "It appears he stood me up."

"I'm sorry to hear that," Felix said with a tilt of his head. "I hope you'll enjoy yourself anyway."

"I'm not," Milo broke in. "We're going to dance. See you later." And before the fox could utter another word, Milo had guided her away.

9

Reid got the call as he was about to leave the station. It was late, the night sky already littered with stars, and his eyes felt like they were sticking to the back of his head. It had been a long day and all he wanted to do was go back to the motel, take a hot shower, and fall into bed.

Diaz and Martinez had come back with talk of a death curse, and Vargas was buying into it. "Curses do not kill people," Reid had retorted angrily. "People do."

The sooner they found out who, the better. This case was getting ridiculous. Voodoo curses. High priestesses. What nonsense. He'd sent them home at five, preferring to write his reports and catch up on paperwork in peace. The only other person at the station had been Dwayne, who was on night duty this week.

His phone buzzed. "Garrett."

"Detective Garrett, this is Control. We have a 10-54 at JT's Bar and Grill in Wynwood."

Jesus.

A 10-54 was a possible dead body. "Any sign of life?"

"No, sir. The officer on the scene says it looks like it's just happened. She's in a dumpster."

"Okay, get the medical examiner and CSI team over there. I'm on my way."

He rang Vargas, but the detective didn't pick up. That was strange. He usually answered on the first ring. Then again, yesterday had been his engagement party, and he'd knocked off pretty early today. Diaz had a family thing, so he called Hamilton. The rookie officer was eager to help, despite the late hour. "I'll meet you there, boss."

Reid glanced up as he ran to his pickup. He was going home afterwards, so he didn't take the squad car. The air was heavy with moisture. Rain clouds hovered, blocking out the crescent moon. It was going to pour down, and Reid wanted to get to the crime scene before that happened.

Wheels spinning, he shot out of the precinct parking lot and sped down the street, siren screaming. The roads were relatively empty, given that it was almost midnight, but Miami never really slept. JT's Bar and Grill was situated on a wide avenue, set back from the street. A crowd had gathered outside.

Shit.

He hoped the officer on duty had cordoned off the area where the body was.

"Detective Garrett." He flashed his badge at the first police officer he saw. "Where is the body?"

"Round the back, sir," the man said, his expression somber.

The dumpsters were always round the back. Reid walked down a wide alley beside the restaurant, studying the group of diners. No one stood out as suspicious. "Take down everybody's name and a contact number," he told the officer standing by a cordon. At least they'd had the sense to block off the crime scene. "That'll get rid of them."

The officer nodded and took out a notebook. Reid didn't stay to watch. He ducked under the plastic tape and approached the area where the dumpsters were kept. The smell hit him first. Sweet and pungent like rotting fruit. It permeated the air as if to deter coming any closer. Reid shook hands with the officer guarding the body. "You were here first?"

"Yeah. Officer Brosner."

"Detective Garrett." He glanced behind the officer to the dumpster. "She still inside?"

"Yeah, I was told not to touch her."

"Sound advice." Reid peered into the metal refuse container, wrinkling his nose. There she was. Pale and placid amongst the piles of offcuts, potato peels, and decaying leftovers, but her eyes... He frowned. Huge, wide, and terrified. Her dark hair spread around her, tangled with what looked like spaghetti and banana skins. "What time did you find her?"

"The restaurant manager called me at quarter past ten," Officer Brosner said. "Apparently, the kid who washes dishes and takes out the trash found her. He's inside with an officer."

"Okay, and why do you think it's recent?"

"The kid said she was still inside at nine when he took his smoke break."

Good. That would help them pinpoint the time of death. They'd have to get the kid's statement.

"All right. Forensics are on their way, and once they're done, we can get her out of there."

The victim was dressed like any other young waitress in jeans and a white shirt. She still had her apron on. It was red and tied around her waist.

"Who is she?" he asked.

"The manager identified her as Sonia Del Ray. She works here several nights a week."

Sonia. Reid grimaced as he studied her young, slender body. What a waste. He scanned her body for injuries but couldn't see any. There were no bruises around her neck, indicative of strangulation. No blood anywhere, so they could rule out a stabbing or gunshot wound. He needed to turn her over. Where was the forensics team?

On cue, he heard a cacophony of sirens and the CSI unit arrived, along with the medical examiner, an austere woman with a military bearing. Reid didn't know this one. Two portable ladders were positioned against the dumpster and a crime scene investigator climbed up to inspect the body. "We won't find much here. Too much contamination."

The ME nodded in agreement. "Let's get her out and then I'll swab her for DNA." Reid watched as Sonia the waitress was lifted out of her smelly resting place.

"We're going to need the contents of this dumpster," another CSI officer said. "Someone's going to have to go through it." Reid was glad he wasn't that someone.

Sonia was laid on a plastic sheet on the potholed ground. Those eyes... The terrified look reminded him of the man they'd found in the glades. A chill shot down his spine.

"Any sign of injury?" he asked the ME, who was kneeling beside the young woman's body. Hamilton arrived and nodded to Reid. Together, they watched as she checked for a pulse. Protocol. It was obvious the waitress was dead. Next, she leaned forward and inspected her neck, then down her arms, and finally her hands.

"No defensive wounds," she remarked, turning her hand over. "There is faint scarring on her inner arms indicative of self-harming."

"Really?" That was interesting.

"They're old though. I'd say at least ten years."

Reid studied the victim's smooth skin, wavy brown hair and lithe body. Early twenties, he guessed. The scarring must have happened when she was very young. "Does she have ID on her?" That would confirm her age.

"Not that I can find," replied the ME, patting her jean pockets. "There's not even a wallet."

"If she worked here, her personal belongings must be inside," Hamilton said. "I'll go and check." He gave the dead waitress a lingering glance, and then headed for the back entrance of the restaurant.

The ME continued to inspect Sonia's body. She felt her ribs, her abdomen and then glanced up at one of the forensic officers. "Help me turn her over." Still wearing gloves, the nearest officer put his hands under the victim's rib cage and together, they rolled her over. "No entry wounds on her back," the ME said.

Reid frowned. "So how'd she die?"

The ME felt the back of her head. "Ah, head wound." Her glove came away bloody. "It's not that deep, I'm surprised it killed her, but there's no other obvious cause of death. I'll know more when I get her back to the lab."

"Could it be drugs?" Reid asked.

The ME inspected the victim's eyes. "I can't see any of the obvious signs of an overdose. She might have been poisoned, but I won't know for sure until I do a tox screen." The sinking feeling deepened. It was just like their other victim. Reid ran a hand through his hair and stared at her face. Two unexplained deaths. Two terrified victims. What were the chances?

"Can we at least close her eyes?" he asked.

The ME nodded and swept her hand over the victim's eyelids. Reid breathed a sigh of relief. "Why did she look so scared?"

"It could be the shock of dying," the ME said with a shrug. "Or she saw something that terrified her before she died."

"Which do you think it is?" Reid glanced up at her.

"The latter."

Reid gave a curt nod. That's what he'd been afraid of.

10

"Do you want to get out of here?" Milo's dark eyes bored into Kenzie's. Her conscience was telling her not to, but then again, if she always listened to her conscience, she wouldn't be where she was today. Still, it might be too obvious if she went home with a man she'd only just met, even if she had no intention of sleeping with him. Her boyfriend's boss, to boot. It would be better if she played it cool.

Milo sensed her hesitation and misinterpreted it. "You'll be pleased you did."

A loud guffaw made her glance up. Sitting at the bar, accompanied by his latest supermodel girlfriend, was the unmistakable form of Salvatore Del Gatto. The Italian-born businessman was even richer than Felix Hammond. It made sense they'd know each other.

The problem was, he knew her.

Or rather, he knew Kenzie Gilmore, the reporter who'd accused Congressman Leonard of cavorting with prostitutes and taking drugs onboard his superyacht. Del Gatto might not recognize her after all this time, but she couldn't take the chance.

"Thanks for the offer, but I'm going to pass." She smiled apologetically, and made her way to the door, careful to keep her back to the billionaire. "I've got an early start tomorrow."

Her dance partner blinked as if he hadn't understood what she'd said. Kenzie got the impression Milo Hammond wasn't used to women turning him down.

"Another time then?" He followed her outside.

"Sure." She was counting on it. Kenzie let her gaze linger on his. "I'd like that."

"You've got my card."

She patted her purse. "I certainly do. Thank you for a lovely evening, and for coming to my rescue."

"Jacob's loss was my gain." He kissed her on the cheek, his lips warm and lingering. She flashed him an enticing smile, then sauntered down the stairs back to her car, aware of his eyes on her back as she went.

"Up to your old tricks, I see."

Kenzie spun around. "Carlisle! Holy crap. You scared me half to death. What are you doing here?"

"Same thing you are, apparently." He gave a wolfish grin. "Extorting information from the Hammond family."

"I–I don't know what you mean."

"Oh, please. Don't give me that, young lady. I know you too well, Kenzie Gilmore, or should I call you Marcy?" He raised an eyebrow.

She sighed. It was pointless hiding anything from Carlisle. Somehow, he always knew everything about everyone. The middle-aged broker specialized in negotiating deals on behalf of his very wealthy and well-connected clients. There were no lines he wouldn't cross. No deal too controversial. He was also a source, and one of her better ones. In return, she published little snippets of information he wanted fed to the public. She had the power to raise a public profile or cast doubt on a rival bidder. A powerful tool for a man like Carlisle. They used each other. It was a symbiotic relationship and Kenzie planned to keep it that way. That's why she never asked questions. It was better if she didn't know.

"Okay, I'm looking into a missing man," she admitted. "I think his boss might have something to do with his disappearance."

"And going home with a suspect is your idea of smart, is it?"

"I wasn't going to go home with him," she hissed.

"Admit it, you thought about it."

"No, I just wanted him to think I was."

Carlisle smiled.

"Besides, if I'm too keen he'll get suspicious."

The broker shook his head. "Kenzie, what are we going to do with you?"

She gave a little shrug. "You know I can look after myself. Now, it's your turn. What do you know about the Hammonds?"

"A lot, but all I'm going to say is these are not nice people. You'd do well to stay clear."

"In what way? Are they involved in something illegal?"

He gave an enigmatic smile. "Kenzie, dear, you know I don't kiss and tell. Just be careful. If they find out you're not who you say you are, there could be consequences."

"What kind of consequences? Like making someone disappear?"

His eyes hardened. "I wouldn't rule anything out."

She frowned. "Can I ask you a question?"

"Sure, although I can't promise to answer."

"Let's say, hypothetically speaking, you're the Hammonds' accountant."

"Risky business." That knowing smile.

"And you found out something you shouldn't."

He frowned. "Like what?"

"Oh, I don't know. Embezzlement, money laundering, that sort of thing."

"That would be dangerous," Carlisle confirmed.

"What if you threatened to go to the police about it?"

He deepened his voice. "Very dangerous."

"Life threatening?"

"Quite possibly. Kenzie, what are you into?"

She exhaled. "Not me. Someone else. I'm just trying to find out what happened."

"Be careful," he warned. "I mean that. The Hammonds are not the kind of people you want as enemies."

"I get it. Don't worry, I'll be fine. Thank you for your input."

At least she knew what type of people she was dealing with. If what Carlisle said was true, it was possible they had something to do with Jacob's disappearance.

"It's always a pleasure, Kenzie. You take care now." And Carlisle withdrew into the shadows, leaving her staring thoughtfully after him.

11

Reid prowled up the road on which JT's Bar and Grill was located, looking for CCTV cameras. There weren't any. Wynwood was a good area, but it wasn't a great area. You'd think someone would have some surveillance somewhere.

"Anything?" he asked Hamilton, who'd just returned.

"I found her bag," he said. "Sonia Del Ray is twenty years old. She's been working at the restaurant for five months. She's a nice girl, a good waitress, and doesn't talk back. Kept to herself, though. Didn't have many friends. Nobody seemed to know her well."

Interesting. Still, she'd only been there five months.

"Got her address?"

"Yeah." He patted his pocket.

"Good."

"What about you?" Hamilton asked. "Any CCTV?"

"Nah, not even the drug store has a surveillance camera."

"Pity." Hamilton shook his head. "The dumpster's not visible from the street, but we might have seen who arrived around the time of the murder."

"What did the staff say? Anyone see anything?"

"Not much," he replied. "The manager thought she'd walked out in the middle of her shift, although he didn't check the back for her purse."

"What about the kid who found the body?" Reid asked.

"He's pretty cut up about it. Poor guy is only seventeen and never saw a dead person before." That was tough.

"When last did he see Sonia?"

"She was still there when he went on his smoke break at nine o'clock. She must have disappeared sometime after that, but he doesn't know when. It was busy, and he didn't see her leave."

Reid studied the outside of the restaurant. The neon sign saying JT's Bar and Grill flashed jauntily as if nothing had happened. "Doesn't anyone around here believe in security?" he grumbled.

"I guess they never needed it before."

Reid leaned against his truck. "We've got nothing to go on."

"We've got her address," Hamilton said. "We could start there." It was the obvious place to begin.

"Someone lured her outside," he said, surveying the restaurant side of the street. "Then they hit her on the head and dumped her body in the trash."

"What do you make of those cuts on her arms?" Hamilton asked, as Reid turned around to scan the other side of the road.

"Traumatic childhood, neglect, some sort of mental health or eating disorder, who knows? There could be any number of reasons."

"We should speak to her parents," Hamilton said, and for the first time, Reid thought he detected a touch of weariness in his colleague's voice.

Enough messing around here. He pushed himself away from the pickup and gave a curt nod. "Yeah, let's go. They need to know she's dead." It couldn't wait until the morning.

A shadow at one of the darkened windows on the opposite side of the road caught his eye.

"Did you see that?"

Hamilton looked around. "What?"

"I'll be right back." Reid took off across the road. The figure disappeared, the blinds hurriedly pulled back into place. He marched up the steps and knocked on the front door. "Police, open up." When there was no answer, he knocked again. "Hello? I saw you at the window. I'd like to ask you a few questions."

After a couple of minutes, the front door opened a few inches. A middle-aged woman in her nightgown peered out at him.

"Good evening, ma'am," Reid said, forcing a smile. "I noticed you at the window. Do you mind if I ask you a few questions?" He showed her his ID badge, holding it steady so she could read it in the dim light.

The woman hesitated. Reid guessed she was wary of the cops. "It won't take long," he insisted. Wordlessly, she held the door open so he could enter.

Reid walked into a dark hallway. He suspected she'd purposely not turned on the light, so she'd see him better outside. "Is there somewhere we can sit down?" he asked.

She pointed to the living room off the hallway. The carpets were threadbare and the furniture worn. Still, he took a seat on an old armchair and waited for her to do the same. Stiff shoulders, back upright, hands clasped in her lap. This woman was clearly uncomfortable with him being here.

"I'll make this quick," he began, hoping she'd relax a little. "I don't know if you're aware, but a woman was murdered across the road earlier tonight. A waitress at JT's Bar and Grill."

"I heard." Her dark eyes were fixed on him.

"Since your house faces the street where the restaurant is located, I was wondering if you happened to see anything suspicious?"

She frowned. "What do you mean by suspicious?"

"Anyone coming and going from the alley, any confrontation in the street, anything unusual." He was betting this woman knew what was usual around here.

"I didn't see who killed her," she said, but there was a hesitation. Slight, but noticeable. Reid took a sharp intake of breath.

"But you saw something?"

"I don't know if it's got anything to do with who killed her," she said, shrinking into herself.

"If you saw something, ma'am, please tell me. It could be important," Reid pushed.

The woman hesitated. "I saw someone in the parking lot. He was dressed all in black, that's why I noticed him."

Reid felt his pulse escalate. "What time was this?"

"I don't know. I'd just finished washing up, so maybe about nine-thirty."

The timing fit.

"Could you describe this man?"

"I just told you, he was dressed all in black, with the hood up. I didn't see his face."

Damnit.

Reid ground his teeth. "But you're sure it was a man?"

A small shrug. "I think so. He was quite tall. Looked like a man to me."

Reid fished for more information, trying to jog her memory. "Did he arrive on foot or was he driving a car or a bike?"

"He was walking. I didn't see no car."

"Did you see him leave?"

"No, sir. After that, I went upstairs to check on my granddaughter. She's seven and her mama works nights."

"I see. Could you excuse me for one moment?"

She nodded as he went back into the hallway to make a call.

Hamilton answered immediately. "Yeah?"

"Could you check if any of the employees are dressed in black, including a hood? I have an eyewitness report of a man entering the premises around nine-thirty and want to rule out any of the staff."

"Understood."

Reid walked back into the living room. "Thank you very much, Mrs.—?" he stopped, waiting for her to give her name.

"Lewis. Verity Lewis."

"Thank you, Mrs. Lewis. You've been very helpful. This is my card. If you think of anything else, give me a call." She gave a cautious nod as she took the card, then showed him to the door.

"I hope you find who did this," she said as he left.

"We'll certainly try, ma'am. You have my word on that."

"None of the wait staff are dressed in black," Hamilton said a short time later. They're told to wear white shirts while on shift." The dark skies were rumbling. Any moment it was going to pour.

"You're sure? You checked everyone."

"Everyone who's there," he confirmed. "I even went through the jackets and tops in the office. Nothing that matches your witness' description."

"Okay, good work," Reid said, his anticipation building. "That means that stranger in black could be our killer."

"Did the woman give a description?" Hamilton asked.

"No, she didn't see his face."

"Bad luck."

Reid didn't want to dwell on it. It was a start. "I'll go talk to the dead girl's parents. Do you have their address?"

"I have the victim's address," Hamilton said. "But I haven't been able to track down her parents. I need to go back to the station for that."

"Okay, you do that while I check out her place."

"You don't want me to come with you?"

"No, we need to notify her parents."

"Okay, boss. See you back at the station."

Sonia Del Ray lived on NW 14th Street, close to the Jackson Memorial Hospital. It was nearly two in the morning when Reid pulled up outside a mustard yellow two-story building. Through the gloom, he could make out several identical buildings and realized it was part of a condo complex.

He climbed out of the car and stared at the numbers on the wall, looking for 4B. A fine drizzle made him glance up. Great. Here it comes, he thought. Sure enough, there was an almighty crash from above and the sky pulsed with lightening.

The drizzle turned into a downpour, and before long, he was soaked. The first block was 1A, and he realized 1B must be upstairs. Ducking between buildings, he searched for number four. There it was, right at the back.

Reid smoothed a hand over his hair, squeezing out the water as he sheltered in the stairwell. It smelled faintly of urine. Leaving a puddle beneath him, he took the steps up to apartment 4B. No lights at the windows, but that wasn't unusual for this time of night.

He rang the doorbell. When nobody answered, he knocked on it, hard. Still no answer. Sonia Del Ray must live alone. He was about to turn away when he heard a shuffling inside. Turning back, he waited on the doorstep.

A hall light came on and then footsteps. Finally, the front door opened, but only a crack. The chain was still on. "Who's there?" asked a female voice.

He held up his ID badge. "It's Detective Garrett from the Sweetwater Police Department. Who are you?"

"Gracie Pulman. Why?" All he could make out were the whites of her eyes.

"Do you know Sonia Del Ray?"

"Yes, I'm her roommate. Has something happened to Sonia?"

"I'm afraid so," he said. "Do you mind if we talk?"

"Oh no. I hope it's nothing serious." The chain was removed, and Sonia's roommate opened the door. As expected, she'd been sleeping and wore a pair of bright pink pajamas with a cartoon character on the front. "What's happened to Sonia?"

"I'm afraid she was murdered this evening."

"What?" Gracie wobbled and clutched the door handle. "You mean she's... dead?"

"Yes."

Her face crumpled. "Oh my God. I can't believe it."

He felt bad for his blunt delivery. In his defense, it had been a hell of a long day. "I'm sorry to have to tell you like this."

"But... but how? What happened?"

"We found her body earlier this evening outside the restaurant where she worked."

Gracie put a hand over her mouth.

"Are you okay?" Reid asked, thinking she might be sick.

"No, I'm not okay." She stumbled into the living room and collapsed on the sofa. Reid closed the door and followed. He noticed the medical equipment on the dining table. "Are you a nurse?" he said.

She nodded. "Yeah, I work at the hospital."

"And Sonia lived here with you?"

"That's right. She moved in about five months ago." Same time as she started work at the restaurant.

"Did you know her prior to that?" Reid asked, curious as to how long they'd known each other.

"No, she responded to an ad I put in the paper. She seemed nice. Quiet, you know? I liked that about her."

"Do you know if she has family?" Reid asked. "We're trying to locate her parents."

"They're both dead," Gracie said. The color was slowly coming back to her cheeks. "Sonia told me they died when she was very young." That would explain why they couldn't trace them.

"I think she might have a brother, though."

"Oh yeah? Do you have an address for him?" He took out a small notepad.

"No, sorry. She mentioned him once, but I got the impression they weren't close. He didn't come to the apartment. I've never met him."

Reid nodded, putting it back in his pocket. "What about a boyfriend?"

Gracie shook her head. "Like I said, she was very quiet. When she wasn't waitressing, she made clothes and sold them at flea markets. She was quite a talented seamstress."

That was news. "Do you mind if I take a look at her room?"

"Sure, no problem."

Gracie led the way to a closed door off the hallway. The apartment wasn't very big, with a galley kitchen and a small bathroom that both women shared.

"Could I ask... Could I ask how she died?" Gracie hovered at the door, watching him search the room.

"We don't know yet," he admitted. She gave a little nod, then to his relief, left him to it.

Reid glanced around the room. On the one side was a table with a sewing machine on it and several offcuts of material. In a box were scissors, machine needles and other sewing paraphernalia. A few clothing items hung on hangers around the room. A bohemian style dress and a flouncy blouse trimmed with lace hung in front of a denim jacket with embroidered patches on it. He didn't know anything about fashion, but they looked to be well made. At some point in her short life, Sonia had learned to sew.

Reid walked over to the dresser. It had the usual feminine items scattered on top of it. Makeup, face cream, hairbrush and mirror. Nothing out of the ordinary. No notes, no letters, no computer.

Reid walked back out into the hall to find Gracie. She was sitting on the couch, her legs curled underneath her. He thought she'd been crying. "Did Sonia have a laptop?"

"No, she was never online. I don't think she even had a social media account."

"That's strange, isn't it?" Reid asked. "For someone her age?"

A sniff. "Not everyone is into social media."

True. "What about her behavior? Was she acting strangely at all, particularly in the last few days?"

"Not that I noticed. We didn't talk much. When she was home, she usually stayed in her room sewing."

"I see." Reid walked back to the bedroom and had one last look around, but he couldn't find a diary, a calendar, or any type of address book with her brother's details. There was nothing that jumped out at him. Deflated, he went back into the lounge. "Thanks for talking to me. I'm sorry to be the bearer of such bad news." He reached into his pocket for another card. "If you hear from her brother, please give me a call." Gracie gave a tearful nod.

Reid turned and walked toward the door.

"Oh, I almost forgot," she said, getting to her feet.

He stopped. "Yeah?"

"This came for her today." Grace squeezed past him and picked up a bulky envelope off the small table in the hall. "She never gets any mail, so I thought it might be important."

"One second." He took a pair of disposable gloves from his jacket pocket and pulled them on. Gracie's eyes widened. "Thanks." He took the envelope and carefully pried the lip open.

Looking inside, his heart skipped a beat. No, it couldn't be. He reached in and pulled out the item. Gracie gasped, while Reid stared in disbelief at what was in his hand.

A voodoo doll. With a pin sticking out of the heart.

12

"KENZIE!" Keith bellowed, his voice carrying over the open plan office. A couple of sympathetic heads turned in her direction.

"Yep?" She poked her head around the door. As usual, his desk was covered with newspapers, documents and used coffee cups. He'd clearly been in a lot longer than she had.

"What do you call this?" He held up her latest article.

"A five-hundred-word piece on Congressman Leonard's Smart Freeway," she retorted. "Why? What's wrong with it?"

He crumpled it and threw it into the wastepaper basket. "Could you at least try to keep the irony out of your tone when you write about him?"

She heaved a dramatic sigh. "He's a corrupt, egotistical, self-centered narcissist. He shouldn't be allowed anywhere near Congress."

"And he's already sued us once, thanks to you," Keith reminded her. "Let's not make it twice."

"Okay, I'll rewrite it."

"Give it to one of the staff reporters if you can't manage an unbiased opinion." He waved an exasperated hand in the air. "This is the *Herald*, not *MAD* Magazine."

Kenzie held back a smile. "That's okay. I'll redo it."

"It's not funny," he retorted. "You're treading a thin line with him – and with me."

"I saw Salvatore Del Gatto yesterday," she said casually, knowing it would get Keith's attention.

His eyebrows instantly shot skyward. "Really? Where?"

"At the Acacia Yacht Club. I was... attending a function with a friend."

It was half true. Keith didn't need to know she was helping Nick look into his brother-in-law's disappearance.

The editor's beady eyes narrowed. "How is everybody's favorite billionaire?"

Salvatore Del Gatto had turned into something of a philanthropist in recent years. Ever since Kenzie's article, he'd changed his ways. Got himself a PR guru and began donating to Florida charities, the Smart Freeway project being one of them. They'd covered it extensively in the Business section of the paper.

Kenzie couldn't wait to delve into the source of those funds, but she'd held back, knowing Keith would blow a gasket if she hinted at any wrongdoing. Until she had absolute proof the two men were engaging in illegal activities, she'd keep her reporter's mouth shut.

"Well. He's making friends and influencing people. He was there with Felix Hammond, do you know him?"

"The shipping magnate?"

"That's the one. He also has a logistics company and an industrial property portfolio." Come to think of it, it was everything a criminal might need to establish a trafficking or smuggling network. The transportation of goods, the ability to bring them into the country, and somewhere to hide them.

And Jacob Peters was his accountant.

Kenzie felt an icy chill slide down her spine.

The Hammonds are not the kind of people you want as enemies.

"If there's nothing else, I'll get back to work." Keith waved her away.

She stopped at Raoul's desk on the way back to her own. "How are you doing on the Congressman's project?"

"He's careful," her research assistant said, glancing up. He had two screens on his desk, in addition to his laptop. One had a continuous news feed running across the bottom, the other, lines of code on a black background flickering across the screen. On his laptop was a Google search results page. How he kept track of so many different things, she had no idea.

It had taken her a while to warm up to Raoul, but ever since he'd helped her uncover the conspiracy behind Maria Lopez's illegitimate child – a stroke of genius on his part – she'd realized how resourceful he was. As a researcher, his skills outshone even hers, and that wasn't something she'd admit easily.

"What about Salvatore Del Gatto?"

"Apart from donating modestly to the cause, he's clean."

"I assure you, he's not." Kenzie rolled her eyes.

"The funds are clean," Raoul rephrased. "The money comes from a legitimate source, and via the charitable branch of his organization."

Kenzie grunted. "What about other sources?"

"I'll keep looking. If there's anything shady going on there, I'll find it."

"There's another name I want you to try," she said softly, glancing at Keith's office to make sure the door was shut.

"Yeah?"

"Felix Hammond."

"Context?" Raoul asked.

"I saw him with Del Gatto recently. I think they might be in bed together."

"Gotcha."

Raoul swiveled around on his chair and got back to work.

While Raoul was looking into Del Gatto, Hammond and Congressman Leonard, Kenzie Googled Marcy Guerrier.

Nothing.

No social media accounts, no passing mentions, and no directory entries. That was weird. Who didn't have a social media presence these days?

Cuba, the woman had said.

Kenzie called a contact who worked at the immigration department. "Stacey, hi, it's Kenzie."

"Kenzie, how are you? How's Sebastian?" Stacey had been his case officer before she'd agreed to foster him.

"He's great," she said. "Settling in really well. I'm so proud of him."

"We're so proud of you. You did a good thing there," Stacey said.

"After what he went through, it was the least I could do," Kenzie replied. "And he's no trouble at all." In fact, he'd saved her life when she'd been attacked, earlier in the year, however she'd never tell them that. She didn't want immigration thinking she'd placed Sebastian in harm's way. "Stacey, I need a favor. I've been given the name of a Cuban immigrant, and I want to check you've got her on file."

"I can't give you any personal information on her," Stacey warned. "No addresses or phone numbers."

"That's okay. Can you check if she's listed? Marcy Guerrier."

"Sure, that I can do. Give me one minute."

Kenzie could hear Stacey tapping away at her keyboard. Eventually, she came back on the phone. "I've found her. Marcia Guerrier. She's in the system."

"Oh, okay." Kenzie bit her lip. She didn't know why she'd thought Marcy had lied. It was just a gut feeling. Turns out she was wrong. "Thanks."

"You said Cuba, right?"

"Yeah?"

"I have her down as coming from Haiti."

Haiti? Kenzie frowned into the phone. Why would Marcy say

she'd come from Cuba, if she'd come from Haiti? It didn't make sense. Unless she was hiding something.

Stacey hesitated, then said, "She arrived last year and claimed asylum. We offered her Temporary Protected Status providing temporary work and relief from deportation. There were special circumstances surrounding her application."

Kenzie felt her pulse tick up a notch.

"What kind of special circumstances?"

There was another pause. "I'm afraid I can't tell you that."

"Was it politically motivated?" Kenzie asked. Special circumstances usually were.

"Yes, but that's all I can say. Her file is classified for her own safety."

That was worrying. What had happened to Marcy in Haiti?

"What about her mother?" Kenzie asked.

"We don't have any information on her mother," Stacey admitted. "Only that she's deceased."

I didn't always feel safe back in my country.

"Sorry I can't be of more help," Stacey said.

"That's okay. You've been great," Kenzie was quick to tell her. She'd just have to get the rest of the story from Marcy herself.

"You're always welcome, Kenzie." They exchanged a few more pleasantries, then said goodbye.

Marcy had lied, but why? That thought occupied Kenzie most of the night. Could Marcy's past have something to do with her lover's disappearance?

And later, a Haitian Voodoo curse is put on her boyfriend? Coincidence? Hmm... She knew what Reid would say about that. Not freaking likely.

Kenzie sighed. This case just got a whole lot more complicated.

13

"There's been a second murder," Reid said, stifling a yawn. He'd been at the station all night, as had Hamilton, although they'd managed to catch a few hours' sleep on the lumpy, second-hand sofa in one of the back offices.

"I'm sorry," Vargas said sheepishly. "I only saw your call this morning."

"It was late," Reid acknowledged. "Don't worry about it." Vargas looked unusually disheveled. His hair was ruffled and his eyes puffy. "You okay?"

"I'm not feeling great today, to be honest. Might be coming down with something."

"Okay, well see how it goes."

Vargas nodded. "What happened last night?"

"Get everyone together, and I'll update the team."

Vargas did as he was told and soon the entire department was gathered in front of the whiteboard. Reid gestured for Hamilton to stand up front with him, while a chagrined Vargas took a seat next to Diaz.

"Morning, everyone. Sonia Del Ray, a twenty-year-old waitress, was found in a dumpster outside JT's Bar and Grill in Wynwood around eleven thirty last night. Time of death was probably between nine-thirty and ten. A staff member saw her when he took a smoke break at nine, so we know she was still alive at that point."

Hamilton nodded. A photograph of Sonia Del Ray stared down at them from the white board. Dyed black hair, haunted eyes, pale skin. It had been taken at the crime scene and didn't do her any favors.

"She had a head wound, but the ME thinks it's unlikely this was the cause of death," Reid said. "There were no other outward signs of an assault. It's possible she was poisoned, but we won't know until we get the autopsy report."

"Just like the other victim," muttered Diaz.

"Yeah, and that's not all," Reid said, his voice deepening. "This was sent to her home address the morning of her death." He reached behind him and held up the voodoo doll housed in a plastic evidence bag.

A muted murmur spread round the room.

Diaz got out of her chair. "Are the two cases related?"

"It's beginning to look that way." Reid turned back to the board, to a photograph of the man found in the glades. The terrified eyes seemed to plead with him. *Find out who did this to me!* He sighed. "We still don't know how our first victim died."

Diaz studied the other crime scene photographs, her eyes narrowing. "Are those scars on her arms?"

"Well spotted, yes. She had a history of self-harming, apparently. Although those scars are quite old and there are no fresh ones, so it seems she wasn't doing it anymore."

"What do we know about her?" Diaz asked.

"Not much," Reid admitted. "Only that she rented a room in Allapattah five months ago and started working at JT's around the same time. Today, I want us to find out everything we can about Sonia Del Ray. Her roommate thinks she had a brother, although she couldn't tell us anything more than that. Let's see if we can track him down."

"What about CCTV?" asked Vargas.

"We checked and there wasn't any on the street," Reid told him with a grimace. "However, a lady across the road thinks she saw a man dressed in black enter the parking lot on foot around nine-thirty. He was wearing a dark sweatshirt with a hood, so she didn't get a good look at him, only to say he appeared suspicious."

"He could be our murderer," said Diaz.

Reid nodded. "If you can pick him up on any of the cameras in surrounding streets, that would be great."

Vargas nodded, eager to make amends. "I'll get on it."

"What about the glades victim?" Reid asked, before he ended the briefing. "Any missing persons reports on him?"

"Nothing," Vargas said with a shrug.

"Someone must miss him," Reid muttered. "Let's keep digging."

Vargas gave a dutiful nod.

The tasks were piling up. "That's it. Let's get to work."

The team filtered back to their desks. Soon, all that could be heard in the squad room was the sound of typing and mouse clicking, with the occasional gasp of the printer as it spat out information that might be useful.

"It's so strange," Hamilton reported, a short time later.

Reid glanced up. "What is?"

His colleague shook his head. "I can't find any reference to Sonia Del Ray prior to five months ago. It's like she didn't exist."

"What do you mean? There must be something."

"I swear, there's nothing." He spread his hands out in front of him. "She applied for a social security number in February, and we have her on the IRA database, but there's nothing before that. No school or college records, no police records."

"Did she change her name?" Reid asked. It was the only thing that made sense.

"Must have. I'll check with the social security agency. If she did change her name, they'll have her previous details on file." He walked back to his desk, scratching his head.

Reid's phone buzzed. "Garrett." He listened, thanked the caller, then hung up. "The autopsy on the glades victim is scheduled for this afternoon," he told Diaz. "I want to be there for that."

"We'll keep working on Sonia," she said.

"Keep me posted. If she changed her name, there must be a reason. We need to know what it is. Could be she was hiding from someone."

"Will do." Diaz turned back to her computer.

The autopsy took place a little after two o'clock that afternoon. Reid grabbed a strong coffee from a nearby pop-up stall and entered the squat, gray morgue building where the lab was based.

It wasn't the cheeriest of buildings, he reflected, as he wound his way down the myriad of corridors to the viewing gallery overlooking the laboratory. The walls were white, bare, and clinical as if any pictures might detract from the awful reality of what went on here. He supposed relatives coming to identify their loved ones didn't want to be calmed by scenic river or mountain shots. They probably wouldn't notice them anyway.

Once seated, he pressed the buzzer and greeted the same medical examiner who'd been at the first crime scene. The diminutive man was suited up, ready to get to work.

The procedure began. Reid watched as the ME inspected the body, starting with the head. He used a surgical magnifier mounted to a stand. "No head wounds," he announced, his voice flat and unemotional.

Not like Sonia. That was one difference between them.

The ME raised the eyelids and inspected the retina. "There is a small amount of petechial hemorrhaging around the eyes," he said, bending in for a closer look. "It's very faint, which is why I didn't notice it before." He tapped the magnifier.

"What does that mean?" Reid asked, although he was familiar with the term.

"It means your victim asphyxiated." The ME glanced up. "But I still don't know what caused it."

"He suffocated?"

"Yes, but he wasn't strangled, and he didn't drown. Those are usually the two main causes of asphyxiation."

"Did someone put a bag over his head, or cover his face?"

"It's possible, although there aren't any indications of that. Usually, we'd see marks around the neck from the bag, or saliva dried at the corners of the mouth. There's none of that."

Reid rubbed his temple. A sleep deprivation headache was setting in. "Did the tox screen come back?"

"We've just got the preliminary one back," the ME said. "I had a quick look at it. There were no known poisons or drugs in his system. I'll check his stomach contents today and take tissue samples, but the bloods showed nothing unusual."

"Damn it," muttered Reid. He'd been sure it was something like that. Still, it might be something uncommon or hard to find, in which case the tissue samples or stomach contents might be more revealing.

"I'll expand the search criteria as well," the ME remarked. "Widen the range, just in case it's one of the rarer toxins." Reid nodded his thanks. The autopsy continued.

"No marks or bruises on his body. No defensive wounds. No cuts or grazes."

Reid gritted his teeth in frustration.

"I'm now going to do the internal examination." He looked at Reid in the gallery from above his glasses. Reid didn't usually stay for this part. Today was an exception. If there was anything there, he wanted to know.

"Go ahead."

The ME nodded, gestured to his hovering lab assistant, and went back to work.

The incision was long and deft, and the ME soon had the victim's torso split open and folded back. Reid tried not to look too closely as he inspected the heart and other internal organs.

"His heart shut down," he commented, probing in the chest cavity. "It's in line with the diagnosis of asphyxiation. When the body doesn't get enough oxygen, it goes into cardiac arrest."

"Maybe he just had a heart attack," Reid said. "It happens." The man was in his mid-forties.

"It does, but there's usually a reason. Either an undiagnosed heart condition or some sort of myocardial abnormality. In this case, there's none of that. This man had a healthy heart."

Reid downed the rest of his coffee in frustration and felt the caffeine rush as it hit his system. His headache eased somewhat. He thought of the amulet around the man's neck. What was it called again? A gris-gris. To ward off evil. He shivered, then put the thought firmly out of his mind. The only thing that proved was that this victim was scared of someone. And that someone killed him.

"What about an ID?" Reid asked.

"I sent you his DNA profile along with the preliminary tox report," the ME said. "His teeth are intact. I'll get the dental analysis done after this, and you'll receive that in due course. You might be able to identify him that way."

Reid sent a quick message to Diaz. "Can you run the glades victim's DNA profile?"

"Already done," she replied. "No hits."

Damn!

He sat back, frustrated. It looked like it was going to boil down to dental records, and that was a shot in the dark. He watched as the ME inspected the stomach contents and took more samples. What the hell had killed this guy? And who the hell was he?

14

"My father has nothing to do with Jake's disappearance," Marcy insisted. They stood outside the door of the upmarket clothing store where the Haitian woman worked. Shoppers and tourists buzzed around them, heels clacking on the sidewalk. The warm sun dried the puddles from the rainfall the night before.

"How can you be sure?" Kenzie asked.

"Because he's in prison and has no idea where I am." For the first time, Kenzie saw a crack in the woman's armor. "No one does."

"It's on file," Kenzie pointed out. "Anyone with a contact in immigration could find out."

Marcy gasped. "Is that how you found out?"

Kenzie nodded.

"Mon Dieu," she muttered, crossing herself. "I hope they don't come for me."

"Who?"

"My father's enemies. He was a bad man, Kenzie. Very bad. I didn't want to be associated with him. I ran away as soon as I could and paid someone to bring me to Miami."

"I understand you're scared." Kenzie regretted telling her anyone with the right contacts could find her. That wasn't strictly true. Stacey had been very careful not to give her any classified information. She should have thought that through before she said anything. "But is there any way Jacob's disappearance could be related to what your father was involved in?"

"I don't think so. My father is in prison and the presidential guard think I'm dead, so do the Haitian police. Our house was burned down after his arrest. Everybody thinks I died in the fire."

"The presidential guard?" There was a lot Stacey hadn't told her.

Marcy's lip trembled. "Papa was one of the president's elite bodyguards. He was very well respected. Then something happened. Someone got to him. I don't know how, but he was responsible for the assassination."

"Not solely responsible." Kenzie frowned. "I heard it was a gang of mercenaries, mostly Colombians, who took out the president."

"It was, but many of the president's top bodyguards were involved. They let in the attackers, they looted the presidential palace. They helped massacre everybody there." Her voice caught in her throat. "None of them were injured in the attack on the president."

Kenzie had to admit, it was very suspicious.

"The police and the armed forces caught most of the mercenaries involved, and my father went on the run." Her eyes filled with tears. "He was guilty, Kenzie. I know he was."

"I'm sorry you had to endure that."

"He was caught and given a brief trial and is now serving life in prison. I was assaulted in the street. I couldn't go anywhere without being harassed. Supporters of the assassinated president threw a firebomb through our window and the house caught alight. I managed to escape, but our housekeeper didn't." Tears fell freely down her face. "Margarita died in the fire, and shamefully, I paid her family to keep quiet about it. I let everyone think it was me who'd died." Kenzie had to marvel at her ingenuity and quick thinking. "Then I paid a man to bring me to Miami. I didn't want to be a refugee, so I went straight to the immigration department and claimed asylum. I thought I would be safe here, that my details would be kept secret."

"They are. My contact didn't tell me anything other than you came from Haiti and there were special circumstances surrounding your immigration. I didn't mean to frighten you. I'm sure you're safe here."

"You think so?" Her brown eyes glistened with worry.

"You know what? I'm going to call her back and make sure they don't give any details to anyone. It might be a good idea if you changed your name too, just in case."

"I'll do that." She sniffed and reached for Kenzie's hand. "Thank you. I'm sorry I lied to you before."

"That's okay. Try not to worry." Kenzie squeezed her hand. It didn't seem like Marcy's father was involved in Jacob's disappearance. The two incidents appeared to be unrelated. "I'll be in touch as soon as I find out anything about Jacob."

Kenzie was on her way back to the office when Nick called. "Can you meet me at Gail's house? There's something you need to hear."

"Of course." She took the next exit and turned around. It had been a few days since she'd heard from Nick and she was wondering what the outcome of his chat with his sister had been.

"Thanks for coming," Nick said when she arrived. "I've spoken with Gail, and she's agreed to talk to you about what happened."

"Okay," Kenzie said. "If she's sure she's ready to talk about it."

"I am." Gail walked towards them, her head held high. "I don't think it's got anything to do with why Jacob disappeared, but it will do me good to talk about it."

Kenzie nodded. "Thank you."

"Follow me." Gail led her into the kitchen and gestured to the breakfast nook. Kenzie sat down and waited for Nick and Gail to do the same.

Nick sat beside his sister, who looked pale, but determined. "I haven't talked about this since it happened," she began, then took a shuddery breath. It had obviously been a traumatic experience for her.

"I was in New York, in my final year at Julliard. We were celebrating our final showcase concert. I was drinking champagne. I remember meeting this man at the bar. He said his name was Jeff." Her eyelids fluttered, but she kept going. "We got talking. He was a salesman, very charming. You know the type?"

Kenzie nodded. She'd come across a few of those in her time.

"Anyway, I started to feel unwell, like I'd drunk too much. As a dancer, I always watched what I drank, so I knew I couldn't be drunk."

Kenzie grimaced. "He'd spiked your drink?"

"He must have, because the next thing I knew, I was in his bed and he was on top of me."

Kenzie saw Nick tense up, his hands curling into fists, but he didn't say anything. Gail continued. "I wanted him to stop, but it was like I was paralyzed. I couldn't get my limbs to work. I couldn't speak properly. It was terrifying." She closed her eyes, as if the memory was too much, then opened them again. "He raped me. It carried on all night."

"I'm so sorry," Kenzie whispered.

"The next morning, the effects of the drug had worn off enough so that I could move. When he took a shower, I got out of there as fast as I could."

"Did you go to the police?" Kenzie asked.

She shook her head. "All I wanted to do was go home." That was understandable, but if she'd reported him, they might have been able to trace him based on DNA samples. "I took a shower and went to bed. I never told anyone what had happened. I just wanted to forget the whole thing."

Kenzie sucked in a breath. "So you never reported him?"

"I spoke to a counselor at the ballet school," she said, looking down at her hands. "But I couldn't remember much. He'd taken me to a motel, the Formosa, I think it was called. I couldn't even remember where it was, I'd been in such a state when I left."

"You knew his name and the motel," Kenzie pointed out.

"If that was his real name," Nick cut in, his voice icy.

True. A man like that would know not to use his real name. It was such a pity Gail hadn't gone straight to the cops, but Kenzie didn't want to berate her, not after what she'd been through. She'd done what she thought best at the time.

"After that, I couldn't let anyone touch me. Jacob was the first. He was so timid and gentle, I trusted him. Eventually, I told him what had happened and that I had a problem with intimacy. He understood, or I thought he did." Nick clenched his jaw.

Gail's eyes filled with tears. "He loved me enough to marry me, even though we'd never been intimate. He said he'd protect me and look after me. I needed that."

It was a male instinct. Kenzie could understand that. How many times had Reid come to her rescue?

"As the years passed, Jacob suggested I go for therapy. He said we'd work towards a sexual relationship, but I wasn't interested. I didn't want to revisit the past, but he couldn't understand that."

Kenzie nodded. Sad, but she got it. Some things were too painful to revisit. Unfortunately, you didn't heal if you ignored them. She knew that firsthand. "Is that when he started having affairs?" she asked.

Gail nodded. "I suggested it. He didn't want to at first, he said he'd rather work on it with me, but I was adamant." A tear ran down her cheek. "I pushed him away. It was my fault he started seeing other women."

Kenzie's heart went out to her. How dare some guy ruin her life like that and not suffer any consequences? One terrible night and this woman would never again have an intimate relationship with a man. The trauma had affected her marriage, led her husband to be unfaithful, and left her devoid of affection. It made her blood boil.

Jeff. The Formosa. She could probably find out the year, even the month the assault happened. That was something to go on. Kenzie bet Gail wasn't the first woman he'd raped. She drummed her fingers on the table, deep in thought. She knew herself, and she wouldn't be able to let this one go.

Nick put his arm around his sister, but she shook it off. "I'm to blame for the breakdown in our marriage."

"It's never that simple," Kenzie said, a bit too harshly. She was just so mad that Gail was blaming herself. "None of this was your fault."

Gail sniffed and dabbed her eyes with the back of her hand. "Thank you."

Kenzie forced herself to calm down. "So Marcy wasn't the first?"

"No, far from it, but Marcy was the first time I felt there was more to it than just sex." She gulped. "I think he really liked her."

Kenzie thought of the feisty woman she'd just met in her tight dress with her sexy curves and luscious dark hair falling halfway down her back. What man wouldn't be attracted to that? Fire and ice. "Not enough to end his marriage, though." Nick said firmly.

Gail shrugged. "He was spending more and more time with her. Usually, he'd come home afterwards, but with her he'd spend the night. I wouldn't see him until the following day after work. That's why I didn't panic when he walked out. I thought he was with her."

"You should have said." Nick gently chastised her.

"I was too ashamed. I knew I'd have to tell you about... about everything."

He sighed and looked at Kenzie. "Do you think this Marcy had anything to do with his disappearance?"

"No, she doesn't." Kenzie shook her head. "I've spoken to her at length about it. She knew about the voodoo doll and that he was worried someone was out to get him. When he missed their date on Friday, she tried calling him, but his phone was already off. She was as concerned as you were."

"Then where the hell is he?" Nick asked.

Kenzie cleared her throat. "There is another possible scenario."

They both refocused on her. "What?" asked Gail, her hand fluttering to her mouth. "Have you found something?"

"Maybe. Jacob's boss, Felix Hammond, is a ruthless, powerful man. It is possible that he was the one Jacob was running from."

Nick crossed his arms. "You think Jacob uncovered something in the accounts?"

"Yeah, either that or he was asked to do something he didn't want to do. By all accounts, Jacob was a good guy."

"He was," Gail confirmed. "He'd never do anything illegal."

Nick again, "Do you think this Felix Hammond threatened him?"

"I think it's possible. Obviously, we can't know for sure. He's not the type you can just ask."

Nick slumped back in his chair. "So now what?"

"There might be a way," Kenzie mused, gazing into the distance.

Nick frowned. "What are you thinking?"

She looked at them both. "I met his son the other day at the yacht club. His name is Milo. Milo Hammond."

Gail's mouth dropped open while Nick stared at her. "You met his son? How did you do that?"

"Let's just say I arranged to bump into him." She gave a secretive smile.

Nick shook his head. "You're incredible."

She brushed off the compliment. "Anyway, I have his business card and I might be able to arrange a date."

"A date?" Nick frowned.

Gail looked worriedly at her. "Is it safe? I wouldn't want you putting yourself in danger."

"That's okay, he thinks I'm Marcy."

They both gawked at her.

"I needed a reason to be there, so I said I was Jacob's mistress, and I was meeting him there."

"What did he say about Jacob?" Gail was hanging onto her every word.

"He was very smooth. He said that he hadn't seen him for a few days. That Jacob hadn't been at work. All true, of course." She gave a little shrug. "I couldn't get much out of him without raising his suspicions, but he lives with his father at the family residence. I was thinking, if I can get into their house, I might be able to have a snoop around."

"How are you going to do that?" Gail asked.

"No." Nick shook his head. "It's out of the question. I don't want you doing that. If this man had anything to do with Jacob's disappearance, he's dangerous."

His concern was flattering, but Kenzie had made up her mind. "I know, but how else are we going to find out?"

Nick hesitated, torn between wanting to support her and not wanting her to put herself in danger. "If you're going to do this, Kenzie, then I want to go with you."

"You can't," she said. "It's a date."

"I can follow you," Nick said, warming to the idea. "I'll be right outside, and if you need me, you just holler. I can ring the doorbell and interrupt. I'll pretend to be a delivery person, buy you some time to get away."

Gail nodded in agreement. "It's safer that way. You can't do this on your own."

Kenzie thought about his idea. It might not be such a bad thing to have backup. It's not like she had Reid to call anymore. "I'll think about it," she said. "I haven't set up the date yet."

"Let me know when you do. I don't want you doing this without me there, Kenzie," Nick said sternly. "I mean it."

She promised, then turned to Gail. "I think it's time you reported Jacob missing. It's been a week now. If he was in hiding, I think we'd know about it by now."

Gail blinked. "You think something bad has happened to him, don't you? You think he's..." She couldn't bring herself to say the word.

"I don't know anything for sure." Kenzie bit her lip. "But you need to get the police involved. They can trace his credit cards, ping his cellphone, and try to find out where his last known location was."

Nick gave a resolute nod. "You're right. I'll take you to the station now, Gail."

The woman nodded. "I'll get my things."

"Do you mind if I take one last look at Jacob's study?" Kenzie asked. "There might be something there that I missed."

"Of course. You know where it is."

Kenzie got to her feet. "I'm sorry it's not better news."

"That's okay. There's still a chance, right?" Gail's expression was hopeful.

Kenzie forced a smile. "There's always a chance."

15

Reid got back to Sweetwater PD to find Vargas' fiancé Shannon there, handing out donuts. She always chose the times he was out to pop in and surprise the team. It was no secret he didn't approve of civilians hanging out at the station.

"Would you like one?" She waved the box in front of his face.

"No thanks." Unlike his colleagues, he wasn't a major donut fan. She shrugged and moved on, and he took a seat in front of his computer.

"How'd it go?" Diaz asked, swiveling around in her chair.

"Cause of death was asphyxia," he said. "But the ME has no idea how it happened. The guy went into cardiac arrest after his oxygen ran out."

"I read an article once about a man who thought himself to death," Shannon was saying.

Reid glanced up, distracted. "What?"

"It's true." She flicked her long red hair over her shoulder, unfazed by his annoyance. "There was a curse on him, and even though that sort of thing doesn't really kill you, this guy believed it did. He was so convinced he was gonna die — that he did." She delivered the end with a flourish, as if it was a foregone conclusion.

Vargas looked nervously at Reid. "Could that be what happened?"

"Don't be ridiculous," Reid snapped. Perhaps he should have had a donut. Too much caffeine and death were making him grouchy. "He stopped breathing. Someone caused that to happen. It was not a Voodoo curse."

Vargas looked suitably chastised. "Perhaps you should go." He put an arm around Shannon and led her to the door. "Thanks for the donuts." A couple of other officers bid her farewell, and then the team got back to work.

"So what now?" Diaz asked.

"They're taking more samples. Maybe those will tell us why he asphyxiated."

"Bizarre," she muttered, shaking her head. "Hamilton and I have done some digging on Sonia Del Ray. It turns out she did change her name, but get this, her original name is redacted."

"Redacted?" He frowned. "What does that mean?"

"Blacked out."

"I know what redacted means," he corrected. "I mean why was it redacted?"

"Off limits. Social Security doesn't know either. Orders from above."

"Witness protection," Reid muttered. At Diaz's surprised look, he explained, "She must be in WITSEC. That's the only reason her name would be blacked out."

Diaz breathed in sharply. "If she is in WITSEC, how are we going to find out who she really is?"

Reid grunted. "Luckily, I know a man."

"Garrett, what can I do for you?" Agent Wilson sounded rushed. Wind echoed down the line, and Reid could hear the DEA section chief's hurried footsteps. "I'm between meetings so I can only give you a couple of minutes."

"Thanks." They dispersed with pleasantries. Theirs wasn't the smoothest of relationships, although they'd worked together to foil undercover agent, Alberto Torres' attempted murder by Maria Lopez and her thugs. Reid cut to the chase. "I need information."

"What else is new?"

Reid gave a snort of acknowledgement. "We've got a victim with a redacted name. We think she may be in WITSEC."

"Shit, really?" He stopped walking. Reid could tell by how quiet it got.

"Yeah, could be one of yours." He had no idea if Sonia Del Ray had ever worked for or with the DEA's office, but he may as well throw it out there. Wilson would need a reason to go digging.

"Drugs involved?"

"Possibly. There were marks on her arms. I can't say anything more at this stage." Not needle marks, but Wilson wouldn't know that.

"What name is she going under?" he asked.

"Sonia Del Ray."

There was a pause. "Doesn't ring a bell. I'll have to look her up in the system."

"Would you mind? Thanks."

A grunt.

"I'll get back to you. Could take a while."

And that was the best he could hope for.

"Boss, I've got something," came Vargas' voice from the other side of the squad room. He was peering over Hamilton's desk.

"What's that?" Reid gave in and grabbed the last donut form the box on his way over. God only knew when he'd get another chance to eat.

"A missing person's report has just been filed at Miami PD,"

Hamilton said, glancing up. As usual, his desk was impeccably neat with not so much as a paper out of place.

"Is it our guy?"

"I think so," the rookie replied. "Here's a picture."

With the click of his mouse, he pulled up the image. It was indeed a healthier looking version of the man in the glades. This man had a smiling mouth, pink cheeks, and a sparkle in his eye. On one hand, he looked nothing like the pale, lifeless victim in the crime scene photograph, but on the other, the features were identical.

"It's him, alright," Diaz confirmed, coming up behind them. "Who is he?"

"His name is Jacob Peters," Hamilton read. "His wife reported him missing a short while ago."

"A week later!" exclaimed Diaz. "Jeez."

Reid just shook his head. "Address?" Hamilton wrote it on a notepad and tore off the top sheet, handing it to Reid. "Diaz." He swung around. "Care to join me?"

"Sure," she said with a nod.

Vargas didn't say anything, but Reid could tell he was surprised at not being asked. Usually, he accompanied the boss everywhere. It wasn't because he hadn't answered his phone the night they'd found Sonia Del Ray's body, although Reid knew that's what his colleague was thinking. "Diaz might be able to form a rapport with the wife," he said.

Vargas nodded, although Reid could tell he wasn't convinced.

Gail Peters was not what Reid had expected. An elegant lady in her late forties, she seemed to float around the room rather than walk. Her striking silver hair emphasized her blue eyes, which he thought were rather cold and guarded.

"I reported him missing this morning," she confirmed, gesturing for them to sit down in her comfortable and tastefully decorated living room. It looked like it had recently been cleaned, and indeed there was a faint smell of furniture polish lingering above the coffee table. "Can I get you some coffee?"

"No, thank you," he said. This wasn't a social call. "I'm afraid we have some bad news, Mrs. Peters."

Her hands fluttered to her face, and she sank down onto an armchair. If she hadn't been standing in front of it, Reid expected she'd have ended up on the floor. "He's dead, isn't he?"

Reid gave a gruff nod. "I'm sorry."

She gave a little gasp, then burst into tears. They weren't noisy, heartfelt sobs like some people when finding out their loved ones were dead, but rather quiet, breathy sobs. This woman was dignified, even in her grief. He imagined she'd give in to her pain later, when she was alone. He admired that about her.

"How did he die?" It was a question he got asked a lot, but he'd been dreading this one.

"We're still trying to figure that out," he admitted. "His body was found in the glades on Friday."

"The glades?" She shook her head. "What was he doing there?"

"We were hoping you could tell us that," Reid said.

"I have no idea." More tears ran down her cheeks.

"Mrs. Peters, I'm so sorry to have to do this, but do you mind if we ask you some questions?"

He glanced at Diaz, who nodded. It was usually an on-the-spot decision whether the grieving relative was up to answering questions, and they both felt Mrs. Peters could handle it.

She sniffed and looked around for a tissue. Diaz handed her one.

"Thank you." She dabbed her eyes, then took a deep, shaky breath. "I'm sorry. It's still such a shock, even though I was half expecting it."

"You were?" Reid raised an eyebrow.

"Yes, he's been gone a week. I knew it was too long. He'd have called or let me know he was okay." She sniffed again. That made sense.

"I'm sorry for your loss," Diaz said gently. "Would you like me to get you anything? A glass of water, perhaps?"

"No, no. I'm okay." Her voice quivered and her hands shook. She didn't look okay, but she was putting on a brave face.

"Excuse me for asking," Reid said, "but why did you wait so long to report him missing?"

"I thought...I thought he was hiding."

"Hiding?" Reid frowned. Diaz shrugged. "Hiding from who?"

"The person who sent him that stupid doll. The one with the pin in it."

"A voodoo doll?" asked Diaz, her gaze shifting to Reid's.

He knew what she was thinking – just like Sonia Del Ray.

"Do you still have it?" Diaz asked.

"No, I—I never actually saw it. Jacob took it with him when he left."

"How do you know about it, then?"

She hesitated. "It's complicated. I asked my brother to look into it for me, and he told me about the doll."

"How'd your brother know about it?" Reid asked.

"You can ask him yourself. He's in the next room."

"Oh, he is?" Reid got to his feet as Mrs. Peters glided across the lounge. "Nick? Would you come in here, please?"

Reid stared at the handsome man who walked into the room. Where had he seen him before? Then it hit him. At the hospital with Kenzie after she'd been attacked.

"You?"

Diaz looked between the two of them. "I'm sorry, do you know each other?"

"Yes, you're the vet."

Nick nodded. "That's right. We met once, a couple of months ago."

Diaz shook her head. "I'm lost."

"He was dating Kenzie," Reid explained.

"Oh." She gave him the once over.

"You say that like it's a bad thing," he retorted.

"How did you know about the voodoo doll?" Diaz asked, getting the conversation back on track.

"Kenzie told me."

"Oh, Lord," she muttered, glancing at Reid, who felt the stirrings of exasperation rising within him.

"Kenzie's involved?"

"Yes, I asked her to look into my husband's disappearance. I didn't want to bother you with it, if he was just hiding out."

Reid breathed slowly through his nose. Of course Kenzie was involved. When wasn't she involved? "Is she here?" he asked.

Just then a door at the end of the living room opened and Kenzie's voice said, "Hello, Reid."

16

KENZIE BRACED herself for Reid's reaction. "I might have known you were involved." Steely gray eyes burned into hers.

"It's nice to see you too," she said dryly. If she didn't know him better, she might be intimidated by that glare.

"Would you care to share with us how you knew about the voodoo doll?" She had to give him credit, he'd retained his line of questioning despite the interruption.

"Yes, I asked his mistress."

"I'm sorry, how do you two know each other?" Gail asked, interrupting.

"We've worked together in the past." Reid shook his head. "His mistress?"

"Yes, Gail and Jacob had an open marriage, you might say."

Gail nodded, and Kenzie read the gratefulness in her eyes. No explanation necessary.

"I see." It was clear he didn't.

"Marcy Guerrier was the last person to see him before he disappeared on Wednesday night," she explained.

Diaz butted in. "That's not true. A Voodoo priestess called Mama

Lucia saw him on Thursday morning. He went to her to ask for protection against the curse."

"What curse?" Gail stared at them.

"That's what the voodoo doll meant," Kenzie explained. "Someone put a curse on Jacob. That's why he was so scared."

"I had no idea." She wrung her hands. "Why didn't he tell me?"

"He must have panicked," Nick said kindly.

"By all accounts, he was extremely anxious," Reid said. "The priestess said he'd begged for her help."

"Oh, God. Poor Jacob." Gail shut her eyes.

"I need to speak to Jacob's mistress," Reid said.

"She didn't have anything to do with his death," Kenzie told him. Nick nodded in agreement.

"Still, I'd like to have a chat."

Kenzie realized Marcy didn't know Jacob was dead. Not officially, anyway. Reid would break it to her. And she'd have to break Marcy's confidence and tell Reid how she came to be in America. "Honestly, she was as worried as Gail was."

His eyes narrowed. "What aren't you telling me?"

"Nothing. I just think it's a waste of time questioning her again when I've already done that. Twice."

"Well, we'll need a statement from her," Diaz cut in, once again cooling things down.

Kenzie shrugged. "Suit yourself." She took out her phone and texted Reid Marcy's contact details and address.

Reid turned to Gail. "Did your husband have a laptop or phone?"

"He took his phone with him," she said, then turned to Kenzie. "You've got his laptop, haven't you?"

Reid scowled at her. "What? I had a look. There's nothing on it."

"I need to check it, Kenzie."

"Okay, I'll drop it off at your place later." Damn. She'd wanted Raoul to have a look at it. On the surface, it was clean. He used it for work, but Hammond Holdings financial software was all online and she didn't have the logins to access it.

"I take it you've searched the house too?" Reid's voice was heavy with sarcasm.

"Only his study. Nothing there either." She didn't mention her theory about the Hammonds. That was a conversation she had to have with Reid in private, once she'd filled him in on the background. Voicing her suspicions now, when he clearly had no knowledge of the victim, would be asking for trouble. Arguing in front of Gail was not something she wanted to do.

"I'd still like to have a look," he told Gail.

"Of course." Gail looked at Kenzie, almost as if she was asking for permission.

Kenzie nodded. "Go ahead. I have to get back anyway. It's getting late."

"I'll give you a ride," Nick offered.

"Thanks." Since they'd come together, she didn't have her car here. As she left the house, she felt Reid glaring after her.

The Everglades was basking in a fiery orange glow as Kenzie drove along the dirt track towards the Gator Inn. She gazed out the window at the shimmering surface of the swamp. It had a strange beauty to it. Menacing, but breathtaking at the same time.

Turning into the parking lot, she spotted Reid's truck. Good, he was here. Their meeting this afternoon had been incredibly awkward. There was so much she'd wanted to tell him but couldn't, not in front of everyone else.

She parked next to him, picked up Jacob's laptop, and got out of the car. The warm air was sticky with moisture. Out here in the swamp, it always seemed damper than everywhere else. Tucking her hair behind her ears, she climbed the stairs to the first-floor walkway, then proceeded along it to Reid's room.

The door opened before she could knock. "Come in," he said. "We need to talk."

"I thought you might say that." She stepped into his room,

surprised by how neat it was. Reid had spread papers out on the small round table underneath the window and was going through what looked like a police case file. Printouts poked out of the folder and his laptop was open on the bed, as if he'd turned around to look something up.

"Take a seat."

Kenzie sat on the only spare chair and put the laptop on the table. "Present for you."

"Thanks." He looked tired. Stubble covered his jaw, and his hair was messy from constantly raking his hand through it.

"Tough case?" she asked.

"You would know," he retorted, not without a degree of sarcasm. "You've been working on it a lot longer than I have."

She sighed. "Look, I'm sorry about that. I didn't know he was dead, okay? Nick asked me to help him track down his brother-in-law. That's all I was doing."

"Nick." His expression was inscrutable. "You guys a thing now?"

"He's a friend. I was helping him out." Not that she needed to explain that to Reid.

He gave a stiff nod, as if he didn't quite believe her. "What did you find?"

"Probably the same as you," she said. "Jacob Peters was working for Hammond Holdings, owned by Felix Hammond, the multimillionaire."

Reid was nodding. "Yes, I know that much. Until this morning, we had no clue who the victim was. There was no ID on the body."

"Hence the next of kin notification."

"Yeah."

"How did you find out?" she asked.

"His wife reported him missing."

"Oh yes. That was my suggestion."

Reid grunted. "They should have done that days ago. Would have saved us a lot of work."

She smiled sympathetically. "I did tell them, but Gail thought he'd gone into hiding. Once I heard that Felix Hammond's business interests weren't strictly legit, I got worried. I told Nick it was time to file a missing person's report."

He frowned. "What do you mean, not strictly legit?"

"There's rumors of criminal activity," she said. "He's pally with Salvatore Del Gatto, which should tell you everything you need to know about him."

Reid raised an eyebrow. "And when you say criminal activity, you mean...?"

"I don't know for sure," she said. "I've got my researcher, Raoul, looking into it."

"Who told you he was crooked?"

"A source," she said cagily. "Although I suspected as much. He owns a shipping company, a logistics company, and warehouses all over Miami. What does that tell you?"

"Are you saying he's smuggling drugs?"

She shrugged. "Or something else. Like I said, I'm still trying to find out."

He exhaled. "You think Felix Hammond had something to do with Jacob Peter's death?"

"I'm considering it. He was their accountant. It's possible he discovered something he wasn't supposed to, or that he refused to cooperate with whatever they were up to."

Reid rubbed his forehead. "I must admit, there could be something there. I'll pay Felix Hammond a visit. If I play my cards right, we might be able to get a warrant to search Jacob's office."

Kenzie gave a little nod. "There's something I need to tell you."

"Oh yeah?"

"Don't scowl at me like that," she said, seeing his expression. "I'm sharing information with you, information you wouldn't otherwise have."

He rubbed his forehead. "Sorry, long day. Make that two days. And it always makes me nervous when you say things like that."

"This is about Marcy Guerrier."

"The mistress?"

"Yeah. She's not involved."

"As I said before, we'll have to ascertain that for ourselves."

"I know, but there's something you should know about her, because I'm not sure she'll tell you, and I don't want you to think she's hiding anything."

He frowned. "What's that?"

"She's an immigrant from Haiti. She was given protected status here last year after her father was arrested. He was part of the militant gang that assassinated the president."

"Jesus." He stood up, his chair falling backwards. "Any more surprises?"

"Yeah, her father's in prison, and nobody knows she's alive. Her house was burned down in Haiti, and she let everyone think she'd died in the blaze, so you can't haul her in for questioning, it might put her at risk. She's trying to keep a low profile and just live her life. She deserves that much."

Reid stared at her. "Not if she had something to do with her lover's death."

"I promise you, she didn't. In fact, she doesn't even know he's dead yet. You get to be the one to tell her, so be gentle, okay? She's had a tough time."

There was a pause as Reid contemplated this. Eventually, he said, "Okay, I'll go easy on her. I still need to talk to her, you understand, if only to rule her out of our inquiries."

"I know, and thanks."

He gave a taut nod. "Any other bombshells you want to drop on me tonight?"

She chuckled. "No, I think that's it. I do have one question, though."

"Shoot."

"How did Jacob Peters die? I noticed you were fairly vague when Gail asked."

Reid hesitated.

Kenzie fixed her gaze on him. "Was it bad?"

"No, nothing like that." He raked a hand through his hair. "He died of asphyxiation, but there was no apparent cause."

"I don't understand."

"Well, the ME confirmed he suffocated, then his heart shut down, but we don't know why. He wasn't strangled or manually suffocated, and there were no known toxins in his body. They're running some more tests."

"That is weird," she said, then her eyes widened as a thought struck her.

"No, don't even say it," he said, reading her mind.

She laughed. "I wasn't going to."

"But you were thinking it. It was not that damn curse that killed him."

"No, but it's what the perpetrators want us to think, right?"

He exhaled. "Right. For a minute there I thought you were going to start sprouting Voodoo stuff."

She shot him a look. "Please, this is me."

He chuckled.

Kenzie grinned. It felt good to be doing this. To be swapping ideas back and forth, talking out a case. There was no denying they worked well together. The problem was it wasn't her case anymore. Her assignment was over. Jacob was dead.

"Do you have the voodoo doll?" she asked.

"Not that one." Then he paused, unsure whether to continue.

"You have a different one?" She frowned, confused. When he didn't respond, she gasped. "Don't tell me you have another cursed victim?"

"A woman," he admitted, easing himself back into his chair. "A young waitress. Also, no cause of death. She has a head wound, but the ME said that couldn't have been what killed her."

"Where's the Voodoo connection?" she asked.

"The doll had been sent to her earlier that morning. It was in her unopened mail."

"She didn't know it had been sent to her?"

"No."

Kenzie pursed her lips thoughtfully. "If she didn't know about the doll, it couldn't have influenced her death. Not in a suggestive way, anyway."

"I thought you didn't believe in that mumbo jumbo stuff?"

"Not in the traditional sense," she started, "but a curse is only powerful if you believe in it."

"She didn't get a chance." Reid stretched his long legs out in front of him. They touched hers under the table, so she shifted them discreetly to the side.

"What does that mean?" Kenzie asked.

"It means she may not have been aware someone was after her."

"Assuming it's the same person who murdered Jacob Peters."

Reid met her gaze. "Assuming that, yes."

Kenzie thumbed her fingers on the table. "Who was she? Any relation to Jacob?"

"Not that we could find," he said. "Mrs. Peters didn't recognize the name when we asked her. It doesn't look like Jacob knew her, and we haven't found any evidence to suggest she knew him either. There's nothing in Jacob's phone records, anyway. We don't have hers."

Kenzie scratched her head. "Maybe she also worked for Hammond Shipping?"

"Don't think so. She worked two jobs, but neither of them was in shipping. She was more of an informal worker. Waitressing and making and selling clothes at markets. Nothing corporate."

"What's her name?" Kenzie asked. Perhaps if she got into Hammond's house, she could look for a connection.

Reid hesitated. "You know I can't discuss an ongoing case with you."

"Come on." She raised an eyebrow. "It's not like we haven't shared information in the past. You know I'm not going to spread it around."

"It's not a story for the *Herald*," he warned her. "I don't want you reporting on this investigation."

"How about after you catch the culprit?" she asked, a cheeky smile playing on the corners of her lips. "Can I report on it then?"

He rolled his eyes. "I'll think about it."

She grinned. "Okay, then I promise. Not a word until you give the go ahead."

"Her name was Sonia Del Ray."

17

Reid was on his way to work when Agent Wilson called him on his cellphone. He put it on speaker. "Your vic's name is Portia Stuckey. She's not one of mine, by the way, but somehow, I think you already knew that."

"Isn't she?" Reid acted dumb.

"No. I hope that helps."

"It does." He thanked Wilson for his time and ended the call. Portia Stuckey. The name didn't ring any bells.

"Let's run her through the database," he told Diaz as soon as he got in. It was still early, and none of the other detectives were in yet. "I want to know why she's in witness protection."

He settled down to work, when he heard an expletive from Diaz. "What have you found?" he asked, looking over. She stared at her screen, apparently in shock.

"Diaz?"

"Sorry, I'm surprised, that's all. I wasn't expecting—" She stopped, then said, "Portia Stuckey was a child killer."

"What?" He leaped to his feet and went over to her desk.

"She killed one of her teachers back in 2016. Stabbed him to death outside his house. At the time of the offence, she was too young to stand trial, so she spent three years in a juvenile detention facility near Jacksonville. She got out six months ago."

"Holy shit," he muttered under his breath. "I was expecting her to be a witness or something, not a killer." He thought of the slender girl lying in the trash heap, scars on her arms. She must have been a very troubled youth.

"There is a brother," Diaz said, scanning the page. "Fred Stuckey. No known address."

"He's probably also in WITSEC," Reid said. Agent Wilson wouldn't give him the details of anyone still alive, and it was pointless asking the Marshals Service. It went against all their protocols, and for good reason. The program was there to protect people. One slip-up could cause their cover being blown.

"He was with her at the time of the murder," Diaz said, reading on.

"Why would she take her younger brother with her if she was planning on killing her teacher?" Reid wondered.

"I don't know, but she took the blame. Said it was all her idea."

Interesting. "Did she say why she did it?"

"He was a jerk who had it in for her. That's the reason she gave when she was arrested."

Reid exhaled. His head was spinning. This new information had added an extra dimension to the investigation, and he needed time to process it. "Okay, so she's been out six months and turns up dead in a dumpster. Is that a coincidence?"

"Are you thinking her past had something to do with her death?" Diaz asked, catching on.

"Don't you?"

"It's possible, but I'm struggling to make the connection with our first victim, Jacob Peters."

"Maybe there isn't one."

"But the voodoo dolls..." She left it hanging.

Reid rubbed his forehead. "Yeah, you're right. That would

suggest the cases are linked. It's too much of a coincidence, otherwise."

"Still, we have to look into it. I'll try to find out some more details about the teacher she stabbed. You never know, it could be someone out for revenge."

"We need to locate the brother, too. If it is a vigilante, the kid might be at risk."

"I'll get right on it."

When the rest of the team got in, Reid briefed them on the latest findings. Their reactions were similar to his.

"She didn't look like a killer," Vargas murmured. "She just looked like a messed-up kid."

"I wonder if her roommate knew," said Hamilton.

"Probably not. She was using a false name. WITSEC made sure she was off the grid due to the negative publicity. She'd been getting death threats. They thought it best to protect her real identity."

"Do you think that's why she cut herself?" Vargas asked.

"Maybe." He wasn't a shrink, but he'd hazard a guess that had something to do with it.

"She's got a younger brother," he told them. "His identity is also redacted. Diaz is trying to find him, but it's not looking positive. The boy has had no contact with his sister for five years."

"How old would he be now?" Vargas asked.

It was a good question. "Fred Stuckey was twelve at the time of the murder. That would make him eighteen now."

"Almost an adult," murmured Vargas.

"He went into care," Reid explained. "As far as I know, he's still with a foster family."

"Do you think the person who killed Sonia knew who she really was? Perhaps it was a retaliation?" Monroe spoke up from the back. "Because if so, we may have to look at the friends and relatives of the teacher she killed."

"Exactly what we're doing," Reid agreed with a nod.

"Except, how is Sonia's death related to Jacob Peters?" Vargas scratched his head. "And how does the whole Voodoo thing fit in?"

That was a question Reid couldn't answer.

He filled the team in on Felix Hammond, Jacob's boss. "We need a warrant to search Jacob's office," he told them.

Hamilton nodded. "I'll get on that."

"I'm going to talk to Jacob's mistress," he told them. That raised a few eyebrows. "She doesn't know he's dead yet. We'll reconvene in a couple of hours and decide on the next steps." They all nodded and got back to work.

Reid met Marcy Guerrier at her apartment. Marcy had the day off, since she was working on the weekend. "How did you find me?" she asked. It had taken him ten minutes of persuading to get her to open the door.

"Kenzie Gilmore gave me your address."

She sucked in a breath. "She said I could trust her."

"You can. Kenzie and I help each other out on occasion. She's a good person."

"But now I'll be in your police report," Marcy moaned. "I know how these things work."

"It won't include your history in Haiti," Reid told her. "Your background will be protected. You'll be noted as Jacob Peter's girlfriend, that's all."

She studied him, an uncertain look in her eyes. It was clear she didn't trust him. "You have my word," he said.

"I'm thinking of changing my name," she muttered. "Kenzie said I should."

"It's probably a good idea," he agreed. "Now, do you mind if we talk about your relationship with Jacob?"

"I guess so." She led him down a dim hallway, through a beaded curtain and into the living room. He glanced around, amazed by the clash of colors. Pink cushions lay scattered on the lime-green, crushed-velvet sofa, while a brightly woven rug rested on a mustard yellow carpet that had seen better days. A low coffee table, chest-style, that looked to be from a local flea market, was covered with fashion magazines, the models' glowing faces smiling up at him.

"Thank you." He sat down. It was overwhelming. He fixed his eyes on Marcy. At least he didn't have to squint to look at her.

"What do you wanna know?"

"When did you meet Jacob?"

"I went through all this with Kenzie. Why don't you just ask her?"

"Because I'm asking you."

A sigh. "Okay, I met him about ten months ago. He came into the shop and we got talking. He was nice. He invited me for a drink."

That tallied with what Kenzie had told him. "Did he talk about his wife at all?"

"Yeah, sometimes."

"Did he ever say he was going to leave his wife?"

"No." Marcy stared at him. "You think she did this? You think she killed him because he was seeing me?"

"Is that such a strange idea?"

"Yes, it's a crazy idea. She isn't the type. Besides, Jake would never have left his wife. He wasn't like that. He just wanted some human contact, that's all."

"And that didn't bother you?" Reid studied her closely. She didn't seem perturbed.

"No, why should it? He's too old for me anyway, I know that. But I needed some company too, you know? And he was nice, he treated me well, and he made me feel safe."

That's what Kenzie had said.

"You didn't want more from the relationship?"

"No. We saw each other two nights a week. Sometimes he stayed over. That was enough for me." There was nothing in her tone that suggested otherwise. "What? You think I killed him now?"

"Did you?"

She shook her head in disbelief. "I was at the store all day Thursday. You can ask my manager." It appeared Kenzie was right. Marcy didn't have anything to do with her lover's death, and it didn't seem like it had any relation to her Haitian roots either.

"What do you know about Voodoo?" he asked her before he ended the interview.

"Voodoo is a way of life in Haiti," she said.

"So you knew what the voodoo doll meant as soon as Jacob showed it to you."

"I knew, but I didn't want to scare him. I told him to get rid of it."

"Did you tell him to go and see a woman called..." He opened a notepad. "Mama Lucia, at Degi Botanica?"

"Mama Lucia is a good woman. Jacob needed protection from the curse, so I sent him to her. She gave him the gris-gris." Marcy scoffed. "But it was too late."

"What do you mean too late?"

"To stop the curse." She shook her head at the tragedy of it.

Reid got to his feet, sending a pink cushion tumbling to the floor. "Thank you." He hesitated. "I'm sorry for your loss."

She gave a brief nod.

Reid was about to leave when he remembered something. Turning, he took out a photograph of Sonia Del Ray. "Do you know this woman?"

Marcy studied it, her eyes widening. "Is she dead too?"

"Yeah." Unfortunately, the crime scene photograph was the only one he had of her. "Do you know her?"

"No." She shook her head. "Who is she?"

"Just someone else we're looking into. We think her death might be connected with Jacob's."

Marcy frowned. "Did Jacob know this girl?"

"I don't know," Reid admitted. "That's what we're trying to find out. His wife doesn't think so."

Marcy shrugged. "Sorry, I've never seen her before."

"Okay." At least he could tick Marcy off the suspect list.

Reid was on his way home when he got a call from Diaz. He was surprised to see it come through on her personal phone, not her work one. "Garrett," he said, putting the phone to his ear.

"Boss, there's something I need to talk to you about."

"You okay, Diaz?" He heard the sound of traffic in the background and realized she was standing outside in the parking lot.

"Yeah, but I've found something you need to see."

"Can't you just tell me?"

"No, not on the phone."

His brain went into overdrive. What had she found that she couldn't talk about in the office? That she had to go outside to make the call? "Did you find a lead?"

"Yeah, something like that. Can you meet me at the Zizi's on your way back into the station?" Zizi's was a coffee shop a couple of blocks from the station.

A bad feeling began building in his gut. "Sure, I've just left Marcy Guerrier's. Meet you in half an hour?"

"See you then." Diaz hung up.

18

Milo Hammond picked up Kenzie outside Marcy's clothing store at seven-thirty. There were two reasons for that. First, it was more believable and second, if she'd met him at the restaurant, she wouldn't have been able to go back to his place afterwards. The real Marcy, safely at home according to Reid, still had no idea Kenzie was impersonating her.

Unbeknownst to Milo, a somber-faced Nick was watching in his Porsche across the road, ready to tail them. Granted, a Porsche wasn't the most unobtrusive of cars, but at least the sleek midnight blue lines would be less noticeable in the dark. He'd assured Kenzie he wouldn't let them out of his sight.

They went to an expensive French restaurant in South Beach. Milo, dressed in a black shirt open at the neck, tailored trousers, and custom-made shoes, was out to impress. Kenzie flirted over her roast parsnip velouté and batted her eyelids through their Côte de Boeuf with dauphinoise potatoes. By the time they got to dessert, he was stroking her arm across the table and rubbing her leg under it.

The bar they went to next was several blocks away, but despite the amount of wine he'd had to drink, Milo seemed fully in control of his senses. Relaxed at the wheel, he drove with an easy, confident style that made her realize it would take more than a few drinks to get him to let down his guard. Kenzie checked her lipstick in her compact mirror and saw the familiar low angled beams of the Porsche not too far behind.

Latin music reverberated down the street and bounced off the brick buildings on either side. "I love this place," he told her. Kenzie was struck with a sudden sense of déjà vu. She knew this club. It was where she'd met Alberto Torres during another undercover op last year. Unbeknownst to her, Torres had known who she was the entire time. He'd played her. Expertly. Was Milo Hammond playing her too?

No. Of course not. She shook off the sudden sense of foreboding. He had no idea she wasn't who she professed to be. Marcy Guerrier, the clothing sales assistant. Jacob Peters bit on the side.

"You okay?" he asked. Shit, her mask was slipping.

She plastered a smile back on her face. "Yeah, I'm great. I love Latin dancing."

His grin widened. "A girl after my own heart."

Cocktails... dancing... and more dancing... The night wore on and Kenzie's feet started to ache. She hadn't worn the best shoes with which to hit the dance floor, and Milo seemed to enjoy grinding himself against her to the thumping Latin beat a little too much.

She'd danced with Torres too. He'd been a great dancer, better than Milo, who was a little too heavy-footed. Briefly, she wondered what Torres was doing now. He'd been relocated after his last scrape with Maria Lopez and the cartel. Poor guy would forever be looking over his shoulder, wondering when they were coming for him. The cartel had a very long memory.

Back off... Or Else.

The message scrawled on her wall served as a reminder. She'd gotten off lightly, all things considered. Finally, she wiped a bead of perspiration off her forehead and suggested they get some air. Enough was enough.

"It's hot in there," she said, once they were outside.

"You're all flustered." He moved a stray hair out of her face. It was an intimate gesture, more so than gyrating against her on the dance floor. Kenzie suppressed a shudder.

"Shall we go?" His voice was low and there was no mistaking his meaning.

"Yes, would you mind dropping me at home? I'm on Devereaux Avenue." She'd agreed with Nick beforehand that she'd give Milo a random address to a block of apartments near the fashion store just in case she didn't want to go back to his place, or vice versa.

"Sure, or we could go back to mine for a nightcap." His gaze was loaded.

She hesitated. It was the moment of reckoning. Thinking about it was one thing, but actually doing it was something else. If she went back to Milo's, she was consciously going home with a man she had no intention of sleeping with, to poke around his house.

It was dangerous, but how else was she going to find out if he had anything to do with Jacob's death? A man had lost his life, and if the Hammonds were responsible, she wanted to know. They deserved to be held accountable. Besides, Nick would be waiting outside. She could leave at any time.

"Sure, why not?" The die was cast.

He put an arm around her waist. "Let's go."

"Wow." Kenzie gazed up at the floodlit white Palladium mansion complete with portico, pillars, and a curving front balcony. "This is your place?"

"Yeah. It belongs to my family. We all live here."

"All?" She'd thought there was only Milo and his father, Felix.

"My sister Charlotte lives in the garden cottage with her family," he explained. "I'm in the east wing, my father has the west."

"Convenient," she murmured.

"I have a place down in Key Largo," he added, as if to stress that he didn't always reside with his father. "It's where I go to escape. Maybe I'll take you there sometime."

She smiled but didn't respond. No thanks. This was it. Her one shot. After tonight, Milo Hammond would never see Marcy again.

"What happened to your mother?"

"She died when I was young." He didn't elaborate.

"I'm sorry." Kenzie exhaled, hit by a pang of consciousness. Her mother had died young too; it changed you.

He shrugged. "I barely remember her."

They went inside. The vast hall was cool, thanks to the marble tiles and high ceiling. An interesting mishmash of steel shapes resembling helicopter rotor blades hung from above, illuminating the entrance. Enormous works of modern art adorned the walls, but Kenzie couldn't identify any of them. The taste was too eclectic for her liking. From somewhere in the house, soft jazz played.

"This way." He headed for the wide staircase that cured upwards to the balcony. "I have my own suite." Of course he did.

Kenzie followed, knowing Nick was outside the automatic gates that prevented anyone else from driving into the grounds. He was a little further away than she would have liked, but it couldn't be helped. At least he was still out there. And they weren't alone. Felix was home too.

Milo led her into a plush lounge complete with a bar and recessed lighting. "Take a seat." He gestured to the leather couch. "What can I get you?"

Kenzie had had more than enough to drink. She'd emptied her last two cocktails into pot plants at the club. "A gin and tonic," she allowed. "But do you mind if I freshen up, first?"

"Sure. Down the corridor to the left. There's also one downstairs if you prefer. It's off the hallway."

"Here's fine." She flashed him a smile loaded with promise. "I'll be right back."

She stepped out into the corridor and glanced right. That was the way they'd come. She didn't remember passing any other rooms to get here. His study must be further down to the left.

Easing off her shoes, she ran along the corridor until she found a closed door. Opening it, she discovered that was the bathroom, so she shut it again, hoping Milo would think she was inside.

There was another door, further down on the right. She tried the handle, it opened. Peering into the darkness, she could just make out a large desk. Bingo. Taking a deep breath, she turned on the light. Heart racing, Kenzie dashed over to the desk and began opening drawers. There were three, all down the right side.

The top one contained stationary, a couple of unused notebooks and a calculator. Nothing of interest there. The second drawer held some papers. Client contracts, by the looks of things. She scanned them, conscious that she didn't have a lot of time. Most were from suppliers from South America. Colombia, Bolivia, Uruguay. Were they important? She didn't know. To be safe, she took out her phone and shot a couple of photographs.

One more drawer to go. She was about to open it when she heard footsteps in the corridor outside.

"Marcy? Are you okay?"

19

Diaz was already there when Reid walked into Zizi's. She'd chosen a table at the back away from the window and was working on her laptop. She glanced up when he arrived.

"Hey," he greeted her, sitting down. She looked flushed, her hair, usually so neat, in disarray. "What's with the subterfuge?"

"You'll understand when I show you what I've found," she said, her face somber. "Remember you asked me to look into that math teacher that Sonia Del Ray killed?"

"Yeah?"

"Well, his name was Ron McDonald. He was a widower. His wife died shortly after they got married. Cancer."

"Uh-huh?" He wasn't sure where she was going with this. "That's terrible, but what's it got to do with our case?"

"Ron McDonald had a daughter. A nineteen-year-old college student who was studying at MIT."

"So?"

"I looked into her. She dropped out of college after her father was stabbed."

"Okay." He watched her stumbling over the words. What wasn't she telling him?

She spun her laptop around. "*This* is Ron McDonald's daughter." On the screen was the smiling face of Shannon Maisie, Vargas' fiancé.

Reid stared at the picture, stunned. "*Shannon* is Ron McDonald's daughter?"

"Yeah."

There was a long pause as this sunk in. A million questions flew through Reid's mind, like why hadn't Shannon said anything? Did Vargas know? Had Shannon realized Sonia Del Ray was her father's killer? Had she had anything to do with the murder?

"Jesus Christ," he whispered, knowing similar thoughts must have gone through Diaz's mind.

"Yeah." Diaz repeated, ashen faced. "What do we do, boss?"

"I need to think about this." His gaze dropped back to the screen. "What do we know about her?"

"She was nineteen when her father was killed, and apparently, she took it badly. One of her professors told me she broke down when she found out and dropped out of college shortly after. It seems his job was paying for her education, along with a financial aid package that she could no longer claim now that he was deceased."

"She couldn't afford to continue at MIT?"

Diaz shook her head. "No, she didn't complete her degree."

"What was she studying?" he asked, although he thought he already knew the answer to that one.

"Computer Science," Diaz replied.

Reid inhaled sharply. "She could be the mole in the department."

Diaz bit her lip. It was clear she'd been thinking along the same lines. "But why would she tell Maria Lopez where Alberto Torres was? What could she possibly gain by that?"

Earlier in the year, they'd arranged a sting operation to capture the notorious cartel boss, Maria Lopez. Reid had sent Vargas an internal email giving him the undercover agent's address, and somehow it had been leaked to Lopez. The ruthless cartel boss had gotten there first, intending to take out Alberto Torres, but law enforcement had swooped in and captured them – or tried to. The resulting gun fight was one he'd never forget. Maria Lopez had lost her life in that fight, along with most of her crew.

"I don't know," he admitted, scratching his head. "Perhaps she wanted to derail the investigation. Perhaps she blames us for not apprehending her father's killer? Maybe she has a grudge against law enforcement?"

Diaz's eyes were huge. "Do you think she found out who Sonia Del Ray was and...and...?" She didn't finish the sentence. She didn't have to. Reid knew where she was going with it.

"We don't know that, yet," he said carefully. But Diaz had gone white. He thought back. "When did Shannon first appear on the scene?"

"About a year ago," Diaz said. "We were working on the Alberto Torres case. Vargas met her in a bar. I remember him telling me."

"Quite a coincidence," muttered Reid, now looking at Vargas and Shannon's relationship from a different angle. "Girl chats up detective in bar, they start a relationship, and shortly after that, information gets leaked to the cartel."

Diaz stared at him.

"What if she hacked into the system? It would be easy with her skills, and Vargas takes his laptop home with him. She'd have access to it."

"Maybe she was trying to find out who killed her father," Diaz whispered.

"I think she already knew who killed him," Reid reasoned. "What she wanted to know was what their names had been changed to and where to find them."

"But even we couldn't find that information. You had to ask Wilson."

"And he tapped the WITSEC database," Reid confirmed. "How

easy would it have been for Shannon to do the same using Vargas' computer?"

"Holy shit." Diaz stared at Reid. "What are we going to do?"

"Nothing for now," Reid said slowly.

"What?" She looked confused. "But—?"

"I want to look into Shannon some more, without her knowledge. If we bring her in for questioning, she's going to clam up, and we don't have any concrete proof that she's responsible for the leaks. She's been very careful to cover her steps. Our IT guys could see the system had been breached, but not by who. Plus, it would destroy Vargas."

Diaz was nodding. "We have to be a hundred percent sure."

He rubbed his jaw. "Exactly. The whole thing might be a terrible coincidence."

"But you don't believe that," she murmured.

He didn't, but he owed his colleague that much. "Keep this to yourself for now," he told Diaz. "I'm going to pay Shannon a visit tomorrow. It's time she and I got to know each other better."

20

"MARCY, ARE YOU OKAY?"

Kenzie held her breath. What now? She couldn't emerge from the study, he'd know that she'd been snooping.

There was a loud knock. "Marcy?"

Another voice. "Milo, what's going on?"

It was Felix. *Shit.*

Now she had both Hammonds to contend with. She glanced at the window. It was one floor up, but it might be her only way out. Before she went, though, she wanted to look in that last drawer.

Darting back to the desk, she pulled it open. What the—? It was filled with mobile phones. Burner phones. They must be. She took one out and shoved it in her purse. She was about to close the drawer when a business card caught her eye. It was a pale blue and faded with age. The corners were tatty, as if fingered regularly. On it, she could make out the picture of a woman. No, not a woman. An angel. The text read: *Coco Botanica.*

Was that a voodoo store?

Pocketing it, she pushed the drawer closed and ran for the

window. It was stiff, but she managed to open it. She pushed harder until it was wide enough to squeeze through.

Felix sounded angry. "What the hell do you think you're doing?"

She didn't catch Milo's reply.

"Can I talk to you for a second?" Felix demanded. There were footsteps as they went back into the lounge.

Kenzie hesitated. If she acted now, she could still make this work without blowing her cover. Carefully, she opened the study door and darted outside.

"She's Jacob's fucking mistress."

Kenzie froze.

"So what?"

"Get rid of her," Felix hissed.

"I don't want to." She could hear the almost pleading stubbornness in Milo's voice.

"She can't be here."

"Why? I like her. Every time I like a girl you want me to get rid of her."

There was a bang, the sound of a fist hitting the bar counter. "Don't be such a spineless lackey." Kenzie slipped on her shoes. "Christ, Milo. We'll talk about it later. Just get rid of her."

Kenzie chose that moment to re-enter the lounge. "Sorry I took so long. Oh, hello, Mr. Hammond. I hope we're not disturbing you?" She gave him her sweetest smile. To her surprise, there was a chihuahua darting around his ankles. "Oh, what a cute dog."

He stared at her for a long moment, then muttered, "Not at all."

Liar.

"It's nice to see you again." She wafted past him on a cloud of J'Adore and went to stand beside Milo.

"Likewise."

Kenzie could feel the daggers whizzing from Felix's eyes, over her head, in the direction of his son.

Get rid of her.

That could only mean one thing. Felix was scared of what she might find out.

"You know, I've suddenly developed a terrible headache," she told Milo with a grimace. "Do you mind if we do this another night?"

He scowled, first at her, then at his father for killing the mood. Kenny G was doing his best to restore it in the background, but it was no use. Resting the back of her hand against her forehead, she turned to Felix. "Would you mind walking me out? I took the liberty of calling a cab while I was in the bathroom. It'll be here any moment."

"But—" Milo fumbled for words.

She turned back to him. "Thanks for a wonderful evening, Milo. I had a lot of fun."

Felix's resting smug face had returned and he waved an arm in front of him. "Of course. Marcy, is it? It would be my pleasure. After you."

Kenzie descended the stairs, the dog's paws clicking on the marble beside her. There was probably going to be an almighty argument between father and son once she was gone. It was clear who called the shots in this family. Felix opened the front door and let her out.

"I'll buzz the gate," he called, as she stepped out into the night.

"Thanks." She turned and gave him a small wave, clutching her purse containing the burner phone tightly against her body.

Nick roared up as soon as the gates shut, and she sighed as she sank gratefully into the Porsche's leather-backed seats. "Thank God. I don't think I could have kept that up much longer."

"Are you okay? Did anything happen?" He cast a worried gaze over her.

"I'm fine. Milo's a bit thrown that I left, but luckily Felix walked in and gave me the perfect opportunity."

"Felix was there?"

"Yep, and he wasn't at all happy Milo had brought me home. If they killed Jacob, it was on his order."

Nick exhaled. "You think that's possible?"

"I don't know. There's nothing to indicate they had anything to do with his death." Yet. She set her purse on her lap.

"You didn't find anything?" She didn't miss the disappointment in his voice.

"I found a couple of things in his desk drawer," she told him. "But I haven't had a chance to look at them yet."

He glanced sideways at her. "What things?"

"A phone, some business cards. Let me take a look when I get home, and we can talk tomorrow."

"Okay." He was tired, she could tell, and she didn't blame him. The poor guy had been sitting in his car the whole time she and Milo were at dinner and the club, then he'd followed her back to the house.

"Thank you, Nick," She leaned across and squeezed his arm. "It was reassuring knowing you were there."

"You're welcome." He looked slightly mollified. "Glad to be of service, although I don't think I could ever be a cop. Stakeouts are so incredibly boring."

She laughed. "Point taken. But thank you. I mean it."

He nodded. "Call me tomorrow."

"I will."

She watched as he turned the car around and drove off, then walked up the path to her front door.

21

It was mid-morning by the time Reid got to Shannon's apartment. He'd made sure Vargas was out of the way, sifting through the contents of Jacob's office at Hammond Holdings company headquarters.

Shannon lived near the Miami Design District in Wynwood, one of the trendier zip codes in Miami, in a modern apartment block with panoramic views of the city. Reid stared up at the blinding white facade with its chrome and glass windows, private gym in the basement and concierge service. Shannon might not have had enough money to complete her studies, but she was certainly doing alright now.

As he walked across the expansive lobby, a thought occurred to him. Maybe she'd been selling inside information to Maria Lopez. How much would that be worth? It would explain how Maria had known that Alberto Torres was still alive, where he was living, and how to find him. The cartel boss had been one step ahead of them the entire time. Now it made sense.

My enemy's enemy.

He should have seen it before. He'd always thought Shannon and

Vargas were a strange match. Shannon was all fiery passion, while Vargas was cool and composed. She was impulsive, he was methodical.

If his theory was correct, she'd been using Vargas the whole time. Reid shook his head. His colleague had real feelings for Shannon, and he was going to be devastated when he found out.

Shannon opened the door after the first ring. Her vivid green eyes widened when she saw who was standing there. "Reid, what a surprise." Then her expression changed to one of concern. "Has something happened to Willie?" She was a good actress, he'd give her that much.

"Vargas is fine. I brought you this."

He handed her an expertly wrapped engagement present, about the size of a shoebox. "It's been in my car for days, and since I was in the neighborhood, I thought I'd drop it off in person. Hope I'm not disturbing you?"

"No, not at all. Come in." She held the door open so he could enter the apartment. "That's so kind of you. I wasn't expecting this."

As he followed her down the hall and into the lounge, he took a good look around. Unlike Marcy Guerrier's place, Shannon's was clean and uncluttered. The neutral palette was soothing, and the recessed lighting was subtle and classy. To his surprise, one entire side of the open plan living dining area was covered in bookshelves. He spotted philosophy books, technology books, and economic books, as well as lots of literary fiction. Given Shannon's vivacious character and love of socializing, he wouldn't have put her as a bookish type of person. Then he remembered she'd studied at MIT. Suddenly a lot of things made sense. The books, the photographs dotted around the room, the sophisticated artwork on the walls.

He studied a smiling group photograph in a silver frame perched on one of the bookshelves. Identical sweatshirts, stone pillars dominating the background, the radiant glow of a carefree student life – not that he'd know. He went straight from school to the Police Academy, but this photograph resembled a recruitment brochure. She was much younger then, fresh-faced with her hair pulled back in a ponytail like Kenzie wore hers. Untainted. Unaffected by the trauma of life.

"College friends," she said, following his gaze.

"MIT. I'm impressed."

Her eyebrows shot up. "You know it?"

"I can tell by the pillars." He couldn't. He'd read it in her file, but she wouldn't know that. "When did you graduate?"

She hesitated. "A while back. Can I get you something? Coffee?"

Avoiding the question. Now why would she do that? Perhaps she was ashamed of dropping out. Maybe she was afraid he'd ask why.

"Yeah, that'd be great." The look on her face told him she was confused as to why he was here. Sure, the gift was a plausible excuse, but it wasn't something he'd usually do, and Reid had a feeling Shannon had him pretty much figured out.

"I hope I haven't interrupted you." He paused in front of the open laptop on the pale pinewood dining table. On the screen were rows and columns of data. A database maybe? Of what, he didn't know.

"I was doing some work for a client, but nothing that can't wait." As she walked past to the kitchen, she pressed the lid of her laptop down.

"What is it that you do again?" he asked, undeterred.

"I design security solutions for businesses," she called from the other side of a rectangular island that divided the living room from the kitchen. "Data protection, encryption, that sort of thing."

Hacking into the police database would be a walk in the park for someone with her skills.

"Impressive. You learn that at MIT?"

"Yeah. Among other things." She reappeared with two steaming mugs of coffee. "Black, isn't it?"

"Perfect." He was impressed she'd remembered, but then he was getting the impression that Shannon didn't miss much.

"You not going into the station today?" she asked.

"No, I'm working on my house, or I was," he said. "I had to get some supplies."

She sat down opposite him. "How's the rebuild going?" Shannon, of course, knew his cabin had burned to the ground and he was living out of a flea-bag motel.

"Slowly, but it's getting there." He took a sip from his mug. "This is great coffee, by the way."

She gave a secret smile. "I know a guy. A Columbian supplier. Willie loves it too."

"Sounds like it should be illegal."

She laughed. "It does, doesn't it?"

"How long have you lived here?" Reid waved his hand in the air. He was no good at small talk – his strength was in the interrogation room – but he had to get the measure of the woman. "It's a nice place."

"Thanks, I like it. I've been here about six months, give or take. Before that I was in Palmer Lake."

"Ah, yeah. I remember Vargas saying." He hesitated. "Now that you guys are engaged, will you be moving in together?"

"Of course." But she didn't meet his gaze. Vargas' place was nothing like this. Reid couldn't picture Shannon giving this up to move into a two-bedroom condo in Westchester.

"It was a great party the other night," he said.

She smiled. "You left early. It got pretty raucous."

He didn't think anyone had seen him go. "I heard. I know Vargas was feeling it the next day."

"We all were." She grinned and tossed her flaming red hair over her shoulder. "But it was worth it. Everyone had a great time."

"Vargas must have been hungover because he missed the call out the next night. That's very unusual for him."

She frowned, but her voice remained even. "That was the waitress who was found in the dumpster, right?"

"That's right. She was so young too, only twenty." He watched Shannon's face for a reaction, but there was none.

"That's terrible. Do you know who did it?"

"Not yet, but we're working on it. We're looking into the woman's background, her friends and family, and so on." There was a flicker of concern, but so slight he could almost have imagined it.

"Well, I hope you get to the bottom of it soon."

"We will." He downed the rest of his coffee in one large gulp, then got up to leave. He'd found out everything he'd come for. "I'd better get back to the building site. Got some stuff to finish off before the rain comes."

She gave a hesitant nod, as if she was expecting something else. When he didn't speak, she also got to her feet. "Okay, thanks for stopping by and for the gift."

"Not a problem. I hope you like it." The sales assistant at the decor shop where he'd bought it had assured him she would.

Shannon walked him to the door. "Thanks again. See you soon."

"I'm sure you will." With a final wave, he left.

One thing he knew for sure was he'd misjudged Shannon Maisie. She wasn't the carefree, effervescent, fun-loving person they all thought she was. Maybe she had been once. He thought of the fresh-faced girl in the photograph. But not anymore.

22

Kenzie picked up the mobile phone she'd found in Milo's study. It was a cheap brand, commonly used for burner phones. Unfortunately, it was locked, so she couldn't get in. There were five missed calls on the display. Someone was eager to get hold of Milo.

Turning it sideways, she realized it was on silent, so she toggled the lever until the sound was on. Next time it rang, she wouldn't miss it. Then she dropped the device into her purse.

Reid might be able to unlock it, but he couldn't use it as evidence since she'd acquired it illegally. Stolen items weren't admissible in court. Besides, he'd be furious when she told him what she'd done. Stupid, dangerous, impulsive. She could picture him berating her, and she'd have to agree. That was one of the more impulsive things she'd ever done.

She fingered the business card she'd found in the bottom drawer underneath the phone. A quick Google search had rendered no results. That wasn't a surprise. Voodoo stores rarely advertised. The address was faded, but she could work it out. Little Haiti.

Picking up her keys, she headed for the door. "Right," she

muttered as she left the house. "Let's see what you were doing there, Milo."

The rusted sign hanging above the front of the store read *Coco Botanica*. This was the place. Kenzie peered through the dirty window but couldn't make out much. The sun reflecting off the glass made it impossible to see inside. She pushed the door open, crinkling her nose. The pungent scent of incense was overwhelming.

"Hello?" There was nobody there.

She looked around. It was a creepy place, with silent statuettes staring down at her, jars of unidentifiable herbs, wooden crucifixes and beaded rosaries hanging on rusted hooks. She shivered, not because it was cold, but because it was that sort of place. Somewhere, in the background, she heard a faint clucking sound.

"Hello?" she called again. "Is anyone here?"

Then she spotted a doorway behind the counter. It was hidden behind a curtain of beads. She pushed them aside, the jangling making her skin tingle.

What on earth was that? An altar? In the middle of the small back room stood a high table with an assortment of stains on it. A ring of candles flickered ominously around the edge. Kenzie instinctively wrapped her arms around herself. The walls seemed to close in on her, the wallpaper peeling upwards as if trying to get away from whatever happened down below.

"What you doin' in here?" came a deep voice, making her jump. A man had appeared through another door, which she assumed led out to the back of the shop. The clucking was louder in here.

"Sorry, I was looking for Mr. Utanga. Is that you?"

He scowled at her, then gestured for her to return to the front of the store. "Who wants to know?" He had a strange accent, a mixture between Jamaican and French. Like Marcy's. She guessed he was Haitian.

"My name is Marcy. I need your help."

Once they were in the front, he turned to face her. Long dreadlocks reached past his shoulders and the flowing robe he wore resembled that of a priest. A Voodoo priest.

Pale blue eyes, so light in color they were almost translucent, studied her. Kenzie got the feeling he was seeing a lot more than just her appearance. There was a sliver of a scar down his left check, and his ear was mangled on the same side. Another victim of violence.

"You want to contact someone on the other side?" His insipid eyes glistened as they caught the candlelight.

Her mind immediately flew to her mother, which was bizarre, since she hadn't thought of her in a while. Not since she'd solved the mystery of her disappearance. "Why'd you ask that?"

He shrugged. "It was just a feeling."

Kenzie shook her head. "No, that's not why I'm here."

His voice rose an octave. "What you want my help for, then?"

"I need—I need you to put a spell on someone." Today she was the disgruntled mistress. The one who'd been promised the world but lied to. The one who wanted revenge. "No, not a spell. A curse."

The man's eyes widened, then his face cracked into a smile. "You 'ad your heart broken, girlie?"

She glared back. "Something like that."

When he didn't respond, she fished in her purse. "I can pay."

His gaze narrowed.

"I'm serious. I want you to cast him. I know you can."

"'ow do you know this?" he demanded.

She fidgeted. "A friend told me. You did it for him."

He sucked in air through his teeth. "Your friend is mistaken. I don't do curses. I only heal."

Kenzie glanced at the bottles of herbs and potions on the shelves. "I want to heal, but the only way I can is if he is dead. Will you help me to heal?"

The man said nothing. The candle fluttered, even though there was no breeze.

Kenzie put two hundred dollars on the counter. "There is more where that came from."

Mr. Utanga stared at it, then back at her. "Do you know what you are asking, girlie? There is no going back from this."

"I know," she whispered.

His voice was a growl. "Tell me which friend."

Kenzie set the faded business card on the table. "Milo Hammond."

Another long pause. Kenzie didn't move. The walls seemed to hold their breath. Even the chickens quietened down.

Eventually, Utanga gave a reluctant nod. "My services are not cheap."

"How much?"

"It will cost you a thousand dollars."

"I'll pay," Kenzie said.

Pale eyes bored into hers. "Bring me something of his. A toothbrush, a hairbrush, a nail clipping. I will try to help you."

"When?"

"Tomorrow. Come at noon and come alone. I will be here."

"Okay. Thank you."

She turned and walked out, leaving the money on the table.

Outside, she breathed a huge sigh of relief. Thank goodness she was out of that creepy place. Mr. Utanga was freaky, and she had no intention of going back there. She'd got what she'd come for. He'd done it. He was the one who'd issued the curse. When she'd mentioned Milo's name, he hadn't flinched. He'd recognized it.

Milo had sent Jacob the voodoo doll. Was it to warn him? To get him to keep his mouth shut? Was it a threat? Had they followed through on their threat and killed him too?

Questions ricocheted through her mind as she drove away.

Kenzie headed towards South Kendall where Nick worked. The animal clinic was right next to Palmetto Golf Course, and as she drove past, she admired the long, smooth green flanked by lush palms and shrubbery. A group of golfers played in the sunshine, enjoying their weekend activity, oblivious to her chaotic thoughts.

Nick met her outside at a pop-up coffee bar across the road. "Have you looked at those items you found in Milo Hammond's study?"

"Yeah." She put them on the table. The phone and the business card. "I can't get into the phone, but someone's been trying hard to get a hold of Milo."

"Five missed calls," Nick said, leaning forward. "I wonder what it's about."

"Who knows?" She shrugged. "There were more phones in that drawer. I'm guessing they're burners for all his sneaky dealings."

Nick's eyes widened. "Shouldn't we go to the police?"

"Yes, we should. Except I can't tell them I stole the phone, can I?"

He grimaced. "I guess not. Won't your friend, Detective Reid, overlook that?"

"I doubt it." While Reid had let things slide from time to time, she highly suspected this wouldn't be one of them. "I'm not supposed to be investigating. This is a police investigation now. Jacob is dead. There's no need for me to keep going on this."

"Why are you?" He tilted his head to the side.

"Because something's not right, and I know the police are stumped. We had a head start on this case, so it makes sense to keep going. If I find anything concrete, of course I'll go to Reid."

"What about the business card?" he asked.

"Now that is an interesting story." She told him about the Voodoo shop, and when she got to the part about the curse, he gasped. "You can't be serious. You're not going back there."

"No, of course not. I just wanted to see if he'd do it, and he did. He's the one who put the curse on Jacob. I know it."

"Kenzie, I really think we should go to the police with this. You've done enough."

Before she had a chance to answer, the burner phone rang.

"Are you going to answer it?" Nick whispered. She stared at it, then made a decision and picked it up. The call connected, but she didn't speak.

A voice said, "Milo? Is that you?"

"Say, yeah," she hissed at Nick.

He bent his head towards the phone. "Yeah."

"I've been trying to get hold of you, man." The caller had a strong Spanish accent. "Where you been? You know what, it doesn't matter. The shipment is on the way. It'll get to you on Tuesday. South Florida Terminal."

"Say, okay," she told Nick. He did as he was told, then she cut the call.

"You don't think they'll be suspicious?" Nick asked, worried.

"No, he'll assume you couldn't talk."

Nick whistled under his breath. "What do you think that was about?"

"I have no idea." Kenzie frowned. "It could be a supplier, I guess, but then why's he calling on a burner phone?"

"He mentioned a shipment," Nick said.

"Milo does run a shipping company," Kenzie pointed out. "It could be nothing."

But in her gut, she knew it wasn't.

23

"Are you going to Sonia Del Ray's autopsy?" Vargas asked when he got in on Monday morning. "It's scheduled for ten o'clock."

Reid was already at his desk, an empty espresso cup in front of him. "No, I've got some reports to write." He looked up as if the idea had just occurred to him. "Why don't you go?"

Vargas had never been to an autopsy before, it'd be good for him. Plus, Reid needed to get him out of the way so he could discuss what to do about Shannon with Diaz, who'd just walked in and was shooting them sideways glances.

"Yeah, if you're sure?" He grinned. "It'll be a first for me."

Reid felt bad going behind his back, but nobody knew about Shannon's connection to the case yet, and he wanted to keep it that way until he knew how they were going to play this.

"Let's hope they can find the cause of death," Reid mumbled.

"I saw the extended tox screen on Jacob Peters came back." Vargas gave him a knowing look. "Nothing concrete."

Reid shook his head. "It must be something untraceable, something we're missing - and before you say anything, it's not the curse, okay?"

"I didn't say anything." Vargas shrugged. "You must admit it's weird though."

That it was.

Reid took a deep breath. "Keep me posted."

"Will do."

He waited until Vargas had left before he turned to Diaz. "Let's get a coffee."

They walked to the nearby pop-up coffee stand. It was a glorious morning. The sun shone down like it hadn't a care in the world. Reid wished he felt as chipper.

"I went to see Shannon yesterday," he told his colleague, whose eyes widened.

"Why?"

"I needed to see her in her own environment, not with Vargas, not being the center of attention."

"And?" She peered at him over her extra shot cappuccino.

"Different person." He explained about the apartment, the books, the security work she did for clients. "There was something extremely complicated on her laptop," he divulged. "Reams of code flashing across the screen. Couldn't make anything of it."

"She's smart, that's for sure," Diaz agreed. "I sent the voodoo doll found at Sonia's to the lab for testing. Hopefully the sender left some DNA on the envelope."

Reid nodded, abstractly.

"But do you think she did it? Do you think she killed Sonia Del Ray?"

"That I don't know. When I mentioned we were looking into Sonia's relatives, she flinched, but that doesn't mean anything. Presumably she knows who Sonia is, if she's as smart as I think she is."

"What did IT come up with?" Diaz asked. "I know you asked them to look into the leak before."

"They could see the firewall had been breached, but they

couldn't tell where the threat had come from. All we know is that it's internal."

"Then she's using Willie's laptop to do it."

"I guess so, unless she's found another way. There's a good chance she's using her own laptop and his logins or commandeering his laptop from hers. I don't know how these things work."

"Has IT inspected Willie's computer?"

"No, only the network. I've got the report back at the station. You can read it."

"We need to take a look at his laptop," Diaz said thoughtfully. "If she's using it to hack into WITSEC or the police database, there must be evidence on there."

Reid sighed. "I hate going behind his back, but I think you're right. The problem is I don't know his passcode."

"I do."

He arched an eyebrow.

She gave a defensive grimace. "What? We sit next to each other. I've seen him type it in a hundred times."

Reid thought about this. "He's tied up at the autopsy all morning. If we're going to do it, now's our chance."

"Who do we know who can help?" Diaz scratched her head. "IT obviously isn't up to the task."

Reid paused, thinking. "I might know someone, but there's no guarantee he can come over now."

"Call him," she said.

Reid took out his phone and called the *Herald's* office.

"Boss, there's a woman on the phone asking for you," Monroe called from across the open plan office a short time later. "She sounds pretty distressed. Gail Peters."

"Put her through." Reid picked up his desk phone. "Mrs. Peters? This is Detective Garrett."

"Oh, thank goodness." Her voice trembled. "I want to report a burglary."

He sat upright. "You've been robbed?"

"Yes, I've just got home and found the front door open. The house is in a mess." She burst into tears. "They've been through everything."

"Are you sure they're gone?" His main concern was for her welfare.

"I—I think so."

"Okay, I'll send an officer over. Don't worry, it's going to be okay."

She sniffed. "What were they looking for? Is this connected to Jacob?"

"Possibly." His first thought was the laptop. It was currently with the forensic tech team, and so far, they'd found nothing. "Don't touch anything. The officer will be with you shortly."

"Thank you."

Reid looked around the station. He couldn't send Diaz, he needed her here when Raoul arrived. Vargas was at the autopsy and Hamilton was out.

"Monroe!" he yelled. The elderly detective looked up.

"Yeah?"

"I need you to respond to a burglary."

He looked surprised. It had been a while since Monroe had been on a call. "Is it in progress?"

"No, the perpetrators have already gone. We'll need forensics there, though."

"Sure, where?"

Reid gave him Gail's address. "It's Jacob Peters' house."

Monroe's eyebrows shot up.

"Get the wife's statement," he said, "and make sure she's okay. She sounded shaken up on the phone."

He grabbed his jacket off the back of his chair. "Will do, boss."

As Monroe left, Raoul arrived. They passed each other at the entrance. Kenzie's researcher strode into the squad room, laptop bag swung over one shoulder, wearing jeans and a gray hooded sweatshirt. He drew curious glances from the other officers, but when Reid got up to shake his hand, they settled down again.

"Thanks for coming." He led the way to a vacant desk on which Vargas' laptop sat. Diaz had moved it to avert suspicion. "This is it."

"Got the passcode?" Raoul asked, once he'd sat down.

Diaz gave it to him.

"How long's this going to take?" Reid asked, checking his watch. They had an hour at the most, until Vargas got back.

Raoul looked up. "Depends on how well he's covered his tracks." Reid had briefed him on the phone. Obviously they wouldn't be able to discern whether Shannon had accessed the police database, as she'd have used Vargas' login. It was the WITSEC database he was more interested in. Shannon would have had to hack into that to get Alberto Torres' address last year, and again to get Sonia's details. Vargas would never have done that, he didn't have access, so it could only be her.

"She," corrected Diaz.

Raoul pursed his lips. "I'll let you know when I find it." Forty-five minutes later, Raoul made an ah-ha sound.

Reid looked up. "Got something?"

"Sure do. Took me longer than expected. Whoever did this knew what they were doing."

He already knew that. "But you've got something?"

"Yeah. This laptop *was* used to access the Witness Security Files Information System. I've got two data stamps. The first time was in October last year, and then again this month."

Reid's heart sank. She *had* used Vargas' laptop. Until now he hadn't been sure, but this sealed it.

"You're absolutely sure?"

Raoul frowned. "Yeah, I'm sure. I can see the search queries. Do you want to know what they were?"

No.

"Yes." He could guess. Diaz shot him a dark look.

"The first was a search for Alberto Torres. It returned one result." He raised an eyebrow, but Reid shook his head. "We don't need to know the details. He's moved on, anyway."

Raoul nodded. "The second search was longer and returned two results."

"What were they?" Reid's heart was in his throat. Beside him, Diaz took a slow breath and held it.

"Sonia Del Ray, real name Portia Stuckey." Diaz exhaled. Reid shook his head. Shit. "And the second result?" Although he already knew.

"Fred Stuckey, alias Blake Fisher."

Blake Fisher. That's the name Sonia's brother had been given. "Is there an address?"

"Sure, I'll pull up the record." His fingers flew over the keyboard. It took seconds before a WITSEC screen appeared. "There you go." Raoul nodded to the address.

Reid wrote it down.

They managed to keep it together until Raoul left.

"Holy crap," Diaz exclaimed, in the small confines of the printer room where they'd gone to talk. "It *was* Shannon. I can't see Vargas hacking into the WITSEC database, can you?"

"He's got some computer skills," Reid said, "but he's not that good."

Diaz couldn't stand still. "Shit, what are we going to do? We can't arrest her, there's no proof she did it. All we know was that it was Willie's laptop that breached the firewall and hacked into the system."

"Vargas would be the one we'd have to arrest," Reid said sourly.

Diaz scowled. "We can't do that. You're going to have to talk to him."

"I can't. What if he tells Shannon?"

She threw her hands up. "What choice do we have?"

Reid turned away. "I hate going behind his back like this, but I can't see any other way. If we tell him, we risk her finding out. She's our prime suspect in Sonia Del Ray's murder."

"You'll have to take him off the case," she murmured.

"He'll suspect something." Reid clawed at his stubble that was now turning into a beard. "What we need is proof."

"The laptop?"

Reid shook his head. "She's too good. You heard Raoul. She didn't leave a trace."

"What about her device?" Diaz asked. "We could get a warrant and ask Raoul to look at that. If it was used to access Vargas' computer or the police database, we've got her."

"We should analyze it," he agreed. "But even if she did use her own laptop, it doesn't mean she killed Sonia. It's still circumstantial."

Diaz perched on the side of the table housing the printer. "Then what are we going to do?"

He thought for a minute. "Nothing, for now. Let's wait and see what the lab comes back with. We might get her DNA off the envelope."

"Like you said, still doesn't mean she killed Sonia." Diaz gritted her teeth. "It's not a crime to send someone a voodoo doll." The printer whirred to life, making her jump. Someone had sent through a print job.

Reid stared vacantly at the paper being spat out of the machine, his mind miles away. "We have another problem."

"The younger brother?" She was one step ahead of him.

"Yeah. Shannon knows his alias and where he lives."

Diaz gave a somber nod. "Do you think she'll go after him? Even though he had nothing to do with the murder?"

Reid looked at her. "He was there when her father was killed. I know Sonia took the rap but..." He left the sentence hanging.

"You think she covered for him?"

"I read the original case file. She was adamant he had nothing to do with it."

Diaz tilted her head to the side. "So what's the problem?"

"Too adamant. I don't buy it." He glared at the pile of paper sitting on the tray. "The kid could have been the perpetrator. We have no way of knowing for sure what went down without talking to him."

Diaz let out a heavy breath. "We have to find Blake Fisher before Shannon does."

Reid gave a somber nod. "And she's already had a head start."

24

It was mid-morning when Kenzie finally arrived at work. Sebastian had had an appointment with his social worker, so she'd taken him to that. It had gone well, they were happy with his progress. Now he was eighteen, they'd said, he could move out. There was no longer any need for a fostering arrangement.

Kenzie had discussed this with Seb on the way to school, and he'd said he'd like to stay, if that was okay. She was still smiling when she entered the building.

Walking to her desk, she noticed her researcher wasn't there. Strange, he was always at his desk. "Where's Raoul?" she asked, popping her head into Keith's office. She could barely see him behind the mountain of newspapers and paperwork on his desk.

"He got a call from your friend, Detective Garrett," her editor said. "Raced out of here with his laptop saying they needed his help. No idea what it's about, but I can't argue with the cops, can I?"

"I guess not." Frowning, she went back to her desk. What did Reid want with Raoul? She tried her assistant's cellphone, but it diverted to voicemail. Giving up, she got to work. There was something she'd been meaning to do, and now seemed like the perfect time. Raoul would be back soon, and she'd find out what he'd been working on then.

First, she googled the Juilliard School of performing arts and navigated to the section where they advertised the final year showcases.

June.

That gave her an idea of the date. Then she called the Alumni Office and said she was trying to get hold of Gail Winslow, in the hopes that she'd agree to an interview for a dance segment they were running in the *Herald*. The secretary was only too happy to give her Gail's contact details. "What year did she graduate?" Kenzie asked. "1998. Got it. Thanks."

Now to find the Formosa Motel. She looked it up online, but there was no website. Not surprising. It might not even be around anymore. Gnawing on her lower lip, she opened her contacts on her phone and searched for Liesl Bernstein. Liesl was a reporter for the New York Times, but she was from Florida. They'd studied journalism together.

"Oh my God!" Liesl exclaimed when she answered the phone. "I was just thinking about you the other day."

"Were you?" Kenzie smiled. They were always like this. Fell naturally into conversation as if no time had passed at all. She really should make more of an effort to stay in touch.

"I read your piece on Maria Lopez. Brilliant stuff, darling. Let's get together soon and catch up. When are you in New York again?"

"Not for a while," she said ruefully. "But thanks. It means a lot." Liesl was a respected journalist in her own right. "I actually called to ask you something."

"Shoot, I'm all ears."

"I'm looking for a guy who stayed at the Formosa Motel back in June 1998. I know it's a long time ago, but I was hoping you could find out if the motel is still around. They might have a record of his name. I've got an address."

"Sure, give it to me, and I'll take a look."

Kenzie gave it to her. "The phone number's out of order now."

"Not surprising after all this time. What's this guy done?"

"What makes you think he's done something?"

"Because I know you, Kenzie. You wouldn't be looking for him otherwise."

"He may have witnessed something, that's all." She kept it vague.

"Alright," her friend said. Kenzie could almost hear the smirk in her voice. "Don't tell me. I'll see what I can find out."

"First name could be Jeff," Kenzie added, "But I'm not sure about that. Might be an alias."

"Intriguing. Jeff, got it. Anything else?"

"He was a salesman. Wouldn't have stayed long. I'm thinking a day or two."

"They might not have records that far back," Liesl said. "But you never know."

"Thanks, I appreciate it."

They chatted for a while and then said goodbye, Liesl promising to be in touch as soon as she knew something.

Kenzie sat back in her chair. It was a long shot, but as Liesl had said, you never knew. She might just be able to find Gail's rapist. What she was going to do with that knowledge, she hadn't yet decided.

Raoul came in shortly after lunch.

"Okay, spill," she said before he'd even had a chance to sit down. "What were you helping Detective Garrett with?"

He took out his laptop and dumped his bag on the floor. "They had a security breach, that's all. Someone hacked into the WITSEC database and looked up a couple of names."

WITSEC? Her mind was spinning.

"I don't understand. Who?"

"I don't know. They didn't say. It was a woman, though."

"A woman?" That was even more intriguing. She knew Reid suspected there was a leak in the department, but the only woman there was Diaz, and it couldn't be her.

A thought struck her. There was another woman who was there a lot. She wasn't an officer, but she would have access to the system. "Which computer were you looking at?"

"One of the detectives. Vargas, his username was."

A chill slid down her spine.

Shannon.

Was she the leak? Had she been the one to give away Alberto Torres' location? No, it couldn't be her. Why would she do such a thing? What did she have to gain?

"Was Reid, I mean Detective Garrett, there?"

"Yeah. He stood right behind me."

"What was his reaction when you told him you'd found the leak?"

"He was shocked. I could tell by his expression. They both were."

"Both?"

"Yeah, him and the female detective, Diaz, is it?"

"Yes." Kenzie realized she didn't know Diaz's first name.

Raoul nodded.

"Was the breach some time ago?" Kenzie asked. Alberto Torres' information had been leaked months ago, because she'd only just started visiting Maria in prison when the cartel boss had asked if Torres was still alive.

"Yeah, the first was last year, the second last week."

Kenzie gasped. "What were the names?"

"You know I can't tell you that." Raoul crossed his arms in front of his bony chest.

"Come on, Raoul. This is me. Reid and I go way back." Or they did.

The researcher pursed his lips. "I'm sorry, Kenz. It's police business. You wouldn't want me sharing your secrets with everyone, would you?"

"You tell Keith everything," she huffed. Why did he have to be so damn discreet? Yet she knew he was right. It wasn't ethical to pass on sensitive police information, particularly about people in the Witness Protection Program.

"That's not fair. Keith's my boss. Besides, he threatened me with dismissal if I didn't tell him." They both knew she was referring to Maria Lopez's illegitimate child.

"Okay, I'll just ask Reid then." Kenzie took out her phone and made the call.

It rang a while before he answered.

"Hi, it's me. I need to talk to you."

"I can't now." There was a roar in the background like he was in a vehicle. "I'm in the middle of something."

"It's important. We need to touch base."

A pause.

"I'll call you back tonight."

"Okay." She had to be content with that.

Reid, as it turned out, did not call her back. She tried several times but got no response. Eventually, she drove out to the Gator Inn to see him. The sun was low in the sky when she turned onto the dirt road flanked by wide canals that led to the motel where he was staying. On either side of the road, the sawgrass was so high it blocked the view of the swamp. It was only the orange glow on the water up ahead that reminded her she was surrounded.

A feeling of nostalgia swept over her as she passed the site of Reid's old cabin. Kenzie slowed to take a look. The construction was in progress. She could see the foundations had been laid and they were starting to rebuild the deck that stretched out over the water.

How many times had they sat on his old wooden rocking bench out on that deck and talked, while watching the eagles swoop from the sky as they caught their prey or hearing the swish of a gator's tail as it sank into the murky green water? Once, they'd even held hands, enjoying the sounds of the swamp and each other.

Kenzie pushed the emotion aside. There was no time for that

now. She'd hurt him, she knew that, and it would take a long time for him to forgive her, if he ever did.

You can't have it both ways.

With a start, she realized there was a dark figure standing on the new wooden deck, silhouetted against the burning sky.

It was Reid.

25

Reid heard car tires kicking up gravel and turned around. He recognized Kenzie's car as she pulled over and cut the engine. Damn, he'd forgotten to call her back.

It wasn't that he didn't want to; it was more that he had so much on his plate, he couldn't think about anything else. The view from his deck always soothed him when things got to be too much, so he'd come here to the building site in hopes it might do the same for him now. It had helped, but not as much as sitting down and watching it with a cold beer.

"I thought that was you." She was smiling, her hair loose for a change, the blonde strands catching the amber light.

"Yeah, sorry I didn't get back to you. I needed some down time, you know?"

Her forehead creased. "You okay?"

He gave a stiff nod. "Long day."

She studied him. "Wanna tell me about it?"

Reid hesitated. He'd love nothing more than to sit and talk like they used to, except there was no house to sit in and Smiley's, next to the Gator Inn, with its loud music and constant theme of breaking bottles and bar fights, was not conducive to a cozy chat.

"I'd better get back," he said, but his voice lacked enthusiasm.

"Well, I need to talk to you, so maybe we can find somewhere to sit down?" At his surprised look, she added, "It's important."

"Okay." If Kenzie said it was important, it usually was. One of the things he'd always admired about her was her gut instinct. She was hardly ever wrong. Besides, he only had his stuffy room at the motel to look forward to.

"How about here?" She pointed to a pile of logs. It wasn't the most comfortable bench in the world, but it would do. They sat down, side by side, both looking out over the glistening surface of the swamp. The water lapped at their feet.

"So, what's up?" Reid asked, breaking one of the few comfortable silences they'd had recently.

"Raoul told me what happened today."

He grimaced. "He shouldn't have done that."

"Don't worry, he didn't mention any names, but he told me he'd helped you figure out who the leak was in the department."

Reid didn't respond, just kept staring straight ahead.

"I guessed it was Shannon."

He turned sharply. "How did you know that?"

"Raoul mentioned it was a woman. After I ruled out Diaz, it could only be Shannon. Then I got thinking, she seduced Willie at the same time we were working on the Alberto Torres case. A chance meeting in a bar. A sexy redhead seducing a backwater cop – no offense. It's a little too convenient."

"None taken." Sweetwater had been backwater then. Somehow, he'd managed to turn it around. Now they had graduates requesting to work there. He almost smiled at the way she said 'we' like they were a team. They had been for a while. A good team, too.

Kenzie hesitated. "What was she doing looking up names on the WITSEC database?"

"You're not supposed to know that," he hissed.

"Well, I do, so it's pointless denying it. You may as well tell me what's going on. I take it Willie doesn't know?"

He sighed and shook his head. That was what was bugging him the most. He had to keep his colleague and friend in the dark.

"When are you going to tell him?"

"Soon. The problem is we can't prove it was Shannon. Until we have something definite, I can't bring her in for questioning."

"But I thought—"

"It's not conclusive. She used Vargas' laptop to hack into the system. It looks like he's at fault, not her."

"Crap."

"Exactly. Until we have more, we can't touch her."

"What about bringing her in for questioning?"

"I want to, but it would destroy Vargas. You know how he feels about her. Besides, we'd have to take him off the case."

Kenzie looked at him. "Jacob Peters?"

"No, the dead waitress."

"I don't understand. What's Shannon got to do with that?"

Reid bit his tongue. Shit. He must be tired. "Diaz linked Shannon to the victim."

Kenzie's eyes grew huge. "No way. How?"

"This goes no further," he warned.

She held up her hand. "Scout's honor."

"I mean it, Kenz. You can't print any of this. It's an active investigation."

"I'm not going to." She looked offended. "None of this was ever for a story."

"It turns out the dead girl murdered Shannon's father."

Kenzie gasped so loudly a startled bird took flight nearby. "You're kidding!"

"I wish I was. She stabbed him multiple times outside his house one day after school. He died before paramedics could get to him."

"Oh my God. Did she serve time?"

"She did. Five years in a juvenile facility. Her younger brother was with her when it happened. They were both placed in witness protection."

Kenzie stared at him. "Hence the database breach."

"Yeah. How's this for a coincidence? Shannon hacks into the WITSEC database and searches for the girl's new name and address. Days later, that same girl is found dead in a dumpster outside the restaurant where she worked."

"You don't think..." Kenzie couldn't continue.

Reid knew how she felt. The words were almost unsayable. Shannon was Vargas' fiancé. One of them. The thought that she could be a killer was unfathomable. Still, he had to consider it. "I don't know, but you can see how it looks."

"Isn't that enough to bring her in?" Kenzie asked.

"She'd just deny it, and Vargas would take the fall. It was his laptop, remember?"

"Oh yeah. Shit."

They were back to square one.

"What about her house? You could get a warrant and search it. There might be something linking her to the dead girl other than the database breach?"

"I went over there under false pretenses to check it out, but I didn't find anything. And if she's involved, she's a good actress. Almost as good as you." Kenzie had the enviable ability to morph into another role when she went undercover. In fact, she was so good at it, he often wondered if she didn't believe it herself.

Kenzie flushed. "Thanks, I think."

"She didn't let anything slip," Reid added. "Not even when I mentioned the waitress."

"I always thought she was smarter than she let on," Kenzie mused.

He gave a curt nod of agreement. "I underestimated her. Should have realized there was something not right about their relationship. I mean, her and Vargas?" He shook his head. "They're so different. I always thought it was strange how they'd fallen for each other."

"It was all a charade," Kenzie murmured. "Poor Willie. He'll be devastated."

Reid nodded. "I know," he murmured.

"Is that where you were this afternoon?" she asked. "At Shannon's place?"

"Nah, we got a line on the younger brother and thought he might be in danger too, but he wasn't at his registered address. The new tenants said he'd left weeks ago."

Kenzie frowned. "Why do you want to find him? You think she'll go after him too?"

"He was there when Shannon's father was killed." Reid hesitated. "There's also some confusion as to who actually stabbed Ron McDonald."

She sucked in a breath. "You mean it could have been the kid brother?"

"I don't know. In the police report, Sonia, that's the dead girl, swears she did it."

Kenzie was nodding slowly. "She could have been protecting him."

"Exactly." He loved the way they were always on the same wavelength. "Fred was twelve at the time."

Kenzie gave a low whistle. "That is very young to be committing murder. Did Sonia say why she did it?"

"He was a jerk who had it in for her, or something along those lines."

"Jeepers." Kenzie fell silent, but he could sense her brain working overtime. The surface of the water changed from burnished orange to a shimmering indigo as the sun dipped below the horizon. Somewhere in the reeds, there was a muted splash.

"What I don't understand is why the killer sent Sonia a voodoo doll?"

"You think Shannon sent it?"

"If she's the killer, then yeah. It makes sense, right?"

"Was it the same kind of doll as the one Jacob received?"

"Identical, right down to the pin in the heart."

Kenzie was shaking her head. "No, that can't be right."

"What do you mean?"

"Well, if she sent that doll to Sonia, she must have sent the first doll to Jacob Peters, and there's no connection between them, is there?"

Reid crossed his legs in front of him. "Not that we can find. Jacob died of asphyxiation, cause unknown, while Sonia died of a brain hemorrhage, according to the ME. Vargas attended the autopsy this morning."

Kenzie tapped her fingers on the log. "Listen, Reid, there's something I have to tell you."

"Here we go," he muttered, glancing sideways at her.

"I know who sent that voodoo doll to Jacob Peters, and it wasn't Shannon."

He jumped off the logs so suddenly it tilted to the side and Kenzie nearly slid off. She found her feet in the nick of time.

"What?"

She shrugged. "I've been doing some investigating of my own."

"I thought you'd given up on that."

"I have. This was a lead I was following up for Jacob's wife."

He crossed his arms. "I'm waiting."

"Okay, well you know Jacob worked for Felix Hammond?"

"The shipping magnate, yeah?"

"Well, I talked to his son, Milo. We became friendly, and he invited me back to his place for a drink."

Reid scowled. He didn't like where this was going.

"It was only one drink," she said, a little too forcefully. "Nick was outside in the car the whole time."

His scowl deepened. He couldn't help it. The thought of Kenzie with that flashy vet made his blood boil. "Jesus, Kenzie. You went on a date with a guy while your boyfriend was in the car?"

"Nick is not my boyfriend."

"He's not?" Reid calmed down a little.

"No, he's a friend. I told you that. Now can I continue with my story?"

He made an expansive gesture with his arm. The flush in Kenzie's cheeks hadn't escaped him. Was she lying about the vet? He hoped not. "Go ahead."

"What I was going to tell you is that I found a business card in his desk drawer, along with a bunch of burner phones."

Reid didn't know whether to be more shocked that she'd searched the study or found the burner phones. "Why does he have a bunch of burner phones?"

"I don't know. I was hoping you could ask him that when you question him."

"I went to his office to have a chat, but he hadn't seen Jacob Peters since the day before he disappeared. There was no cause to bring him in for questioning."

Kenzie made an annoyed sound with her tongue.

"I can't manufacture a reason," he told her.

"What about the burner phones?"

"It's your word against his."

Kenzie took the phone out of her pocket and set it on the log between them. "There's your reason." Reid stared at it. "You stole a phone from his study?"

"Wouldn't you?"

"No, not without a warrant. I can't use this, Kenzie. You know that."

Sighing, she reached for it, but he was quicker. "I'm still confiscating it."

She smiled. "It's locked, I can't get in. Although it did ring earlier today, and I answered it."

"You answered it?"

"Yeah."

"What was the call about?"

"A shipment." She shrugged. "Someone with a Spanish accent

telling Milo Hammond the shipment was on the way and would arrive on Tuesday. I don't know who it was."

"A customer, I'm guessing."

"Probably."

He put the phone in his pocket. There was no need for an evidence bag since everyone had been handling it, and it wasn't going to be used as evidence.

"Anyway, back to the voodoo doll," she said.

He nodded.

"The card I found was for a voodoo shop in Little Haiti. Weird place. Out of the way, not your usual tourist store. The man who works there, Utanga, casts curses on people. He charges a thousand dollars for the death curse."

"Holy shit!" Reid erupted. "A thousand bucks for a lot of mumbo jumbo."

"Yeah. Pretty much. Anyway, get this... When I mentioned Miles, he didn't bat an eyelid. Miles Hammond sent the voodoo doll to Jacob Peters, not Shannon Maisie."

26

KENZIE WATCHED as Reid paced up and down in front of the logs, the water almost touching his shoes. He looked tired. The dark stubble, the shadows under his eyes, the taut muscles in his jaw. "Are we saying that Shannon didn't send Sonia the doll?"

"No, I'm saying that she didn't send it to Jacob. Miles Hammond did. And he got it from the Voodoo priest. I'm sure of it."

Reid paused, hands on his hips. "Surely the dolls were sent by the same person?"

"What reason would Miles Hammond have to send Sonia a voodoo doll?" Kenzie asked.

"I don't know." He spread his hands. "That's what I'm trying to figure out. There's no connection between them."

"Okay, well if he did, it would have come from the same place, right?"

"Yeah, I guess so. Your Voodoo priest. What's his name again?"

"Mr. Utanga."

"Do you have his address? I'm going to bring him in for questioning."

"I'll text it to you." She got out her phone. "He's creepy, though. I'm warning you."

"This whole case is creepy. Mysterious deaths, voodoo dolls, curses." He shook his head. "I can't make any sense of it."

"Smoke and mirrors, in my opinion."

Weary eyes tangled with hers. "You saying it's all a distraction?"

She waved a hand in the air like a magician. "Why not? Make it look like a curse to distract from what's actually going on."

"It's working," he growled, clearly frustrated. "The Voodoo priest must know who bought the dolls. He could lead us to our killer."

"Or killers," Kenzie said. "If it's the same person. The only problem is cursing someone is not a crime."

Reid gritted his teeth. "I wish we had more manpower on this. There are too many angles. We've got Shannon's involvement, the Hammonds, Gail's burglary, and now this Voodoo priest."

"Gail was robbed?"

"Yeah, this morning. Monroe went out to oversee the forensic team. They took a bunch of prints, but I doubt they'll find anything. It looks like a pro job."

"Anything taken?"

"No, nothing Gail can see. My guess is they were after Jacob's laptop."

"That's the most likely scenario," Kenzie agreed, biting her lip. "You didn't find anything on it, did you?"

"Not yet, but if Raoul didn't, there won't be anything to find."

"True, but the perpetrators don't know that. Maybe they were being overly cautious," she suggested.

"Who? The Hammonds?"

"Maybe. Whoever killed him."

Reid made a disgruntled sound in the back of his throat that closely resembled an angry bear. "This has been the most exasperating case I've ever worked on. Nothing freaking makes sense."

"How about letting us help?" Kenzie suggested, feeling sorry for him.

He frowned. "What? How can you help?"

"We'll look into Sonia and her brother. Raoul has some time on his hands. He might be able to trace him for you."

Reid studied her, his eyes searching her face. "He'd do that?"

"Yeah, of course. Send me Sonia and her brother's real names, so we can get going on that. I know Shannon's name, and you mentioned her father was Ron McDonald?"

"Yeah, I'm guessing she changed her last name to escape the publicity."

Kenzie pursed her lips. "Makes sense."

Reid paused for a moment, contemplating her. "What's in this for you?"

"Why does there always have to be something in it for me? Why can't I do this out of the goodness of my heart?" She pretended to be offended.

"Because I know you, Kenzie."

"You've already given me an exclusive, remember? I'm gonna hold you to that."

At his look, she added, "Once you catch whoever did this, of course."

"I'm glad you added that," he muttered.

"What about the Hammonds?" Kenzie asked. "Do you want us to do some digging there?"

"We already looked into them. They seem to be above board. We checked out their business interests, all of which appear legit. Admittedly, we didn't dig very deep, but on the surface, they seemed fine."

Kenzie gazed out over the swamp. "On the surface, everything always looks fine."

He acknowledged the truth of that with a little nod of his head.

"Leave it with us," Kenzie said. "I'll let you know if we find anything."

He looked at her, his gaze softening. She felt her stomach lurch. Only Reid could make her feel like this. "Thanks, Kenzie. Appreciate the help."

She covered her feelings with a grin. "Makes a change, doesn't it?"

He couldn't help but smile at that.

"I'd better go," she said. "It's getting late." Without the sun, the water shimmered in inky darkness in front of them, and the bird calls had been replaced by the cry of cicadas.

As Reid walked her to her car, his phone rang. He held up a finger. She paused. "Garrett." He listened intently for a few minutes, then fist pumped the air. "Yes!"

"What is it?" she asked.

"They've discovered what killed Jacob Peters."

Kenzie raised her eyebrows. "Yeah?"

"He *was* poisoned. The ME found a minuscule needle mark underneath his big toenail."

"Ouch!" She grimaced.

"Thank God for that. We're not going crazy. I knew there was a logical reason."

Kenzie agreed, not that she'd ever thought his death resulted from a curse. "What's the poison?"

"That's the strange part. It was snake venom."

"Snake venom? Why was that so hard to find?"

"Because it's not one we've seen before. There was no record of it on the poisons database. Apparently, it's from an extremely venomous species found in Africa — called the Black Mamba."

"The Black Mamba," Kenzie whispered. "Sounds ominous."

"It is. The ME said a tiny drop can kill you within minutes. I don't have all the facts, yet, but he's sent through a report." He looked at her. "Which of our suspects do you think might have access to an African snake?"

"Utanga?"

"Exactly."

Reid made a call. "Dispatch, I want to put out a call for Samuel Utanga, a Voodoo priest living in Little Haiti." He gave the address of the store Kenzie had texted him. "Let's pick him up tonight."

He turned to her. "I've got to go."

"Of course." She watched as he jumped into his pickup and sped off while the dust curled around her.

27

It was a dark, clear night. The moon, the slimmest of crescents, provided a muted source of light, not helped by a cluster of stars deadened by the city lights. On the bright side, it didn't look like it was going to rain.

"There's an eclipse tomorrow," Diaz said, glancing up.

"Really?" Hamilton looked excited. "I've never seen an eclipse before."

"They were talking about it on the radio this morning."

The arrest team consisting of Reid, Vargas, Diaz and Hamilton were parked across the road from Coco Botanica.

"It looks empty." Vargas adjusted his body armor as he surveyed the small, rectangular brick structure with its peeling paint and dilapidated awning. There wasn't a flicker of light visible through the dirty glass window.

"Utanga rents the property behind the store," Reid informed them. "He's lived there since he arrived in Miami seventeen years ago." They'd all been briefed on the suspect. "Let's check out the store first and make sure nobody's there before we move on to the house." He didn't want Utanga to escape, or worse, double back on them and take them by surprise.

They moved forward, keeping low, holding their weapons steady. Reid hoped they wouldn't need them, but you never knew. In situations like this, it could go to hell in a matter of seconds. They had to be prepared for all eventualities.

They surrounded the store and Diaz peered through the window. "Nobody there." She tried the door, but as expected, it was locked.

"Take a look inside." Reid ordered. Their arrest warrant allowed them to gain entry to Utanga's property, including the store.

A firm kick from Hamilton sent the door flying inwards. Reid was the first person in, gun drawn. Diaz slipped past him, her flashlight illuminating the room. Rows of silent, righteous faces glared down at them from the shelves.

"Christ, that's creepy," Vargas muttered, entering behind them. A stale smell of incense hung in the air.

Diaz stepped behind the serving counter on which was an ancient cash register. "There's a door here. I'm going in." Hamilton backed her up. She poked her gun and flashlight through the jangle of beads that hung over the door. "Clear."

"Right, let's proceed to the main house." Reid didn't want to waste any more time in the store. He ushered them out, then pulled the broken door shut behind them.

They crept around the shop and up to the ramshackle house behind it. In the yard, they found an empty cage carpeted with chicken feathers.

"Animal sacrifices," muttered Vargas with a shudder.

"Seriously?" Hamilton's eyes were so wide Reid could see their whites in the darkness.

"Not anymore. It's empty." Had Utanga flown the coop too? Reid surveyed the house, but it was dark. "Come on, let's see if anyone's home."

They snuck up to the small, single-story dwelling. Like the shop, it was in dire need of a paint job. The porch was dry and cracked, the walls were peeling, and the front door was a noncommittal gray.

Reid gestured for Vargas and Diaz to go around the back in case Utanga tried to make a run for it. Once they'd disappeared around the house, he rapped on the door.

"Samuel Utanga? It's the police. Open up." When executing an arrest warrant, they had to announce their presence in order to give the resident an opportunity to open the door. In Reid's experience, no guilty person ever willingly did that when they knew it was the cops outside.

"Force it down," he ordered.

Hamilton, who Reid had recently found out used to play soccer for a junior national team, kicked it open, popping the flimsy lock. The door swung inwards, rebounding off the wall with a hollow thud. Both men stepped into the darkened hallway, guns drawn.

"Samuel Utanga?" Reid called.

No response. The only sound was the floorboards creaking as they inched forward. Reid gestured for Hamilton to take the first room, while he proceeded down the hallway to the next. The beam from his flashlight bounced off the claustrophobic paisley wallpaper, showing him the way.

Pushing open the door, Reid found himself in the main bedroom. It didn't look lived in. There was a dirty mattress on the bed, no bedding and no pillows. He checked the closet. It was empty. Not so much as a hanger. Shit. Utanga was in the wind. "Clear!" he yelled.

"Clear," came Hamilton's accompanying call.

They proceeded through the house, checking the bathroom and kitchen. Utanga was nowhere to be seen.

"He's gone," Hamilton said, shining his flashlight around the surprisingly large kitchen.

"Yeah, I'd say he's been gone for a while." The house was bare, but Reid couldn't figure out if he'd taken most of his furniture with him, or this was all he ever had. He suspected it was probably the latter.

Hamilton tried the light switch, but nothing happened. "Power's off," he said. The beam of his flashlight roamed around the room, illuminating a wooden table, but no chairs, a silent refrigerator, and an industrial-sized steel basin.

A chill ran down Reid's neck. There was something eerie about the house, even though it was vacant. The condition of the place made it feel neglected, and he couldn't shake the feeling that something bad had happened here. Hamilton felt it too, because he shivered and said, "This place is creepy."

Opening the fridge, Reid grimaced. A bottle of milk that had seen better days was reeking on the top shelf but other than that, it was empty. He turned around, his flashlight beam roaming like a spotlight across the room. When he got to the sink, he froze.

God, no.

Was that what he thought it was?

Moving closer, he angled his light into the deep sink.

Blood. Lots of it.

It coated the bottom and was splattered over the countertop and wall behind.

"Hamilton," he hissed, his pulse racing.

His colleague joined him at the basin. "Yeah?"

"Look."

The uniformed cop followed the trajectory of the beam to the sink.

"Holy shit, is that—?"

"Blood. Yeah. Get the CSI team over here. We need to lock this place down."

"Shit, okay. I mean, yes, boss." He pulled out his phone to make the call.

There was a pounding on the back door. Reid unlocked it. Vargas and Diaz were waiting outside. "He's gone." The two detectives holstered their weapons.

"You sure?" Vargas peered over his shoulder into the dark interior.

"Yeah, place has been cleaned out, but we found blood in the sink."

"Jesus, really?" With that news, they both took a step backwards. They knew better than to contaminate the place more than they already had.

"Yeah, Hamilton's calling forensics. Cordon off the property. This is now a crime scene."

28

Kenzie could not sleep. Too many questions were swirling around in her mind. Had Reid completed the raid? Was Utanga in custody? Had he said anything about who'd bought the voodoo dolls?

She closed her eyes and felt the anticipation grow. Nope, she wasn't going to get any rest tonight. Throwing back the covers, she got up and padded down the hall to her office.

She'd just sat down at her computer when she heard Sebastian come out of his room. "You okay, Kenzie?"

She turned and smiled. The teenager stood in the doorway, a concerned expression on his face. His English had improved immeasurably over the last few months, thanks to the classes he'd been taking. A smart kid, she'd realized he could do pretty much anything when he put his mind to it.

"Yeah, I'm okay. I just couldn't sleep. How come you're still awake?"

He shrugged. "I was playing my game."

In some ways he was a typical teenager, in others, an old soul beyond his years. What he'd been through... the trafficking, losing his mother, starting over in a new country, knowing nobody. It had been tough, which was why she'd offered to take him in.

"Why can't you sleep?" he asked. She sensed he wanted to talk.

"I've got a lot on my mind."

"Is it work?"

"Yes." Amongst other things.

"Are you trying to catch another bad guy?" Once, soon after he'd moved in, she'd explained what she did for a living. *"I couldn't be a cop, so I catch bad guys another way. I investigate them, and I write about them. That way everyone gets to know what they've done."*

"Yes, the only problem is they're very clever, and I can't prove they did anything wrong." She didn't discuss the intricacies of her work with him. He'd been through enough in his young life, but she did give him a rough overview, so he understood what being a reporter entailed.

"Did they hurt people?"

She hesitated, then nodded. "I think so."

He gave a firm nod. "Then you must stop them." One thing she'd noticed about Sebastian was that he had a strong sense of right and wrong, which wasn't surprising given his traumatic past.

She smiled at the simplicity of it. Sometimes having a language barrier broke things down to their most basic form. "I will. I've just got to figure out how."

After Sebastian went back to his room, Kenzie tried to focus on the Hammonds. She pulled up the photographs she'd taken in Milo's study, zooming in to them on her screen. They appeared to be supplier contracts.

Avicola International, Panama.

Operandora Agro, Venezuela.

AGCS, Colombia.

The inventory listed a range of agricultural products, mostly fruit and vegetables.

She thought back to the phone call. The voice had been Spanish.

The shipment is on the way.

Had the man on the line been from one of these companies, or was he someone else? A port official, a harbor master, the captain of a cargo ship? If only she could trace the call, but she hadn't noted the number and now the phone was with the forensic tech guys. Had they looked at the call logs?

Not knowing anything was killing her.

She heaved a sigh and opened Google, typing in the first company on the list. A corporate website came up displaying a banner with mud-covered tractor wheels on it. She scrolled down the page and found contact numbers and CEO details. Seemed legit.

It was a similar story for Operandora Agro in Venezuela. They supplied a range of farming equipment and machinery and had various export options. Again, there was a page with contact details and a sales team.

When she got to AGCS, Colombia, the search result was a little different. The website was basic at best, with only one homepage. At the bottom was a contact email address that read: admin@agcscolombia.com. No names, no physical address, no merchandise. Interesting.

She pondered this for a while, then went back to the results page. There was nothing else on the company at all. It appeared to be a shell corporation, and when she tried to find out who the directors were, she found yet another shell company.

Definitely sketchy.

Stifling a yawn, Kenzie logged off her computer. If she didn't get some sleep, she'd be a zombie tomorrow. The one thought that consumed her as she dozed off was whatever the Hammonds were shipping in from the Colombian company, it wasn't agricultural equipment.

29

The first thing Reid did when he got back to the station was put out a BOLO for Samuel Utanga. The CSI team had arrived at the abandoned house and were collecting samples of the blood in the kitchen.

Jacob Peters didn't have a scratch on him, and Sonia Del Ray only had a head wound, so who did it belong to? Was there a third victim they didn't know about?

"Got him," Monroe called. He was on night duty and had been monitoring the search effort on the police radio. "A couple of cops on patrol found his station wagon parked in an alleyway next to a property three blocks from his store. "According to dispatch, it's his sister's house."

"Fantastic," said Reid, grabbing his gear. "Let's go pick him up."

"They're waiting outside for you. They won't go in until you get there."

"Good."

"I didn't know he had a sister," said Diaz. "It hadn't come up on the search."

"Could be she's using a married name," said Monroe.

Diaz nodded. It made sense.

"You're not going to notify Vargas or Hamilton?" she asked as they blue-lighted it back to Little Haiti. The streets were mostly deserted at this time of the morning.

"Nah, let them get some sleep. They'll need it tomorrow."

"What about you?" she asked him. "How are you doing?"

"I'm okay. I'll take a nap after we have him in custody."

They pulled up outside a house similar to Utanga's rented one, although this one was in a slightly better state. Painted pink, there was a matching awning and an assortment of potted plants outside the door.

"Colorful," Diaz remarked.

Reid didn't reply, his eyes were on the window, lit from the inside. "Late to be up, don't you think?"

"Yeah." She followed his gaze. As they watched, a shadow moved across the window.

"That's him," Reid murmured.

Diaz signaled for the two officers to go around the back to cover the rear entrance, then they crept up to the front door, weapons drawn.

Reid pressed the buzzer and waited. At Diaz's raised eyebrow, he held up a finger. He was not going to go in guns blazing and give this guy a chance to get away. To his surprise, the door opened. A woman stood there in her nightgown, hair in some sort of turban. She sounded tired. "Yes?"

"Ma'am, my name is Detective Garrett from the Sweetwater Police Station. We'd like a word with your brother, Samuel Utanga."

"Samuel's not here," she said, too quickly for Reid's liking. "What do you want with him anyway?"

"We want to question him in connection with two homicides." He went for the shock effect, hoping it would scare her into complying.

"He didn't do nothing wrong."

"We're not saying he did, ma'am. We just need to talk with him. Can we come in?" He stepped forward, but she didn't budge.

"I told you, he ain't here."

"I saw him through the window," Reid told her in a calm voice. "If you don't open the door, we'll have to arrest you for perverting the course of justice. Do you want to spend the rest of the night in jail?"

Her pupils dilated as his words registered, then she took a hesitant step backwards. Reid pushed the door open and marched into the house, gun in hand. He wasn't taking any chances.

There was no need.

Sitting in the lounge, like he didn't have a care in the world, was Utanga. A faint tang of marijuana hung in the air. Reid quickly surveyed the room, expecting more resistance, but there was nobody there. Just the suspect, reclining in an armchair, legs crossed in front of him.

He holstered his weapon, although Diaz did not. If Utanga made any sudden moves, she had him covered. "Mr. Samuel Utanga. You're under arrest."

"For what?" The suspect rose to his feet, leaning heavily on the arm of the chair. He wasn't a young man, probably mid-sixties with dreadlocks and a scarred face. It was a face that had seen hardship, however, it was the eyes Reid found most disconcerting. So pale they were almost opalescent, they seemed to see everything and nothing at the same time.

"On suspicion of the murder of Jacob Peters and Sonia Del Ray."

The Voodoo priest shrugged. "I don't even know who these people are."

"When you get to the station, I'll remind you." Reid reached for his handcuffs. Utanga didn't resist.

"You're wasting your time," he said as the cuffs were clicked on. "I didn't kill these people."

Reid didn't reply. Instead, he led the suspect outside, past his shocked sister, to where an officer was waiting beside a squad car.

"Take him to Sweetwater Police Station and book him."

. . .

"Everybody here?" Reid asked when he got to the station the next morning. He'd grabbed a couple hours of sleep, but still felt like death warmed up.

"Yup," confirmed Diaz, who looked annoyingly fresh despite having the same amount of sleep as him. His eyes were gritty, and he was sure his hair was sticking up at all angles. He hadn't had time to shave, and his face felt itchy and rough.

"Good, let's have a quick meeting before we question the suspect."

They all gathered around his desk. Diaz pulled the whiteboard over.

"Glad you got him," Vargas said. "You should have called us." Hamilton nodded in agreement.

"It wasn't necessary," Reid replied. "Two patrolmen found him and assisted with the arrest. Better you got some sleep."

"You didn't," said Monroe, taking in yesterday's jeans and his creased T-shirt. The older detective didn't have to be here, having been on night duty, but he was a veteran cop and didn't want to miss anything.

"I'm okay. Let's start." He pointed to a photograph of Utanga that Diaz had just pinned to the whiteboard under SUSPECTS. Even in an image, his eyes seemed to stare straight through you.

"Did he resist?" Vargas asked, gazing at the picture.

"No, practically handed himself in. In fact, I think he was waiting for us at his sister's house."

"Strange," said Hamilton.

"As you know, we found a great deal of blood at his residence. CSI is on the scene so hopefully we'll get the results soon. I've asked them to expedite them since we have the suspect in custody."

"Before we question him, have we found Fred Stuckey yet?" Reid glanced around at his team.

"Not yet," said Vargas, who'd been overseeing it. "Still looking."

Reid grunted. Maybe Kenzie would come up with something. She was good at this type of thing.

"Okay, can we keep going with that? We really need to talk to him." Maybe Raoul would come up with something. Vargas gave a nod.

Reid turned to Diaz. "Ready?"

Vargas looked taken aback. Reid knew he'd been expecting to sit in on the interview. "Diaz was the arresting officer," he explained.

The detective nodded, although his shoulders slumped. Reid sighed internally. It couldn't be helped. It was best to keep Vargas out of the mainstream investigation in case there was a problem later. He didn't want any evidence they gathered to be inadmissible in court because of his association with Shannon.

"Stand by for fact checking," he said. "I need you to be on this and keep an eye out for those blood results. They promised me a DNA check against our victims first thing this morning."

"I told you, I don't know those people." Utanga sat in the hardback chair, seemingly unfazed. Reid and Diaz sat opposite him, the police report containing photographs of the victims open on the table. Above their heads, the red light of a surveillance camera flashed intermittently to indicate it was filming.

The interrogation was being recorded on the Sweetwater server so the team could watch from their desks. It was a handy new feature that IT had rolled out a couple of months back. Personally, Reid thought it was about time Sweetwater caught up to the rest of the Miami police departments.

"But you agree this item is from your shop." He took the voodoo doll sent to Sonia out of an evidence bag and placed it on the table. The pin was still sticking out of the chest.

Utanga's pale gaze swept over it. "I sell those types of dolls, yeah. But I can't say for sure it's from my shop."

It was a good answer. Unfortunately, there was no way of checking that. No DNA or fingerprints had been found on the doll.

"You're denying you sent them to the victims?"

"Yes, I'm denying it. I sell them. I don't mail them out." He chuckled. "I'm not online."

Fair point. Reid took a photograph of Milo Hammond out of the folder and slid it across the table. "What about this man? Do you know him?"

Utanga stared at it for a long time.

"Take a good look," Reid said.

Eventually, Utanga whispered, "He looks familiar. I think he's a customer."

Reid sat up straighter. "He came into your shop?"

"I think so, if it's the same man."

"Could you confirm when this was?"

"I don't remember exactly. A few weeks ago."

"Did he buy one of the dolls?"

"I don't know. My memory isn't so good these days."

Reid gritted his jaw in frustration. "Okay, but you'd remember if he bought two voodoo dolls, wouldn't you?"

"Sure. Nobody buys two voodoo dolls, not unless..." he broke off.

"Not unless they wanted to curse two different people?" Diaz broke in.

Utanga's gaze fixed on her face.

"Did this man ask you to curse someone?" she pushed.

Utanga sucked in a breath. "I don't do that."

"We know you do."

A scowl. It made the silver scar down the side of his face more noticeable. "How do you know?"

"Someone told us."

He laughed, a hoarse sound that didn't go beyond his throat. "I knew she was five-O."

"Who?" asked Diaz politely.

"That woman. The blonde one. As soon as she came in, I knew." Diaz glanced at Reid. He'd told her Kenzie had gone to see Utanga.

"I don't know who you mean," Diaz said smoothly. "Let's talk about the death curse. Did this man ask you to cast it?"

No answer.

"Did he pay you to curse someone?" Diaz repeated.

Utanga stared at the table for a long moment, then nodded. "Casting is not a crime."

"No, except the person you cursed is dead."

A shrug. "It was a death curse."

"Are you admitting you killed him?" Diaz stared into his colorless eyes.

"Who?"

"This man." Reid tapped on Jacob's photo.

"I didn't kill no one. If he's dead, it was the spirits." He glanced upwards, as if they were in the room with him. Reid was beginning to wonder if Utanga was all there.

"What about this woman?" Reid pointed to the photo of Sonia. "Did that man ask you to curse her too?"

He shook his head. "I never seen her before."

Reid ground his jaw. Two identical dolls, but one curse. One buyer. One victim.

"Did anyone else purchase a voodoo doll recently?" he asked.

"People come to me for all sorts of reasons," he said. "Some come for love, some for revenge. Your friend came for healing." He nodded at Reid.

"My friend?"

"The blonde woman." He chuckled to himself. "She's smart, that one."

Reid was momentarily thrown. "How do you know she's my friend?"

Another shrug. A chill shot up his spine. Did Utanga know who Kenzie was? Was she in danger?

"Mr. Utanga," Reid said. "Did this woman buy a doll from you?"

He held up his phone. Diaz glanced at him in surprise, but he made sure that the screen was angled away from the camera.

The suspect leaned in to take a better look. "I'm sorry, I don't have my glasses with me."

Reid held the phone closer. The Voodoo priest shook his head. "Nah, I think I would have remembered if she'd come into my shop." His lips curled back in a smile.

Relieved, Reid put his phone away. Beside him, he sensed Diaz relax. Perhaps Shannon hadn't sent the voodoo doll to Sonia, after all, which begged the question, who had?

But he couldn't focus on that now. Changing the line of questioning, Reid said, "I want to talk about the blood found in your house."

"Blood?" He seemed genuinely surprised.

"Yeah, in the kitchen sink. We found a large amount of blood there. Who does it belong to?"

The Voodoo priest broke into a wide grin. "Nobody."

"What do you mean, nobody?"

"It's chicken blood."

Reid blinked. "Chicken blood?"

"Yeah, in Voodoo we kill chickens to honor the gods. It's a Voodoo practice."

"I know it's Voodoo practice, but—" He broke off, unsure what to say next. Chicken blood, for fuck's sake.

Needing confirmation, he spun around and looked up at the camera. A moment later, his phone buzzed. Hamilton had sent him a text.

Lab confirmed. Animal, not human.

Shit.

Utanga was leaning back in his chair, still chuckling. "I told you, I ain't done nothing wrong."

Reid grimaced. Nothing they could prove, anyway.

Diaz shook her head, gathered up the photographs and slotted them back in the folder. They had no choice but to let Utanga go.

30

Kenzie woke up with the sun streaming through her window. She glanced at the time and leaped out of bed. Crap, she had to get to work. She needed to talk to Raoul about Hammond Holdings and what she'd discovered last night. Hopefully, he'd be able to find out some more about those shell companies.

Sebastian had already left for school, so Kenzie rushed around getting ready. Grabbing a banana, she shoved it into her backpack and pulled the door open. She was about to step outside when she saw the bulky, brown package on the doormat.

"What's this?" she murmured, bending to pick it up. It was addressed to her, but there was no postmark. It had been hand delivered. A chill shot down her spine as she gave it a gentle squeeze. She knew exactly what this was.

With shaking hands, she ripped open the package. Sure enough, inside was a voodoo doll with a pin stuck into its chest. Hands shaking, she took out her phone and dialed Reid's number. It went straight to his voicemail.

Clearing her throat, Kenzie left a message. *It's me again. Sorry to disturb you, but I've received a voodoo doll too. Found it on my doorstep this morning. Thought you should know.*

If the priest was still in custody, perhaps Reid could quiz him about this one too. The overriding question, however, was who had sent it? Had Milo Hammond ordered a curse be placed on her too?

Kenzie rushed into the Herald building after battling to find parking. The two elevators were hovering around the fifth and sixth floors, so she took the steps two at a time.

"Are you watching the eclipse this afternoon?" Katya, the climate editor asked as she reached her floor.

"Um, no. Probably not," she panted. "When is it?"

"Quarter past three. Don't miss it, it's going to be a good one."

"Kenzie!" bellowed Keith, as she walked in, still trying to catch her breath. She glanced at Raoul, then back at her boss. He beckoned her over. Sighing, she changed direction and went to his office.

"What's up?"

"This is much better," he said, waving the article she'd redone in the air. "Professional, non-biased reporting. Just what I like to see."

"Great. Can I go, because..."

"Hang on. What are you working on at the moment?"

She paused. "Why?"

"Because I've got something for you."

"Oh?" Her heart sank. All she wanted to do was talk to Raoul and find out what the Hammonds were up to.

"I want you to cover Emmanuelle Lenoir and Warner Sullivan's wedding. It's high society, and there's bound to be questions about Emmanuelle's links to the cartel."

"It's in New York." Kenzie frowned.

"Yes, two weeks away, so start prepping."

"Okay, but Keith, I might have something."

He raised his eyebrows. "Go ahead. I assume this is from your police contact?"

"Indirectly. I've been looking into the disappearance of a friend's brother-in-law. He worked for Felix Hammond. Remember I mentioned him the other day?"

"He was with Salvatore Del Gatto, right?"

"That's right." Keith had an excellent memory for interesting tidbits of information. "Well, a couple of days ago the brother-in-law turned up dead—" She didn't get a chance to finish.

"Dead? Jesus. What happened?"

"He was poisoned."

Keith's gaze darkened. "Is Hammond involved?"

Kenzie frowned. "What makes you think that?"

"He's a slimy character."

Kenzie nodded. "He is friends with Del Gatto."

Keith grunted.

"As is Congressman Leonard, I might add."

Keith raised a hand. "Do not go there, Kenzie. You know my position on the Congressman."

"Okay, fine. Anyway, a couple of days later, another woman, a young girl, was found dead. Head wound. The police think the murder is related to the first victim." She purposely left out the names because as much as she liked Keith, she couldn't trust him to keep the story to himself. He'd gone behind her back before and published a story she was working on.

"Why do they think it's connected?"

"Because both victims were cursed by a local Voodoo priest."

"Seriously?" He shot her an incredulous look. "That's what the police are basing this on? Voodoo."

"It's not as far-fetched as it sounds. Both victims were sent a voodoo doll with a pin stuck through the heart before they died," She neglected to mention she was sent one too.

His eyebrows shot up. "I suppose it makes for a good story."

She couldn't argue with that. Wasn't much fun being on the receiving end, though.

"And your Detective Garrett is working the case?"

"He's not my Detective Garrett."

"You know what I mean. Your source, your confidant, your special friend. Whatever you want to call him."

He used to be.

"Detective Garrett's working on it, yes. He's promised me an exclusive, but only once the perpetrator is behind bars."

Keith clapped his hands. "Great work, Kenzie. Keep me posted. I want to know the minute you have something."

"Will do."

His desk phone started ringing. He reached for it, picked it up, then covered the mouthpiece. "Sorry, gotta take this. Make sure you do some preliminary work on the wedding. It'll be the story of the month."

Kenzie left his office and made a beeline for Raoul's desk. "We have to talk," she said, pulling up a chair. "It's about Hammond Holdings."

He leaned back and stopped typing. "Tell me."

Where to start?

"Okay, so you know I went on a date with Milo Hammond the other night?"

"I didn't, no." He raised an eyebrow, adjusting his glasses. "How'd that go?"

"It didn't, not really. I did find a bunch of contracts, though. All companies in South America."

"Oh yeah?" His gaze didn't move from her face.

"I did an online search. Most of the companies appear to be legit, except one. AGCS, Colombia. They had a shifty website with a generic email address. The owner is a shell company out of Bogota, set up by another shell company."

"Does sound dubious," he agreed. "What do they sell?"

"That's the thing, I don't know. I couldn't find any product details."

"Give me the URL. I'll look into it."

She wrote it down for him. "I think something fishy's going on,

Raoul. I can feel it in my bones. I don't know what it is, but the Hammonds are neck deep in it."

"Leave it with me, Kenz."

She went back to her desk and called Reid again, but he didn't pick up, so she tried Diaz instead. It diverted to her voicemail. Giving up, she turned her attention to what Congressman Leonard had been up to. It seemed his extensive modernization project at PortMiami was paying dividends. The largest cargo ship to ever visit Florida would be arriving there next week before heading east to the Suez Canal.

The arrival of the massive container ship, which could carry 15,000 containers, would break the record for the largest ship ever to dock there. Thanks to Leonard's expansion projects, ships of this size no longer had to bypass Miami. The press release she was reading mentioned more jobs for truck drivers, more hours for the longshoremen who discharged and loaded the ships, and a general benefit for the community.

She frowned. No doubt this was thanks to Del Gatto's charitable donations. She wondered what Del Gatto was getting in return.

"Kenzie," hissed Raoul. She glanced up. He was bouncing up and down in his chair.

"What?" she asked, going over.

"You gotta see this." He had so many windows open on his computer that she wondered how he kept track of what he was doing. "Look."

"What am I looking at?"

"I managed to trace one of the shell companies back to a man. Leonardo Antonia Herrera."

"Who's he?"

"Herrera is a front man for the paramilitary organization, CLF."

She scrunched up her face trying to remember where she'd heard the name before. "Aren't they a narcotrafficking guerilla group?"

"The Colombian Liberation Front. Yeah." His gaze met hers.

Kenzie hesitated. "Are we saying the Hammonds are trafficking drugs into the country?"

Raoul shrugged. "Drugs, gold, people. Who knows? All I can say is it isn't agricultural produce."

Kenzie gave a low whistle. "This is bad."

"Hammond Holdings have got the perfect setup." Raoul continued. "I mean, think about it. They use their shipping contacts to import the goods into Miami. They have their own logistics company to transport them and warehouses to store them in."

Kenzie stared at him. "But to pull off a racket like that, they'd need to bribe customs officials, wouldn't they? It's not as simple as just bringing in illegal goods and loading them onto trucks."

"Most of their business is legit," Raoul said. "The smuggling is a profitable sideline."

The shipment is on its way. It'll be there Tuesday.

Today was Tuesday.

She got up. "I've got to go."

31

It was time. Reid needed answers and he was hoping Shannon would give them to him. Besides, he couldn't keep side-lining Vargas. The detective needed to know what was going on.

"I can talk to him, if you like," Diaz offered.

"No, it needs to come from me."

She nodded.

Reid took him out for a coffee, to the same place he'd met Diaz. This time they sat by the window, the sunlight streaming in across their table. It was a bright, breezy place, with air conditioning easing the humidity.

"Is there something wrong?" Vargas asked, as they got their coffees. This was very unusual behavior by the boss, Reid got it. Vargas was right to feel nervous.

"I needed to talk to you about something," he began, his own hands beginning to sweat. "And I thought it best to do it away from the station."

"Okay." Vargas waited, his coffee untouched.

"It's about Shannon."

Vargas' eyes widened, then he nodded. "I know, I'm sorry. I'll talk to her."

"Huh?"

"I know you don't like her coming into the station unannounced. She means well, but she doesn't get that it's off limits to civilians."

"It's not that," Reid said, quickly.

"Oh, what then?" His forehead creased. "Has she said something?"

"It's more what she's done." Reid wondered how the hell he was going to tell his colleague his fiancé was the leak.

"What has she done?"

Reid took a steadying breath. "It's come to our attention—" God, he couldn't sound more formal if he tried. "That Shannon has been using your laptop to hack into the WITSEC database."

A heavy silence fell across the table. It took a moment for his words to filter through Vargas' shocked brain. "I'm sorry, what?"

"It was Shannon who leaked Alberto Torres' name to Maria Lopez and the cartel. It was Shannon who discovered Sonia Del Ray was actually Portia Stuckey."

Vargas blinked at him. "It can't be," he whispered. "She'd never do something like that."

"Well, your laptop was used to hack into the WITSEC database on more than one occasion," Reid explained. "And I know you didn't do it."

"I'd have no idea how to," he replied.

"But Shannon does."

He was silent for a moment. Eventually, he said, "I don't believe it. Why would she do something like that?"

"Because Sonia murdered her father."

Vargas shook his head. It was a lot to take in.

"Sonia Del Ray stabbed Shannon's father when she was at college in Boston," Reid explained. "She served five years in a juvenile detention center before relocating to Miami under the witness protection program."

"When did you find this out?" he asked.

"A couple of days ago. We didn't tell you because... Well, because you can see how it looks."

"Shannon did not kill Sonia Del Ray," Vargas said, getting to his feet. "I'm sorry, boss, I usually trust your gut instinct, but you've missed the mark with this one."

"Sit down," Reid said.

"She was with me the night Sonia was murdered. We were in bed together."

Reid had been pondering this. "I called you that night. You didn't pick up."

"I was asleep."

"Exactly. Since when do you sleep through a call out?"

Vargas ran a hand through his hair. "Are you saying she drugged me?"

"I don't know but think about it. You were dead to the world. You missed my call and came in the next morning feeling like shit. What does that tell you?"

"That I was hungover from the night before."

"Maybe."

Vargas stared at him for a long moment. "I think I've heard enough." A few heads were turning. Reid had never seen Vargas angry before, but he was quietly fuming now. His hands had balled into fists, and he was as stiff as a mannequin.

"We had your laptop analyzed," he said.

"You did what?"

"We had to. We had to know for sure."

Vargas sank slowly into his chair.

"If you didn't do it, who did?"

Denial was written all over Vargas' face.

"I'm bringing her in for questioning," Reid said. "I just thought you should know."

"Is this why you've been sidelining me?" he asked.

"To a certain extent," Reid admitted. "I'm afraid I'm going to have to take you off the case until this is resolved."

Reid could almost see Vargas' brain working overtime. "Was it Shannon's photograph you showed Utanga in the interrogation?"

He gave a nod.

"You think she sent that voodoo doll to Sonia, and then met her at the restaurant and killed her? Do you really think Shannon is capable of something like that?"

"You tell me," Reid said quietly. "You know her best."

"For fuck's sake." Vargas got to his feet again. "I've had enough of this bullshit."

"Detective, I need you to hand in your badge and gun," Reid said. He hated saying it, but he couldn't have Vargas out there trying to prove his fiancé's innocence. This case had got way too personal for him, and he'd become a liability.

Without another word, Vargas unlipped his badge and laid it on the table, then he took out his weapon and did the same.

"Don't go near Shannon," Reid warned him. "You could be seen as an accessory."

Vargas just gave him a hard look and turned and walked out of the coffee shop.

"Shannon's here," said Diaz, when he got back to the station.

"Great, thanks. What about Vargas?"

She shook her head. "How'd he take it?"

"Not well." He put their colleague's service weapon and badge down on the desk. "He stormed out."

Diaz grimaced. "I'll give him a call and make sure he's okay."

"Which room?"

"Interrogation Room Two."

"Why am I here?" Vargas' fiancé demanded as Reid stepped into the room. "I haven't done anything wrong. You can't arrest me without a reason."

"Sit down." He gestured to the chair bolted to the floor.

"No, I don't want to sit down. Where's Wille? I want to talk to Willie!"

"He's not here," Reid said. "And technically, you're not under arrest."

"Then what's stopping me from walking out of here?"

"Nothing, but we will arrest you if you try."

She shot him an exasperated look.

"You can call a legal representative, if you'd like."

"How do I know if I need one when I don't know why I'm here?"

Fair enough. "You're being questioned in connection with Sonia Del Ray's murder."

She frowned. "Who?"

It was a good act, but he wasn't buying. "Do you want a lawyer or not?"

"No, I don't need one because I haven't done anything."

"Okay, fine." He sat down on the cold, metal chair and placed the folder he was carrying on the table. Her gaze immediately flew to it.

"Won't you sit down, Shannon, and let's talk about why you're here."

Reluctantly, she eased into the chair. Somehow, she still managed to look in control. Chin up, shoulders back, hands clasped loosely on the table in front of her.

"How long have you and Detective Vargas been together?" Reid started at the beginning, creating context, framing the interview.

"Nearly a year," she replied.

"And how did you meet?"

She frowned. "You know how we met."

"I'd like to hear you tell it." He wanted the chance meeting on the record. It would show how she'd chatted Vargas up in a bar, thereby establishing the first contact.

"We met at a wine bar in Brickell."

"Did he come up to you, or did you engage him?"

"I can't remember. I think he offered to buy me a drink." Reid was quite certain Vargas had bought her a drink, but only after she'd initiated contact.

"Out of the blue?" he asked. "Or did you say something to him first?"

"I really can't remember. What does it matter?" But the gleam in her eyes told him she knew exactly what his game was. Shannon Maisie was not easily fooled.

"It doesn't." He changed the subject. She wasn't going to admit she'd chatted him up first. "Could you tell me where you went to college?"

Her eyes narrowed. "You know I went to MIT. I told you the other day when you were in my apartment." Another smart move. She was showing that he might have a conflict of interest too.

"You did, but for the record, could you tell me what you studied?"

"Computer science." She tossed her wavy red hair over her shoulder. It was then he noticed how made up she was. Her hair was shiny and lustrous, her bronze eyelids shimmered in the harsh fluorescent lighting, and her coral lipstick matched her silk blouse.

The arresting officer had said she'd been reading on the sofa when they'd arrived. With a start, he realized she'd been expecting this. No, she'd prepared for it.

His impromptu appearance at her apartment had aroused her suspicions. Shannon was too smart to believe he was there delivering a gift. She knew he was on to her, and that this moment was coming. All he'd done was give her time to get her story straight.

Reid opened the folder and took out a photograph. "Do you know this woman?" He slid it across the table toward her.

She glanced down, then shook her head. "No."

"Are you sure? Take another look." Shannon wasn't going to make this easy for him. She looked at it again, but there was no recognition on her face. Once again, he was amazed by her ability to lie. If he didn't know better, he'd have believed she really didn't know who Sonia was.

"I'm sorry, I don't know who this is."

"Her name is Sonia Del Ray," he supplied.

"Is that name supposed to mean something to me?"

"I thought it might, seeing as it's the name you looked up on the WITSEC database two weeks ago."

She blinked several times. "I did what?"

Damn, she was good.

"You know, when you hacked into it from Detective Vargas' laptop."

There was a long pause, then she said, "I'm sorry, detective, but you must have me confused with someone else. I have never used my fiancé's laptop. I have a powerful one of my own."

That was what he was hoping she'd say. "How do you explain your fingerprints all over it?"

She scoffed. "I helped him install an antivirus program not so long ago. When it comes to computers, Willie often asks for my help." She smiled disarmingly. "His skill set lies elsewhere."

He didn't doubt she had helped him. Shannon had thought of everything.

"Detective Vargas' device was used to access secure information from a federal database. As you've acknowledged yourself, he does not have the skillset to do that himself, so it could not have been him."

"And I do, so it must be me? Is that what you're saying, detective?"

He gave a sardonic grin. "Is that a confession?"

"No, it is not." Emerald green mixed with steely gray. "That's quite an assumption, detective."

"You can see how it looks though?" He leaned back in his chair. "You chat up Detective Vargas in a bar and the two of you start dating. Before long, you're going steady. Then information from a federal database is leaked to one of the biggest cartel bosses in Miami. Shortly after that, you receive several large payments."

At her surprised look, he added, "Oh yeah. We checked your bank statements."

Her shoulders stiffened. "You had no right."

"We had every right. You're a suspect in a homicide."

"I told you, I don't know that woman." She nodded at the photograph still lying face-up on the table, Sonia's face, pale and waxy against the damp asphalt of the parking lot.

"Sonia Del Ray murdered your father."

Her eyelids flickered, but she held her cool. "My father died five years ago."

"I know, outside his house in Tampa. Sonia Del Ray was the teenager who stabbed him."

Shannon shook her head. "No, you're wrong. The person who stabbed him was a student named Portia Stuckey. She's in a juvenile facility in Jacksonville."

Reid had to admit, she was convincing.

"Not anymore," he informed her. "She was released six months ago and moved to Miami. She was going by the name Sonia Del Ray."

Shannon stared at the image for a long time. "I didn't know," she whispered. "I swear, I didn't know."

Reid frowned. She seemed legitimately upset. Could he have been wrong about her? No, he mustn't fall for her act. Everything pointed to her. It had to be her.

He took a deep breath. "You know what I think happened?"

She raised an eyebrow.

"I think you knew Sonia had been released and had moved to Miami, but you didn't know where. You decided the only way to find her was to hack into the WITSEC database and get her new name. How were you going to do that?"

Shannon sat silently watching him.

"Miami PD was out of the question, as they have tighter security, tougher protocols. So, you chose a backwater police department, and you watched and waited. One day, you saw Detective Vargas go into a bar. He was alone. This was your opportunity. You chatted him up and then seduced him. He was easily taken in by your charms."

He saw her hand tighten on the table. He was getting to her.

"Once you had access to his laptop, you hacked into the WITSEC database to look up Sonia's name, except maybe you couldn't find it. Perhaps it wasn't there or hadn't been updated yet. Since you were in, you looked up Alberto Torres' new whereabouts. You knew Maria Lopez was looking for him, so what did you do? You told her he was still alive. How am I doing?"

Shannon sat as still as a wax figure. "It's all supposition," she said. "You're looking for someone to pin this on, and I'm it."

Reid clenched his jaw. "How do you explain the fact that your fiancée's laptop was used to hack into a system containing Sonia Del Ray's name and a week later, she turns up in a dumpster? That's quite a coincidence."

"I can't, but perhaps you should look into setting up a stronger firewall. I can help you with that if you like?"

He couldn't believe the audacity of the woman.

"Shannon, you're in a lot of trouble here. You had access to Detective Vargas' laptop. You knew how to hack into the system, and you had a reason to want Sonia Del Ray dead. That gives you means and motive. We could arrest you right now."

"No, you can't." She sat up straight. "I have an alibi. I was at Willie's house the night Sonia was found in the dumpster. He'll vouch for me."

32

"Kenzie Gilmore." Kenzie flashed her press pass at the kiosk manager at the entrance to the South Florida Container Terminal. "I'm writing an article on Congressman Leonard's new modernization initiative. I'd like to take a look around."

He stared at her photograph, hesitated, then said, "Pull over."

She dutifully did as she was told. "You need a photo ID pass," he said. "Follow me." She got out of the car. The small security hut was equipped with a camera and computer, and five minutes later, she had a lanyard around her neck with her name, occupation, and photograph on it.

"Stay clear of the loading dock," the guard said. "We've got a big one in at the moment."

She smiled her thanks. "Will do."

As Kenzie drove down the service road, the sky suddenly dimmed, as if someone had dialed down the sun. "What the—?" She looked out of the window. The eclipse! Of course. Quarter past three. It couldn't be better timed. The darkness would help with concealment, just in case she needed any.

'The big one' turned out to be a massive cargo ship docked at the side of the terminal. Not only was it long, but it was also piled with multi-colored containers several stories tall. Was that the ship that the man on the phone had mentioned?

It'll be with you Tuesday. South Florida Terminal.

As far as she could see, there was only one ship at the dock. At the end of the road was a commercial parking lot, so she pulled in and watched as a production line of trailers drove up to the side, were loaded with a container, then drove off again.

Taking a pair of binoculars out of the glove compartment, she tried to read the logo on the side of the containers. HH.

Bingo.

Starting the car, she followed one of the trailers back down the service road until it turned into an enormous container yard. Rows upon rows of contains stretched in front of her, as far as the eye could see. How was she ever going to find her way out of here?

As she drove, she realized the rows were marked with letters and numbers, like a grid system on a street map. Currently, the trailer was trundling down South D. She followed at a discreet pace, until it turned off into West 28. It continued for another two hundred yards, then came to a stop. Kenzie turned into West 26 and cut the engine. Getting out of the car, she poked her head around the corner to see what was going on. A stationary container crane with a claw descended and lifted the container off the trailer, placing it strategically on top of another container, also with the HH logo on it.

How many containers would they be unloading? She'd noticed the cargo on the ship belonged to a range of different logistics companies, so hopefully not too many more. They'd already unloaded about thirty containers, at a rough count.

"Excuse me, what are you doing?" came a male voice behind her. She spun around and saw his eyes drop to her lanyard.

"I'm Kenzie Gilmore, from the *Miami Herald*," she said, holding it up. "I'm doing some research for an article I'm writing on Congressman Leonard's modernization project."

He frowned. "What are you doing in the container yard? This is off limits."

"I'm taking photographs of the cranes unloading the trailers," she said, pointing in front of her. "Not only is it fascinating for our readers, but I believe you've acquired a bunch of new cranes?"

He relaxed somewhat. "Yeah, that's right. We got more gantry cranes, that's what they're called," he added for her benefit. "As well as more cargo space. I suppose you noticed the new touchless gate kiosks at the entrance. That's for truckers to move safely and efficiently through weigh-in-motion scales. It's made things a lot smoother."

"Interesting," Kenzie said, taking out her notebook. "I believe there's an environmental aspect to the project too?"

"Yeah, that's right. It's quieter and cleaner for our neighbors. Did you know we're the first container terminal in the US with a 100% electric fleet with zero emissions in the container yard?" He puffed out his chest, proud of the fact.

"I did not know that. Can I quote you on that?"

He preened even more. "It's not my words, you can read it in the latest PortMiami magazine. There are some free copies in the administrative building. That's where we take all our guests."

"Thank you." Kenzie smiled at him. "I'll be sure to stop by when I'm done here."

He hesitated. "You're not really allowed to be here."

"Would you mind if I walked down to the crane to get a few close-ups? I won't be long, then I'll be out of your hair."

"Well, I suppose it's okay."

"Thank you."

She flashed him a smile and waited until he'd walked away, before she got a pair of bolt cutters out of the trunk. A weird twilight fell over the yard, as the eclipse progressed. Day turned into night, as if time had been sped up. When she got to the containers, it was almost completely dark. The lights dotted around the yard must have been on a timer, because none of them came on. She had to use her phone flashlight to see where she was going.

The trailer drove off, high beams carving a path between the containers, but she was betting the next one wouldn't come down until the sun came back out. She was right, the yard stayed quiet.

"Let's find out what you're bringing in," she muttered, approaching one of the containers. The bolt cutters were heavy, and it took a bit of muscle to bite through the heavy-duty steel container lock. Prying open the door, Kenzie glanced around to make sure nobody was in earshot. It was still pitch dark, so she didn't worry about being seen.

Inside, it was even darker, if that was possible. By the light of her phone, she could make out big wooden crates stacked on top of each other. Some of them had a green agricultural logo stamped on them, while others had a red military-type seal on the front.

No contest. She pried open one of the red stamped crates and peered inside. It looked like it was filled with straw. Her heart sank. Probably eggplants or something. Dipping her hand into the crate, she felt around amongst the straw. Her fingers connected with something hard and cold. The shape was almost... she was sure it was... A handgun.

Holy crap, was this what they were smuggling? Arms?

She dug around the crate some more and pulled out several other small caliber handguns. A Glock 19 and a SIG Sauer P226, amongst others.

Pulse racing, she stared at the weapons. Evidence. She needed evidence. Using her camera phone, she took several shots of the different guns, including the ammo. Then she sent them straight to Reid.

A sound outside the container made her freeze. The sky was getting lighter again, the eclipse was receding. It was time to go.

She placed the weapons back into the crate and replaced the lid, although it wasn't nailed in as before. It would have to do. She turned to leave, but as she was about to step outside, the container door slammed shut.

"Hey!" she yelled, thumping on the side of the container. "Hey, I'm in here."

There was no reply.

"Hello!" She tried again, but she was wasting her time. She was trapped.

33

Reid felt his phone buzz but ignored it. Shannon had been placed in a holding cell after the interview, but he couldn't leave her there indefinitely. "We can hold her for twenty-four hours, then we'll have to let her go."

"The house search didn't turn up anything either," Diaz told him. "We found no evidence that she was passing information to Maria Lopez, or that she even knew about Sonia Del Ray. The tech department is going through her phone and laptop now."

"She'd have used a burner phone to contact Maria," he said, "and her laptop will be clean. There's no way she'd leave it lying around if there was incriminating evidence on it." Shannon was way too smart for that. "Vargas is lucky he doesn't have any computer skills, otherwise he'd be our prime suspect."

Diaz smiled, although it was tinged with sadness. "I tried calling him, but his phone was off."

"He'll take a while to get his head around it," he said. "When I told him, he was shocked. He didn't see it coming at all."

"No, why would he? He's in love."

Reid felt bad for Vargas, he really did, but it was better his colleague found out now, than after they were married.

"Do you think she ever had any intention of marrying him?" Reid asked. "Or was she just continuing the façade long enough to find Sonia?"

"Or her brother," Diaz added. Then she sighed. "I don't know. He proposed to her, so perhaps she had to say yes in order to finish the job. I don't think she'd have agreed to marry him otherwise."

Poor Vargas. "Where are we on Fred Stuckey?"

"The US Marshals Service is still refusing to give us his whereabouts. They want a full report, and if they think the threat is credible, they'll intervene themselves. Either way, we're kept in the dark."

"Ugh." Reid turned away in disgust. "By the time we send them a goddamn report, it could be too late."

"Let's keep Shannon in until tomorrow," Diaz said. "That'll give us more time to find him ourselves."

"Agreed. I'll give Kenzie a ring. She said Raoul was going to look into it for us. He might have something by now." He pulled out his phone. "Oh, that was her messaging me."

Opening her message, he stared at the photograph of the crate of guns. An uneasy feeling churned in his gut. What the hell was she up to now?

"What is it?" Dias asked, seeing his expression.

"Kenzie's sent me a photograph of a crate of guns." He turned the screen around so she could see. "No explanation. Nothing."

Diaz frowned. She knew as well as Reid that Kenzie never did anything without a reason. "Strange. Where is she?"

"No idea. She left a voicemail earlier." He dialed into it and listened, his gut twisting with every word. "Fucking hell," he growled, hanging up.

"Reid?"

"She received a voodoo doll this morning. It was left on her doorstep."

Diaz paled. "That is not good."

"No, it's not, and I've been too damn busy to answer her calls." He dialed her number and waited for it to ring.

Please pick up.

"Reid?"

"Kenzie, thank God." Relief washed over him. "Are you okay?"

"Um, no not really." Her voice sounded tinny, like she was in an enclosed space.

The uneasy feeling came back. "Where are you?"

"In a shipping container at the South Florida Terminal. I'm locked in."

"What are you doing there?"

"I was checking out a Hammond Holdings container, and I found guns in it. Reid, I think they're trafficking guns into the country."

"I got the photos. Are they from the container you're in now?"

"Yes, someone shut the door. I'm trapped, Reid. I can't get out."

He signaled to Diaz to grab her stuff. "Okay, don't panic. I'm on my way. Where in the South Florida Terminal are you?"

"South D, West 28. I don't know which container. It's one of the ones with HH on the side."

"Okay, hang tight. Diaz and I are on our way. Call me if anything changes."

"Will do. Thanks, Reid. Hurry."

"Let's go," he said to Diaz, who had already pulled on her ballistics vest and was checking her service pistol.

"Ready!"

They headed for the exit. "Hamilton, organize backup and send it to the South Florida Terminal at PortMiami!" he shouted over his shoulder. "I'll call you with the exact location."

The police officer nodded and immediately reached for the phone.

Siren blaring, they raced downtown and took the causeway to the SFT. The security guard at the gate let them in after a brief flash of Reid's badge. "Which way to South D, West 28?"

"That's South D over there, fourth one in. Keep going down until you get to West 28." It sounded simple enough. They turned into South D and accelerated down the service road until Diaz yelled, "Stop! That's West 28."

He reversed and turned left into the narrow row of containers. "Where the hell is she?" he said. They drove on until Diaz gave a shout. "That's her car!"

Stopping, they saw a bunch of containers with HH stenciled on the side. Reid switched off the engine. "That must be them."

"Kenzie!" he shouted, but there was too much background noise. "Let's split up," he suggested. Diaz nodded. The HH containers were grouped together, so it didn't take long to walk between them. There were about forty in total – and he banged on every one of them.

He called her phone again, but she didn't pick up. Diaz shot him a worried look. Neither of them wanted to think what that meant.

"Kenzie!"

No answer.

Shit.

"What do we do now?" Diaz asked.

"Keep listening. I'm going to call her again. Her phone is on, it might lead us to her."

They walked up and down the containers until Diaz shouted. "This one!"

"Can you hear her phone?" he asked.

"No, but it's been forced open. Look." The metal lock had been sliced in half. Bolt cutters. No doubt Kenzie's doing. Grabbing the handles, he pulled them down and turned them outwards, opening the heavy, metal container doors. They shrieked apart.

Inside smelled musty, a little like a stable. There was straw scattered all over the ground. He glanced around and a light caught his eye. Bending down, he picked up Kenzie's phone. "She was here," he said.

Three missed calls, all from him in the last half hour. There was one from Raoul, at three twenty-five. Her assistant must have called her while she was here, but she hadn't answered. That gave him a rough timeline. Still, the container was empty. No crates. No guns.

And no sign of Kenzie.

34

KENZIE SAT PINNED against the side of a utility van, fighting to stay upright. The two thugs who'd kidnapped her had said very little before they'd manhandled her out of the container, zipped plastic ties around her wrists, yanked the hood over her head and chucked her into the back of the van.

She'd landed awkwardly, scraping her knee on something sharp on the vehicle base. It stung, but that was the least of her problems. She'd dropped her phone in the tussle, so she had no way of contacting Reid, or anyone else for that matter, and she was upset with herself for being caught.

How had they known she was there? Had she triggered an alarm of some sort? That was the most likely scenario. Not a port alarm though, because then she'd be in the guard's hut right now explaining herself. This must have been an alarm connected to Hammond Holdings.

Kenzie tried to map their route in her mind. Up the row of containers, right turn onto the main service road, slowing through the gates.

"Help!" She kicked out against the side of the van. "Hello, can anyone hear me? Help!" She screamed as loud as she could, but the van kept going. No one came to her rescue.

Shit, now what?

The back of the van stank of oil and exhaust fumes. Momentarily defeated, Kenzie leaned back against the side and tried to take stock. Where were they going? All she could hear was traffic sounds, the occasional horn honking, and the low grumble of tires on tarmac.

At least ten, fifteen minutes passed. It was hard to tell blindfolded. Not being able to see the passing of time made it harder to fathom. They'd left the main hub of the city and were heading out of town. The traffic quietened a little, became less chaotic, the grumble became a murmur. She thought their speed had increased, like on a freeway.

Ten minutes later, or thereabouts, the van veered off the freeway. They were nearing their destination. Kenzie tensed as they took a series of sharp turns, where she had to dig her heels into the base of the van so not to go skidding across it. Her knee was pounding where she'd grazed it, and her jeans felt wet. Her mother had warned her about rusty nails, but again, that was the least of her worries.

Finally, the van came to a stop. The traffic sounds had dimmed to a distant hum. The doors opened, and fresh air surged in, replacing the exhaust fumes. Thank God. She took some deep breaths and the queasiness that had been creeping up on her disappeared.

Strong arms reached in and pulled her out of the van. "Okay, okay," she said. "You don't need to be so rough." It didn't help. They hauled her across what felt like concrete or tarmac, and into a shaded area, possibly a garage or warehouse. The hood over her head wasn't completely opaque, and she could tell there was more light in here. Natural light from several large windows.

They led her to a chair and forced her to sit down. "Let me speak to Hammond," she said.

There was a pause.

Her hands, which had been bound in front of her were now unclipped, but before she had time to move, they were refastened around the arms of the chair. Her ankles, they tied together. Once she was secure, they removed the hood.

Kenzie squinted against the light. They were in some sort of industrial garage, along with several trucks and other vehicles. "Didn't you hear me? I want to speak to Hammond."

"Which Hammond?" asked a voice.

She turned her neck to see Milo appear from a side office. "You'll do."

He grinned and nodded to the thugs who moved away. They'd probably taken up positions at the entrance, in case she tried to get away, although how she was going to do that, she had no idea. Twisting her wrists didn't help, the ties only dug into her skin. Her ankles had more mobility, but tied together, she couldn't do much.

"What am I doing here?" she demanded.

"I should be asking you that question," he said. "You were the one caught breaking into my container. I could have you arrested."

"Why don't you? Call the police. Call them now."

He chuckled. "I don't operate that way. I prefer to keep my security..." he paused, "in house."

She swallowed. "Does your father know I'm here?"

He scoffed. "Felix doesn't know shit about what I do. He thinks he does, but in reality, he knows nothing. He's just an old fool."

Kenzie studied him. Gone was the meek, smooth talking, spoiled rich boy from before, and in his place was a hard, ruthless criminal. He'd been playing a part too. Pretending to do what he was told, running daddy's company, but in fact, he was trafficking arms into the country. "So Felix doesn't know about your profitable sideline?"

He smirked. "Of course not. Felix might bend the rules occasionally, but he'd never go this far. He doesn't have the balls."

Interesting. If anything, Kenzie would have called it the other way round. Shows how wrong she'd been, and how calculating Milo was.

"What were you doing in my container, Kenzie?"

She gasped at her name. He laughed. "What? Do you think I

didn't find out who you were? Poor Marcy couldn't believe you'd impersonated her. I'm sure that's against the law too, you know."

She glared at him, but his cool gaze didn't wander. "What did you do to Marcy?"

"Relax, she's fine, although she did tell me all about you. Kenzie Gilmore, the reporter from the *Miami Herald*."

Shit.

"It was you. You sent me that voodoo doll."

He laughed. "You should have heeded the warning. Now answer my question."

The front of the garage was still open. They must be very confident no one would find them here. Did they have her phone? Did they know she'd spoken to Reid and given him her location? How long would it take him to get to the port and discover she was gone?

She needed time. Reid would guess the Hammonds had taken her. He'd visit Felix, who'd be oblivious to what was going on. Would he guess Milo was the one calling the shots?

"I took a look in your study when I was at your house." If she could draw this out, there might be a chance Reid would find her before — before Milo killed her.

Milo's eyes hardened. "I knew you were up to something."

"I found a burner phone. Several actually, but I only took one."

"It was locked. They all are. You'd never get into it."

"I didn't need to. You got a call from a man in Colombia. He confirmed the shipment was on its way and would be here Tuesday. He even gave me the location. It wasn't hard to figure out that you were in bed with the rebels."

"Clever, aren't you?" He scowled at her. "But also stupid. You came down to the terminal to investigate by yourself. You gave your real name to security."

She couldn't argue with him there. "That was a mistake."

"Indeed. Too late now though."

"What are you going to do with me?"

"I can't let you live, obviously. You must see that. You could blow my entire operation. Luckily for me, you came alone, not even your office knew where you were."

"How did you—?"

"I checked. I'm not going to bump you off if the world knows you came to see me, am I? Give me some credit."

He must have called the office. Keith wouldn't have had a clue, but it didn't matter. Reid knew where she'd gone. He'd find her phone and work out what had happened. He'd find her.

Please let him find her.

"Did you kill Jacob Peters too? Did he find out what you were up to?"

"Jacob." He paused. "Now there's a mystery. Convenient, but still a mystery. How his body ended up in the glades, I have no idea." He shrugged. Kenzie frowned. What did that mean?

"How did you get the poison?" she asked.

He frowned. "What poison?"

Was he playing her again? She couldn't be sure. One thing she'd realized was Milo was an excellent liar. Even better than she was. "Jacob was poisoned. He was injected with snake venom."

He looked surprised. "Was he really? Poor guy. I never took to him, he was too much of a people pleaser for my liking. Always did what he was told. No initiative."

A guard marched up, a serious expression on his face. He whispered something into Milo's ear.

"What?" he exploded. "Already? How did they know?" Then he whirled around. "*You* told them, didn't you? You called the cops?"

She may as well admit it. At the very least it would wipe that smug look off his face. "Obviously. I'm surprised it took you so long to figure it out. I even sent them a photograph of the guns. You're busted, Milo. The police know all about your little operation."

His eyes narrowed. "They won't find anything. They're there now, searching, but we've moved the merchandise already. You're too late."

Her heart sank. "Still, they know you've got me. If anything happens to me, you're the first person they'll come looking for."

"Wrong. They'll go to my father." He choked back a laugh. "Felix Hammond will be taken in for questioning. I'm the spineless lackey, remember? I do what daddy tells me to do."

He had a point. Would they think to look at Milo, or would they assume Felix was the mastermind behind the trafficking scheme, like she had?

"Why guns?" she asked, desperate to keep him talking. "You're buying from the Colombians. Why not drugs?"

He scoffed, momentarily diverted. "The drugs market is oversaturated. Everybody's bringing in drugs. Did you know there's a gun shortage in America?"

The look on her face must have given her away, because he said, "Really. Thanks to Covid, there's a massive backlog of license processing, coupled with additional gun control measures thanks to the recent school shootings, so it's become harder to buy weapons on the open market."

"So you're supplying them on the black market," she finished.

He gave a gleeful nod. "Exactly. We get them from the Colombians, Ecuadorians and Venezuelans who seem to have more than they know what to do with. Don't ask me how they get a hold of them. Corrupt military officials, arm caches, hijacked shipments. They keep the assault rifles, obviously, and the other more useful items, and sell the handguns. We're happy to partner with them."

Milo's phone beeped, and he glanced down. "Shit."

At Kenzie's curious gaze, he added, "There are law enforcement officers at my house, questioning my father."

"It won't be long now," she said with more bravado than she felt.

"It'll still be too late for you." He put his phone away and pulled out a gun that had been hidden in the back of his jeans. "Enough talking, Kenzie Gilmore. It's time to say goodbye."

35

Reid, accompanied by Diaz, Hamilton, and several uniformed officers, pulled up in front of the Hammond mansion. Tall, wrought-iron gates prevented them from racing up the driveway. He pulled up alongside the control panel and pressed the buzzer.

"Detective Reid Garrett," he barked at the voice that answered. "I have a warrant to search these premises. Let us in or we'll take out the gate."

"That won't be necessary," said the voice, and the large, metallic gate swung inwards.

"Nice pad," Diaz remarked dryly, as they drove up the short driveway towards the Romanesque pillars and ornate portico at the front of the house. The rest of the property stretched out lazily in both directions, gleaming in the afternoon sun. "Be a pity to lose it all."

Reid was out of the car almost before he'd turned the engine off and was marching up to the front door. It opened before he got there.

"I'm Felix Hammond," said a genteel man in his sixties, with silver hair and riveting blue eyes. "What can I do for you officers?"

"Mr. Hammond, you're under arrest for suspected kidnapping, arms trafficking, and money laundering."

"Excuse me?" He seemed genuinely startled.

"I'm afraid you'll have to accompany us down to the station. We also have a warrant to search these premises." Reid strode past Hammond into an enormous hallway with double vaulted ceilings, a crystal chandelier and modern art on the walls.

Diaz took out her handcuffs. "Put your hands behind your back, sir."

He complied, although he was shaking his head. "I haven't kidnapped anybody."

"You haven't seen this woman?" Hamilton showed him a photograph of Kenzie.

"Marcy?" His eyes widened. "Has she gone missing?"

Reid hesitated. "Marcy?"

"Yeah, she introduced herself as Marcy Guerrier, the late Jacob Peters' girlfriend."

Reid's head was spinning. Of course, Kenzie had been undercover. How could he be so stupid? She'd never use her own name when investigating a suspect.

"I see. Well, have you seen her?"

"No, I'm afraid not. Last time I saw her, she was here with my son, but she said she had a headache and left rather suddenly. I walked her out myself."

"When was this?" Reid asked.

"Friday, I think." He frowned. "When did she go missing?"

"Today, from one of your containers at South Florida Terminal."

"One of my—?" He shook his head. "What was she doing in one of my containers?"

"Looking for these?" Reid showed him the picture of the handguns.

He scrutinized it. "I don't recognize those crates, and I certainly didn't import any guns."

"Well, someone did," Reid said. "These were in a Hammond

Holdings container and came off a ship that docked earlier this morning."

He fell silent, but his eyes stared unseeing past Reid. "Do you know who did?"

"No idea. It must be some sort of mix-up. Our business is one hundred percent legit."

"Even the part your son runs?"

He fell silent again.

"Where is your son now?" asked Reid.

"I have no idea. I don't keep tabs on him. He's a grown man."

"Could he be at work?"

"Maybe, I don't know."

"Could you call him and find out?"

"You want me to entrap my own son?" He gave a snort. "He hasn't done anything wrong. None of us have."

"Sir, someone in your organization has been trafficking weapons from South America into this country. Kenzie found out about it. Now who could have kidnapped her?"

"Not my son."

"Then help us prove it."

Felix Hammond sighed and nodded toward his handcuffs. Reid gave Diaz a nod. She undid the cuffs, and he reached into his pocket and pulled out his phone. "Give me a minute."

They watched as he looked up a number, then dialed it. "He's not picking up."

He called again and spoke to a receptionist. "Claudia, is Milo there? No? I see. Thank you." He shook his head. "He's not at the office."

"Where else could he be? Do you have a list of warehouses or properties that he could store trafficked goods at?"

"Well, yes. We have lots of—"

"I need a list."

"I'll have to go to my office." Diaz and Hamilton accompanied him, while Reid waited in the hallway. The uniformed officers conducted a quick search of the house. "She's not here, sir."

Diaz came back with the list. Hamilton was leading a re-cuffed Hammond by the arm. "There are too many for us to search," she said.

"Get the local police units involved," he barked. "I want all those properties searched. Now. We'll take the ones closest to us." She had to be somewhere.

"Yes, boss."

Reid only hoped he wasn't too late.

Kenzie felt the cold, steel barrel press against her temple and froze. "You don't want to do this, Milo," she whispered. "You'll be wanted for murder."

"I already am, according to you." He laughed, slightly manically. "What does one more matter?"

"Of course it matters."

His phone beeped. Kenzie took advantage of his diverted attention and twisted away, flinging the chair over on its side. She kicked out, connecting with his legs. He fell backwards, landing on his backside. The gun went off, the bullet embedding itself harmlessly in the ceiling.

"Damn it," growled Milo, getting up. Two of his security guards came running.

"It's okay," he told them, brushing himself off.

"Boss, the merch is here," one said as Kenzie heard the rumble of approaching trucks. "Shall we tell them to unload it?"

Milo glanced at his phone. "No, bring the trucks in. We may have to move it again soon."

"What about her?" the other one asked.

Milo glared at Kenzie. "Put her in the office. I'll deal with her later."

Thank God.

Kenzie went weak, and if she hadn't been sitting down, may even have collapsed. She'd literally just dodged a bullet.

The two thugs picked her up off the floor, chair and all, and carried her into the office. If her situation wasn't so dire, it would have been comical. Behind her, the garage sprang to life. The trucks inside were moved out, and the ones that had just arrived were driven in. In the back were the crates of trafficked weapons. If only she could get a message to Reid.

She looked around the office. It was pretty standard, with a desk, a chair, and several filing cabinets. Wall shelves contained rows of lever arch files, their spines tatty and well-used. The desk, which had an inbox stacked with paperwork and a mug holding pens and pencils, was one of those modern metal ones with extendable legs. Perhaps Milo liked to stand and work. She stared at the legs. Where the join was, there was a screw that was partially protruding. If she could get close enough, she might be able to use one of them to snap her ankle ties.

Milo was still outside talking to his men. The drone of the truck engines meant no one would hear her if she scraped the chair over to the desk. Using her feet, she bumped and dragged it as close as she could get, then she lifted her legs and tried to catch the plastic tie on the protruding screw. It took several attempts, but she finally managed it. It held fast for a few seconds, then snapped apart. Her legs were free.

Now what? Her wrists were fastened to the thin arms of the office chair. Wiggling them didn't help. While there was some give, she didn't have the strength to break the arms off the chair. Perhaps the hard metal desk would work? It would be noisy, but it was worth a shot. She didn't have many other options.

Standing up, she brought one of the chair arms down hard on the desk. It cracked but didn't break. Once more should do it. Kenzie repeated the process until the arm snapped away from the chair back. Yes! She slid her wrist along and out.

Reaching over the desk, Kenzie grabbed a letter opener out of the mug containing the pens and pencils and rammed it under the plastic tie on her other hand. It cut into her skin, but she pushed harder until that too snapped. She was free!

Kenzie opened the office door and peeked out into the garage. It was potent with exhaust fumes from moving the heavy trucks around. She ducked down and ran behind one of the trucks. Just in time, too, for seconds later, she heard footsteps striding into the office, and a voice shouting. "She's gone!"

Milo came running. "What? Find her!"

Shit.

Kenzie kept going, darting behind trucks, until she was at the back of the garage. There was nowhere else to run. The fumes were strongest here, and she longed to get outside and breathe fresh air. Boots approaching sent her scurrying into the back of a truck. Perhaps she could hunker down and they wouldn't realize she was there.

"Check the trucks," came Milo's order.

Kenzie broke out into a sweat. She was done for. The vehicle bounced as a large man climbed onto the back. Crouching behind a crate, she hardly dared to breathe. Please let him not find me, she prayed.

Unfortunately, God wasn't listening.

"Got her!" came a yell, as a rough hand grabbed her by the hair.

"Hey!" She kicked and wriggled as he pulled her unceremoniously out of the truck. It felt like her scalp was on fire. "Let go."

But he didn't. He pulled her all the way to the front of the garage and threw her on the ground in front of Milo.

"Nice try, Kenzie," he said. "But I've had enough of your antics." He turned to the thug. "Hold her still. Let's get this over with."

Her heart was about to beat out of her chest. This was it. She was going to die here in this smelly garage at the hands of Milo Hammond. A sob caught in her throat, but she refused to cry. She wasn't going to give the prick the pleasure. Instead, she glared up at him.

"They will find you, you know. You won't get away with this."

He shrugged, pointing the gun at her head. "You'll never know."

Kenzie closed her eyes.

Was that sirens? She opened them again, listening hard. Milo had heard them too because he glanced uncertainly at the guard.

"It's too late," she whispered. "They're here."

But were they coming for her? Or would they drive past and fade into the distance again?

Reid, please...

The unmistakable dual-toned wail of police sirens got louder. Her heart sang. Yes! They were coming for her.

"Fuck," hissed Milo, his face contorting with rage. He wasn't as invincible as he thought.

The guard looked uncertain. "What do you want to do, boss?"

"Let's get out of here," he growled. "Bring her with us."

The last thing Kenzie remembered was the butt of the gun coming down on the side of her head. After that, everything faded to black.

36

"KENZIE? KENZIE, CAN YOU HEAR ME?" Reid scooped her up in his arms, frantically feeling for a pulse. She opened her eyes and gave a little groan. He felt weak with relief. Thank God, she was alive.

"Reid? Is that you?"

"I'm here. I've got you."

She relaxed, her head falling back against his arm. "I thought you weren't going to make it in time."

"Of course I made it," he said softly. "I'll always find you, you know that."

She smiled. "Did you get him? Did you get Milo?"

"Yeah, he's in custody. We've rounded up the rest of his men too."

"The guns are in the trucks," she murmured, her head still against his arm. Her eyes flickered open. "Did you find them?"

"We're searching the vehicles now," he said. "Shh... don't talk if it hurts."

"I'm okay, it's just a bump on the head." She tried to sit up.

"Easy."

She gripped his shoulder and pulled herself upright. He grimaced at her stubbornness. "I want you to get checked out."

"I will, but I can't lie here forever. The fumes are making me feel sick. Can we go outside?"

"Sure."

A paramedic rushed up, and together they supported Kenzie as she walked outside. She took several deep breaths. "I feel better already."

"Take a seat in the ambulance," Reid ordered. "I want them to make sure you're okay." Thankfully, she did as she was told.

The paramedic inspected her head. "You've got quite a bump."

"He hit me with his gun." Reid gave a tense nod. The murdering scumbag would pay for that and for his other crimes. He'd make sure of it.

"Look at me," said the medic. He shone a flashlight into her eyes. "Not much of a concussion. You're lucky. I'll get you an ice pack, and then you should probably go home and rest."

"I'll take you back," Reid said.

"How did you find me?" Kenzie asked, as he drove her back to Bay Harbor Island. It was dark, the moon having disappeared altogether, but the route was well lit, and he had no trouble navigating the evening traffic. Milo Hammond would be booked and held in a cell overnight. They'd interrogate him tomorrow. He wasn't going anywhere. Right now, he wanted to make sure Kenzie was okay.

"Process of elimination," he said. "We got a list of all the warehouses owned by the Hammonds in the Miami area, triangulated Milo's phone – stupid bastard didn't turn it off – and took an educated guess. Luckily, it was the right one."

She gave a little nod. Glancing over, he noticed her eyes had filled with tears. It wasn't like her to get so emotional. "You okay?"

"When he had the gun to my head, I thought I was going to die."

He reached over and squeezed her thigh. "Not on my watch."

Her watery smile made his heart sing.

"Did you speak to Felix Hammond?" she asked.

"He didn't know anything about it," Reid told her. "It seems Milo had masterminded the whole thing."

"He said he didn't kill Jacob," Kenzie said. "He didn't seem to know about the poison."

"You asked him?"

"Yeah, he didn't deny it either, he just seemed confused by the whole thing."

"Don't worry about that. We'll get it out of him during the interrogation." Milo Hammond didn't know what was coming. "I found your phone in the container," he said, handing it over to her. "Thanks for the pictures. Those will help when we prosecute him."

"Thanks." She glanced at the screen. "Five missed calls from Raoul."

"He's probably worried," Reid said. "You should call him back."

She dialed his number, holding the phone to her ear. "Hi. Yes, I'm fine. Reid found me...You what? Seriously?"

"What?" mouthed Reid, glancing over.

"Okay, send it to me. Thanks Raoul. Yes, I promise I'll call you later."

"What's happened?"

"He's found an address for Fred Stuckey."

Reid gave a sharp inhale. "He has? Where?"

Her phone buzzed, and she looked at the message. "Westview, not far from here. We could go there now."

"No, you've got to get home. You need to rest. I'll head over there after I drop you off."

She glanced at him. "What about Shannon?"

He hesitated. "We had to let her go."

"You brought her in for questioning?" Reid had forgotten she wouldn't have known any of this.

"Yeah, we know she was the one who hacked into the WITSEC database, using Vargas' computer. We know she's been passing information on to the cartel, and we know she used it to find out Sonia Del Ray's name and location. The problem is we can't prove any of it."

"What about the voodoo doll? Did she send it to Sonia?"

"We don't know that either. A search of her apartment turned up nothing. There isn't a shred of evidence against her."

Kenzie gnawed on her lower lip, a habit she had when she was thinking. "She covered her tracks well."

"She was extremely careful, and the only laptop she used to break into the system was Vargas'. She didn't seem to have an issue with blaming him for the breach."

"Bitch," Kenzie whispered in a rare display of hostility. "Poor Willie. How's he taking it?"

"Not well, from what I can gather. He hasn't been back to the station since I told him."

"Probably best to get him out of the way."

"Shannon will be looking for Fred Stuckey." He gripped the steering wheel with both hands. "Now she's out, she'll want to track him down."

"Why didn't she do it before?" Kenzie asked. "If she knew where Sonia was, she must have gotten Fred's details too."

"Fred moved from the address WITSEC had on file. Like us, she probably went to the wrong place."

"If Raoul can find him," Kenzie said without preamble, "she will too."

"Yeah, agreed."

Kenzie turned to face him. "So what are you waiting for? Let's go."

"I'm taking you home."

"I'm fine. Let's go find Fred before it's too late."

"Are you sure? You weren't looking so hot an hour ago."

"I bounce back fast," she said. "Besides, I'll stay in the car. Let's go find him. Every moment counts."

He couldn't deny that.

"Okay," he said, turning the car around. "Let's go get Fred."

37

Fred Stuckey was living in a student rental apartment near Miami Dade College's North Campus, according to Raoul. "How did he find him?" asked Reid.

"He did some sort of student enrollment search and found him that way," Kenzie explained. "Given his age, he thought it likely he'd be studying somewhere."

"Smart." Reid pulled into one of the vacant bays outside the neat, two-story apartment block. "Which one is his?"

"Number 3," Kenzie said, studying the doors. There were four on the lower level and four on the top. She pointed to her right. "Must be that one."

"I think it's probably a good idea if you wait here," Reid said as he opened the door.

She nodded. "Yeah, happy to sit this one out."

Reid walked up to the door, scanning the parking lot. Most of the bays were occupied, and there was a cluster of mopeds and bicycles at the far end. It wasn't yet ten o'clock, and lights were on in most of the windows. He hoped Fred would be home.

Reid pressed the buzzer and heard its shrill ring echo inside the apartment. A short time later, there was shuffling as someone looked through the peephole. Reid held up his badge. "Police, open up."

The door opened and Reid faced a tall, well-built youth in track pants and a T-shirt that said Junior Athletics League on the front. "Fred Stuckey?"

"Er, no. I'm his roommate, Zack."

"Is Fred home?" Reid peered behind him into the apartment.

"Nah, man. He had a rehearsal, but he should be back soon."

"Rehearsal?"

"He's a theater studies major."

"Ah."

"What do you want with him?"

"We'd rather discuss that with him," Reid said, giving a nod. "Thanks."

"No problem." He shut the door.

Reid was walking back to his pickup when he heard the distinctive sound of a gun being cocked. He froze.

"Turn around and keep your hands where I can see them."

Shannon.

He put his hands up and turned around. Inside the car, he saw Kenzie shuffle down in the passenger seat. "Shannon, what are you doing? Put the gun down."

She gestured to the pickup. "Get out, Kenzie. I see you there."

Kenzie opened the car door, her hands in the air. Shannon gestured for her to come around and stand beside Reid.

"You don't have to do this, Shannon," she said.

"Kenzie's right. Put the gun down and we'll talk."

She stared at him defiantly. "Why? So you can arrest me? I told you, I didn't kill Sonia."

He took a step closer to her. "How did she die, then?"

"Give me your gun."

He didn't move.

"Now!" Her arm straightened as she aimed the pistol at him.

Reluctantly, he took his gun out of his holster and put it on the ground. "Okay, easy."

"Kick it over to me."

He did as she said. The gun scraped across the asphalt. Shannon kicked it further away, under a car where it wouldn't be easy to retrieve.

"How did Sonia die, Shannon?" Reid asked. "I know it was you who killed her."

Her voice caught in her throat. "It was an accident."

"What happened?"

The hand holding the gun shook. "I went there to talk to her, to confront her. She killed my father and ruined my life. I had to drop out of college because of her. Why should she get a fresh start while I had to suffer? I wanted the world to know what she'd done."

"She served time for her crime."

Shannon snorted. "Five years in a boarding school. You call that a punishment? How about losing your friends? Having to stay in a hovel? Working two jobs just to survive?"

"I'm sorry it was so tough for you," he said.

But she wasn't listening. "I wanted to shame her. I told her I was going to tell the world what she'd done, that she couldn't hide from the truth."

He let her finish her rant, then said, "Tell me what happened."

"The murdering bitch went for me. She physically attacked me, hitting and clawing at me like a wild thing. I pushed her away... she fell... hit her head." Shannon stared desolately into the recent past. "I thought she was stunned, maybe concussed, but when she didn't get up..." She took a shuddering breath. "I felt her pulse. There wasn't one."

Kenzie exhaled beside him.

"Why didn't you call us?" Reid asked. "Call Vargas?"

She arched an eyebrow. "I knew how it would look. I'd hacked into the WITSEC database, found the person who killed my father and now she was dead. I panicked."

"So you threw her body in a dumpster?" His voice was disbelieving.

"I didn't know what to do. She was just lying there, bleeding. All I could think about was hiding her body before anyone saw her."

He shook his head. "You should have called an ambulance."

"She was dead." Her voice was flat. "Besides, when you follow the chain of evidence, it leads to me. I've been with Willie long enough to know how these things work."

He didn't have an answer for that.

"What about the voodoo doll?" he asked. "Did you send that to her?"

She gave a little nod. "Willie told me about the doll that was sent to Jacob Peters. I thought if I sent an identical one to Sonia, you'd think it was the same killer."

That was exactly what had happened. They'd been convinced the two cases were linked, when in fact, they weren't related at all. Shannon had been playing games with them.

"If you didn't intend to kill Sonia, what are you doing here with a gun?"

Her eyes had a fanatical gleam in them. "Before we fought, Sonia admitted she hadn't killed my father. It was her younger brother, Fred. He was only twelve at the time, so she took the blame. At first, I didn't believe her, then I decided to find out for myself, so I came to confront him."

"Why don't you put the gun away and we'll ask him together?" Kenzie suggested, talking for the first time. "There's no need for anyone else to get hurt."

Shannon turned on her. "You don't think I'm going to turn myself in, do you? Nobody's going to see this from my side – and I'm not going down for murder."

"You don't know that," Kenzie replied.

"Yes, I do."

"That's for the courts to decide," Reid said. "But if you get yourself a good lawyer, it'll probably be a manslaughter charge."

Her eyes narrowed. "I'm not prepared to take the chance."

At that moment a bicycle turned in and a young man got off. Shannon immediately turned the gun on him. "Fred Stuckey?"

He gasped when he saw the gun. "N—no, I'm Blake. Blake Fisher."

"Don't lie to me. That's not your real name. I know who you are."

He frowned. "Then why are you asking?"

She glared at him, taking two strides forward.

"Shannon," warned Reid. The kid was only about eighteen, not much older than Sebastian. "You're scaring him. Put the gun down."

"I want some answers." She stopped a few feet away from Fred.

He paled. "What answers?"

"Did you kill Mr. McDonald?"

He blinked several times in rapid succession. "Who are you?"

Her voice was a blade. "I'm his daughter."

Fred glanced at Reid, as if asking permission.

"Go ahead." Reid gave a firm nod. "It's okay, you can tell the truth now."

Fred put down his bike, then slowly looked up at Shannon. "Yeah, it was me. I stabbed him." He covered his face with his hands and emitted a strangled sob, as if it was a relief to finally let go of the secret he'd been carrying around for years.

Shannon stiffened. "Why? Why would you do such a thing?"

Fred turned hostile, wet eyes to Shannon. "He was raping my sister."

Kenzie gasped.

"Bullshit!" erupted Shannon, turning red.

"I saw them," Fred whispered. "I met her after school one day and I was early. He'd kept her back after class. I watched them through the window. He had her bent over a desk and was... was..." He couldn't finish.

Reid gritted his teeth.

"I was only twelve, but I knew what was going on. She was crying. It wasn't consensual."

Of all the explanations, Reid had not been expecting that.

"That's crap." Shannon marched up to him, the gun less than two feet from his chest. From that distance, she wasn't going to miss. "Tell them you're lying," she shouted. "My father was not a rapist."

"He was," the youngster spat back, oblivious to the weapon aimed at his center mass. "I knew something was wrong, even before that. Portia would come home and go straight to her room. She lost weight. She began cutting herself. Our parents didn't know what to do." That explained the scars on her arms.

"Did she tell them what was going on?" Kenzie asked.

"I don't know. I don't think so." He puffed up his eighteen-year-old chest. "I decided to take matters into my own hands."

Reid's head was spinning. Sexual assault, self-harming, psychological trauma. Why the hell didn't Sonia plead self-defense? She'd have had a case. Except the teacher was dead. He couldn't confess. He couldn't corroborate her story. She'd have felt useless, powerless. Worried no one would believe her. Maybe she hadn't been thinking at all, her only instinct to protect her brother. "What did you do?"

"I took a knife from our kitchen drawer and waited for Mr. McDonald outside school. I followed him home and when no one was looking, I stabbed him in the back."

Kenzie cringed.

"How did your sister get there?" Reid asked.

"She followed me. I think she saw me take off after him. I didn't know she was there, but she saw the whole thing. After it happened, she ran over and took the knife from me. She told me to leave, but the neighbor came out and started screaming."

Reid knew what happened next. It was in the report. The neighbor called 911 and Sonia confessed to the murder of Mr. McDonald, her math teacher. She was arrested on the spot.

"*She* was the victim," Fred insisted. "And she paid the price."

"I don't believe you." Shannon's voice was hoarse with emotion.

"It's true."

They glared at each other, the gun hovering between them. A set of headlights shone bright as another vehicle pulled up. Shannon stared at it, horrified.

Vargas got out. He took one look at the standoff and began walking towards his ex-fiancé. "Shannon, what are you doing?"

Reid had to admire his calmness.

She gazed at him, then back at Fred. "He's telling lies about my dad."

Vargas kept walking. "That's no reason to shoot him."

The gun wobbled as her voice cracked. "Don't come any closer, Willie. I don't want to hurt you."

"You're not going to hurt me," he said. "I know you. You're not a killer."

"You don't know me." She masked a sob. "I'm not who you think I am."

"Yes, you are. You may have had an agenda, but there are some things you can't hide, Shannon."

Her eyes filled with tears, but she didn't drop the gun. "It's over, Willie. I used you. Don't you get it?"

He flinched but kept moving toward her. He held out his hand. "Give me the gun."

"No," she cried, oscillating wildly from Vargas to Fred to Reid and back again. "He has to pay. How can you kill someone and not pay the price? It's not fair."

"No, it's not fair," Vargas said, standing in front of her. Now she had the gun pointed at his chest. Fred took a step backwards. "Shannon, look at me."

She shifted her gaze to his. "It's going to be alright. We're going to bring him in too."

Her arm wavered. "You are?"

"Yeah, we're all going in together, aren't we, boss?"

Reid nodded. "That's right."

"I'm sorry," she whispered, tears falling down her face.

Vargas kept his cool. "I know. Give me the gun."

When she didn't move, he wrapped his hand around it. "Let go, Shannon."

With a sob, she released the gun.

Reid let out a slow breath. It was over.

38

It took a few days before Kenzie felt herself again. The bump on the head must have been harder than she thought. Seb was helpful, making breakfast, ordering takeout, and keeping an eye on her.

Nick had called several times, but she hadn't felt up to talking to him. The one person she wanted to call, hadn't. To be fair, he had his hands full with Milo Hammond and Shannon both in custody.

Eventually, she called him.

"Kenzie, how are you feeling? Sorry, I've been meaning to call, but—"

"It's okay," she said, hiding her longing. "I know you're busy."

"Yeah, I haven't been home in days." He sounded weary, his voice heavy with fatigue. She imagined his face, rough and unshaven, and had a sudden urge to kiss it.

"What's happening? Has Milo confessed to killing Jacob?"

"No, but we charged him with the murder anyway and for your attempted murder." The fear she'd felt having the gun pressed against her head came back. She shivered.

"What about the voodoo doll? I know he sent it to Jacob."

And me.

"Yeah, it was supposed to be a warning. Jacob had been asking too many questions. It was Milo's way of quieting him down. He knew how superstitious Jacob was."

"But he denied poisoning him?"

"Yeah, but the state prosecutor thinks we have a case. And he admitted to trafficking arms as well as shipping unauthorized weapons, so we've got him for that, too. He'll be going away for a long time."

"He deserves it." Although something didn't feel right. She couldn't explain it. "Don't you think it's strange he didn't admit to murder?"

"Not really. Trafficking is a much lighter sentence than murder."

True. Perhaps she was overthinking it. The man was ruthless. He hadn't flinched when it came time to pull the trigger. If Reid hadn't arrived when he had... She dreaded to think what would have happened.

"Do you want to get together when things quiet down?" she asked, before she had time to think. She hadn't forgotten his arms around her at the warehouse. Strong, supportive, oddly gentle.

There was a pause.

"I'd like that."

A warm glow spread through her. "Great."

They said goodbye, and Kenzie went into the kitchen to make herself a coffee. Then she'd get dressed and go into the office. She'd promised Keith some background on Emmanuelle and Warner's upcoming nuptials, and she was behind schedule.

Her phone bleeped while she was pouring the coffee. Putting it down, she pressed the speaker button. "Hello?"

"Kenzie, it's Liesl." Her reporter friend sounded rushed as always. A car horn tooted in the background.

"Liesl, how are things?" With everything that had happened, she'd almost forgotten about Gail's rapist and the favor she'd asked the New York Times reporter.

"I looked into your witness," she said, getting straight to the point.

"He was there, at the time you mentioned. The motel kept computerized records, as it turns out. I got a name for you."

"Yeah?" Her pulse ticked up a notch.

"Jeff Dooley."

"Jeff Dooley." She tried the name out for size, rolling it around her tongue. "Great work."

"That's not his real name," she added, as if Kenzie hadn't spoken. "I looked him up, and Jeff Dooley was a leather worker in Queens."

"Was?"

"Yeah, I talked to his wife. She's in her fifties now. Jeff died five years ago from asbestos poisoning. He never worked in sales, and he was sick for a long time."

Kenzie frowned. "You don't think it could have been him?"

"It's unlikely. This guy was five foot four and prematurely balding. Didn't you say your witness was six foot and blonde?"

"Yeah." Looked like a high school quarterback, was how Gail had described him.

"Not your man."

"Right." Kenzie's heart sank. So much for that. "Well, thanks for trying, Liesl. I appreciate it."

"Always a pleasure, Kenz."

"Let's get together next week," she said before hanging up. "I'm covering Warner Sullivan's wedding for the *Herald*."

"Lucky," she scoffed. "Our entertainment editor is handling it. He's over the moon."

"Lunch on me?"

"Definitely. Call when you get here."

"Will do."

Kenzie hung up and stared into space. Gail's rapist had stolen another man's name. That meant they must have known each other, or at least met each other. If she had time, she'd look into it when she was in New York next week.

. . .

Her phone rang again. It was Nick. She may as well fill him in on what had happened, although she was sure the police would have updated Gail.

"Hey, Nick."

"Kenzie, how are you? Gail told me what happened. I'm so glad you're okay."

"Thanks. I'm just glad they caught him."

"Same. I know it's closure for Gail."

"That's good. Listen, I'm about to head into the office."

"Let me take you out for dinner," he said quickly, before she had time to brush him off. "It's my way of saying thank you for what you did for Gail."

"That's not necessary," she said.

"I insist. It's the least I can do after all you've been through."

Maybe dissecting the case with Nick wouldn't be such a bad thing. She hadn't had the opportunity to go over it with Reid, and she needed a bit of closure of her own. Talking through what had happened would be good for her. She'd been moping around the house long enough.

"Okay," she said. "Where should we meet?"

"How about my place? I'll cook for us."

"I didn't know you cooked?"

"There's a lot you don't know about me." He was smiling, she heard it in his voice.

A relaxed dinner at his place sounded better than a noisy restaurant. She wasn't sure her head was up to that yet. "I'll look forward to it. What time?"

"How does eight o'clock sound?"

"Perfect, text me your address and I'll see you later."

Nick lived in a modern, multi-level house in Coral Gables. She'd known he was successful, but this was something else.

"Wow," she breathed, as he took her out onto a terrace overlooking a well-maintained garden and azure swimming pool. Lit from below, it sparkled like a sapphire set in the green baize of the lawn.

"I'm glad you like it." He handed her a glass of wine. "It's a lovely evening, shall we sit outside?"

"Sure. What smells so good?"

"Garlic prawns. You do eat shellfish, don't you?" He flashed her a worried glance.

She laughed. "Yes, don't worry. There's not much I don't eat."

"Woman after my own heart."

They sat on the terrace and watched as the sky turned from indigo to black. The stars came out, twinkling invitingly. It was a lovely evening, she only wished she were spending it with Reid, rather than Nick. Then she felt bad for thinking that. Nick had been nothing but nice to her. He was attentive, he called regularly, he was successful. He just didn't make her heart leap like Reid did or make her catch her breath when she looked at him.

"How are you feeling?" he asked.

"Fine. It took a few days for the concussion to wear off, but I'm okay now."

"Good. What an ordeal. Gail told me how you'd found the weapons and been kidnapped. How did you get away?"

"The police arrived," she said, leaving out the sordid details. She didn't feel like rehashing the part where she'd nearly been shot in the head.

"Thank goodness. Your friend, Detective Garrett?" Was that a flash of irritation in his tone?

"Yes, along with the rest of his team. They arrested Milo Hammond and his thugs and confiscated the illegal weapons."

"I heard. Hard to believe it was Felix Hammond's son who was behind the trafficking scheme."

"I know. I suspected his old man, myself. He seemed too suave for his own good, and the way he bossed Milo around, it wasn't exactly fatherly."

"No wonder Milo wanted to get his own back," Nick said. "He was probably tired of being flattened."

"There's one thing that doesn't make sense, though," Kenzie mused.

"Oh yeah?"

"Milo denied killing Jacob. He didn't seem to know about the poison."

Nick raised his eyebrows. "Perhaps he was lying so as not to incriminate himself."

"Could be." She paused. "I got the impression he was confused by it, though." She shook her head. "Anyway, it doesn't matter. What with Jacob's disappearance, and his shifty dealings, it makes sense that he'd want him out the way."

"What about the voodoo connection?" Nick asked. "How did that come into it?"

"I think that was a scare tactic," Kenzie said. "Again, he hasn't said anything about it, but Utanga, that's the Voodoo priest, confirmed that Milo had been in the store."

"He was warning him off," Nick said.

"Yeah, except he died the day after he received the doll. That didn't give him much chance to heed the warning."

"Perhaps Milo grew tired of waiting and just wanted him gone."

"Maybe." She shrugged. "I guess we'll never know." At least the mystery of the second voodoo doll that had been sent to Sonia was solved. That was a genius move on Shannon's part. It had confused the hell out of the police.

"I'd better get the lamb out of the oven," he said. "And the prawns are ready."

Kenzie followed him into the lounge-kitchen. Everything was spacious and modern and clean. A dining table had been set with plates, napkins, and cutlery. Thankfully, he hadn't gone so far as to light a candle. This was a friendly get together, not a date.

She perused the room while he attended to dinner. "You've got some interesting things," she said, admiring a wooden statuette on the sideboard. "Is this from the Pacific Islands?"

"Africa, actually," he said. "A few years ago, I went to West Africa on a wildlife and conservation course. It was fascinating."

Looking at the statue, Kenzie could see it was indeed more African than Pacific Islander. "I'm sure it was. Did you see the big five?"

"I saw a lot of things. They're doing a lot to conserve endangered species out there." He turned and smiled. "Do you want to take a seat? Dinner is served."

She was about to sit down when her phone rang. It was Reid.

"Excuse me," she said, getting up again. "I won't be a moment. I've got to take this."

He nodded and began to dish up.

She took it out on the terrace. "Hi."

"Kenzie, it's me. How are you feeling?"

"I'm fine. Back to my normal self."

"That's good." He hesitated. "We've been doing some digging into your friend, Nick the vet."

"Oh yeah?" Her voice was guarded. How could she tell Reid she was at his place right now? He'd misunderstand. After all they'd been through, she didn't want to give him the wrong impression. Damn, why had she agreed to come?

"Yeah. It was something Felix Hammond said. A couple of months back, your friend Nick took legal action against Hammond Holdings, but it was dismissed."

She frowned. "Legal action? What for?"

"Several years back, Felix Hammond bought shares in a logistic company operating in the Florida area. He then sold off the assets until the company was worth nothing. The owners were forced to sell, and he picked it up at a bargain price. It seems it's not the first time he's employed that tactic."

"Okay, but what's that got to do with Nick?"

"The logistics company was owned by his parents. A short time after they went bust. His father shot himself, and his mother drank herself to death a year later."

"Oh my God," she whispered.

"Yeah, and get this, he recently got back from a trip to Nigeria. Didn't the ME say that snake venom was from Africa?"

Kenzie went cold. "Reid, I have to go. I'll call you back."

She cut the call.

No way. It couldn't be...

He was a vet. He'd know how to extract snake venom. He'd been to Africa. He had the statue on his sideboard. When she'd mentioned Jacob had been poisoned, he didn't bat an eyelid. How had he known about it when the police hadn't released that information?

"Kenzie? Is something wrong?"

She swung around. "No, nothing's wrong." But she could tell he didn't believe her.

"Was that your friend Garrett?"

"Yeah, he was just checking up on me."

Nick took a step closer. "Was he?"

"Yeah." She brushed past him into the lounge. "Let's eat. I'm starved."

He grabbed her arm.

She turned, heart hammering.

"You know, don't you?"

She bit her lip. "Know what?"

"It's written all over your face."

She didn't reply. The grip on her arm tightened. The next thing she knew, there was a prick in her neck, and she felt herself falling.

39

When Kenzie opened her eyes, she was in Nick's house, lying on the island that separated the kitchen from the living area. Somehow, he'd tied her arms and feet to the four corner legs so she couldn't move. Her mouth was dry and her head was spinning.

"You're back." Nick's face drifted in and out of focus in front of hers. "I'm sorry about that. I had to use a horse tranquilizer. It was the only thing I had on hand."

She swallowed. He was crazy. "You killed Jacob."

"Correct. Well done. I knew you'd get there eventually."

"But why?"

"Why do you think? He was going to leave my sister for that slut."

"Marcy? No, he wasn't."

"She tell you that?" He scoffed. "You shouldn't be so gullible, Kenzie. He broke it to Gail a few weeks ago. Said he'd tried his best, but he didn't love her anymore. He'd found someone else to make a life with."

"I don't believe it," she rasped, but deep down, she knew it could be true. Marcy had played it down, but there'd been glimpses. She'd just chosen to ignore them.

"I know. She was so much younger than he was, but he was in love. I'm sure you know what that feels like." He smirked down at her. "That's the reason you broke it off with me, isn't it? Detective Garrett?"

She didn't reply. How on earth could she have been so blind? The signs had been there, but she hadn't seen them.

"Gail came to me in tears. Jacob was everything to her, always had been. He was the only man she trusted."

"You knew what had happened to her?"

"I knew. What she didn't tell you was that she had an abortion."

Kenzie gasped. "The fucker impregnated her. I seduced her friend after she'd left college, and she told me everything."

Poor Gail. How awful for her. It was bad enough that she'd been raped, but to fall pregnant and have to have a termination. It was too terrible for words.

"I tried to find him, of course, but he'd moved on. He was some sort of salesman."

Under a false name. Kenzie didn't mention her conversation with Liesl.

"But why kill Jacob?" she whispered.

"Gail would have been left with nothing in the divorce. She didn't have any assets of her own. She was a dancer, for Christ's sake. They don't earn much."

"You could have helped her." He had money, buckets of it.

"I did help her," he said. "Now she'll inherit everything and can claim on his life insurance."

"What about Milo Hammond?" Kenzie remembered what Reid had said about the Hammonds destroying his parents' business.

"Well, there is the added bonus of seeing Milo Hammond go to prison." He chuckled, a hollow sound that made her skin crawl. "I suppose you know about my parents?"

"Yes."

"He destroyed them. They were devastated when the business folded. Everything they'd worked so hard for over the years. Their life's work. Gone in an instant. All because of them." He spat the word.

"You thought you'd kill Jacob and blame it on the Hammonds?"

His eyes gleamed. "It was a good plan. Come on, admit it."

Insane.

"I wanted them to lose everything, just like my parents had."

"Did you know about the illegal arms?"

"No, but I knew they were up to something. I'd been watching them for some time. I must thank you for that. I'm sorry you got kidnapped, but it worked out pretty well in the end, don't you think?"

That was debatable.

"It was you who gave him Utanga's business card," she whispered. It had been bugging her how that had ended up in his desk drawer.

"Very good, Kenzie. Yeah, that little yappy dog of his was sick. Sometimes the herbs help. I encouraged him to get in touch."

"And he ended up buying a voodoo doll to send to Jacob."

"A bonus." His eyes were shining. "I couldn't have planned it better myself."

Unbelievable. She had to admit, he was an expert manipulator. Her eyes drifted to the African statue on the sideboard.

"You're probably wondering about the snake venom," he said, holding up a glass vial with a milky liquid in it. "I got it from Africa on my last trip. Black mamba poison. I was fascinated by it."

Kenzie stared at the vial, her stomach clenching. It was hard to breathe.

"The black mamba is one of the most poisonous snakes in Africa," he continued. "A tiny drop will render you completely paralyzed in twenty minutes."

He wasn't going to... He wouldn't...

"It's not a very nice way to die," he continued, his voice taking a far-off quality. "The paralysis starts at the head and works its way down. There is excessive salivation. The victim becomes weak with heavy limbs. Sometimes there is tingling around the lips and tongue, which spreads to the entire body. It's the same in animals, by the way."

Kenzie didn't want to hear any more, but he was getting into his stride. "There is excessive sweating and muscle twitching. Nausea and vomiting. Then the descending paralysis starts." He looked almost gleeful at this prospect. "First, the eyelids don't open, then the pupils stop working, so vision is affected. Next, the jaw locks and the tongue becomes stiff. The victim slurs as if intoxicated. Swallowing is difficult. When the paralysis moves to the chest, that's when it affects the breathing."

Kenzie closed her eyes. "Stop. I've heard enough."

Nick continued as if she hadn't spoken. "At this stage, if the victim isn't placed on a ventilator, they will die. When there is no more oxygen, the heart stops. In adults, death occurs in between one to four hours."

Perhaps her time was up. Maybe she'd been meant to die in that warehouse, and Reid's arrival had just given her a brief respite. Maybe this was fate. She'd never believed in fate before, but she was starting to...

"The best part is, it's completely untraceable. There is minimal tissue damage at the site of the bite, or in our case, the injection, and no indication of poison in the body. It's the perfect murder weapon."

Nick pulled out a syringe and stuck the needle into the vial. Kenzie watched as he drew up the liquid. Her chest rose and fell in rapid succession. She didn't want to die. If only she'd told Reid where she was, but she hadn't. This time no one was coming to get her.

Reid called Kenzie back, but she didn't pick up. That was weird. Why had she cut him off? He'd recognized her tone, too. She was working on something, a lead. A horrible suspicion began to gnaw at him that he couldn't let go.

"Diaz," he called. "Get me Gail Peters' number."

They'd been at the station all day, interrogating Milo Hammond and verifying his story. Once they'd confirmed his alibi for the day of the murder, Reid knew it couldn't be the shipping executive who'd killed Jacob.

It was Felix, who'd voluntarily come in for questioning, who'd told them about the lawsuit. Diaz had asked if he knew of anyone who held a grudge against them, and Nick Murray had been top of his list.

"She's with Monroe," Diaz said with a grin. "He went to her place an hour ago."

"What?" Reid scratched his head "What's Monroe doing at her place?"

"Remember he responded to the burglary? Well, apparently, they hit it off, and she invited him over for a home cooked meal. It's kinda cute, really."

Wow, he hadn't seen that coming, but it worked in his favor. "Okay, good. Get Monroe on the phone."

"Is something wrong?"

"I've got a gut feeling, and I hope I'm wrong, but we need to check it out."

Diaz got Monroe on the phone. "Sorry to interrupt your dinner," she said. "The boss wants a word." She handed Reid the phone.

"Hey, could you ask Gail if she knows where her brother is right now?"

"Sure, hang on." The elderly detective put him on hold. A few seconds later, he was back. "Home, as far as she knows. He said he was cooking dinner for Kenzie."

"Shit, really?"

"Yeah, what's wrong."

"What's his address?"

Reid heard Gail talking in the background. "Coral Gables. Why?"

"Can you get there? I think Kenzie's in trouble." It would be quicker for Monroe to get to Coral Gables than him. Sweetwater was at least forty minutes away.

"Yeah, we can leave now. It'll take fifteen minutes, at the most."

"Okay, I'll send a unit for backup. Nick's the killer," he added, before Monroe could ask for more details. "He's the one who killed Jacob Peters."

"Holy shit."

"Get over there, pronto."

"On my way."

40

"No, Nick. Please," Kenzie pleaded as Nick prepared the syringe of poison.

There was no empathy on his face. "I'm sorry, Kenzie. It can't be helped. You know too much."

"So does Reid," she said. "Killing me isn't going to make a difference."

"He can't prove a thing," Nick said with a shrug. "Just because I traveled to Africa doesn't mean I'm a killer."

"When they find my body, they'll know."

He shook his head. "They won't find your body. I'll make sure of that. I'm not going to make the same mistake I did with Jacob. The gators were supposed to finish him off. They usually do."

She remembered his receptionist tell her he worked one day a week at a wildlife sanctuary in the glades. Damn, why hadn't she seen through his smooth façade before?

"Why did you get me involved?" she asked. "You called me, remember? You asked me to look into Jacob's disappearance."

"I knew the trail would lead you to the Hammonds. You were my catalyst, Kenzie. You put everything in motion."

She felt sick. He'd manipulated her like a puppet, and she'd fallen for it.

"I'm sorry this is so painful," he said. "But I don't own a gun. Don't believe in them." She spluttered at that. How ironic could you get?

"If it's any consolation, it'll be over in an hour or two. You've got a small frame, so it shouldn't take long. I'll be here to hold your hand, you won't die alone."

God forbid. He'd lost the plot a long time ago. She saw that now. Had he always been this way?

He raised the syringe, then held her arm steady. "It's a tiny prick."

Just then a female voice said, "Nick, put it down."

Gail.

Her brother glanced up in alarm. "Gail, what are you doing here?"

"Put the injection down," came another voice, male this time. Kenzie couldn't see who it was, but she recognized it. "Or I'll shoot."

Nick hesitated.

"For God's sake, Nick, put it down. For me." Gail's voice again. How had she found them? Then she knew. Reid. He'd realized something was up. Oh, thank God.

Nick paled, then lowered his arm. She heard the syringe clatter to the floor. A plainclothes man with a gun rushed over and forced his hands behind his back. It was the elderly cop from Sweetwater PD. Monroe.

"Nick Murray, you're under arrest for the murder of Jacob Peters and the attempted murder of Kenzie Gilmore." As he said the rest of the Miranda rights, Kenzie burst into tears. She couldn't help it. For the second time in a week, she'd nearly lost her life.

Gail rushed over. "Kenzie, are you alright?" Her nimble fingers grabbed a kitchen knife and cut the ties that bound her to the kitchen island. Free at last, Kenzie rolled off onto the floor. Her legs wouldn't support her.

Gail held her as she sobbed. The rest of the night was a blur. More law enforcement officers ran in and took Nick away. Monroe and Gail stayed with her until she felt strong enough to stand up by herself.

"I always knew he wasn't quite right," Gail admitted, running a shaking hand through her hair. "My parents knew it too, but they doted on him, so nothing was ever done about it. He was always the more driven, the more successful of the two of us, but he lacked empathy."

"He's a psychopath," Kenzie whispered.

"Undiagnosed, but yes. When we were young, he used to hurt me, then feel bad because he'd made me cry. He couldn't understand emotions."

She shook her head. "I'm sorry."

"As we grew older, he became incredibly protective. I never told him what happened at dance school, but I got the feeling he knew."

"He found out from one of your friends," Kenzie said. There was no point in telling her he'd seduced them.

She gave a sad nod. "It makes sense. He could charm anyone, he had that way about him."

Like many psychopaths, he'd learned the art of manipulation. Charming people was part of his persona. She was a prime example. He'd taken her in hook, line and sinker.

"My parents' deaths affected him badly. He went to pieces. I was quite worried about him."

"I heard about the legal action."

"When it was thrown out of court, he was angry. I've never seen him that angry. He vowed to get even with the Hammonds."

"Why didn't you say something?" Kenzie asked. Monroe sat beside her, holding her hand. Kenzie wondered when that had happened. "You knew we were looking into them."

"I don't know." She shook her head. "I wasn't sure of the extent of it. Also, Jacob worked for them, so they may have had something to do with his death." Her eyes filled with tears. "I can't believe it was Nick."

"He thought Jacob was going to leave you," Kenzie explained.

"He was. I should have told you that too, but I was too ashamed." Monroe gave her hand a squeeze.

"It's okay," he said. "You don't have to explain."

"I know it's my fault," she said. "I drove him away. I refused to get help, and he was so patient with me. For years, he put up with my inability... well, you know. Then he met Marcy and I think he wanted more from a relationship. I can't blame him, really."

"It wasn't your fault," Kenzie said softly.

"I've decided to go and see someone," she said, wiping her eyes on the back of her hand. "It's time. I don't want to carry on like this." She glanced at Monroe. "I've let it ruin my marriage, and I don't want it to ruin the rest of my life."

Kenzie saw the sparks flying between them and knew Gail would be alright. "I think that's a great idea, Gail. And very brave of you."

Monroe nodded in agreement.

The CSI team arrived and soon officers clad in white suits were hovering all over the house. "I think it's time we left," Monroe said. "Kenzie, do you need a lift home?"

Weariness seeped into her every pore. "Is Reid coming?"

"No, he was on his way when he heard Nick was being transported back to the department to be booked."

She nodded. Reid would want to interrogate him in person. He'd never liked Nick, and now he had the upper hand. "Does he know what happened?"

"Yeah, he's been fully briefed."

Monroe and Gail dropped her off on their way back to Gail's. Monroe was heading back to the precinct, but Kenzie heard Gail promising him a raincheck for dinner. She was happy for them. Gail needed a hero in her life, and Monroe was just that. After all, hadn't he just saved her life? Or rather, Reid had just saved her life. Again.

41

Kenzie had just climbed into bed when the doorbell rang. What now? She couldn't handle seeing anyone else today. To her relief, Seb went to open it. A moment later, she heard Reid's voice. "How is she doing?"

Except Reid.

Pulling on her robe, she walked into the lounge. "I'm fine." She smiled at Seb, who said goodnight to Reid and went back to his room.

Reid strode up to her. "Kenzie, I'm sorry I couldn't come before now. I wanted to but—" he shrugged. "I've got to get back to the precinct, but I needed to make sure you were okay."

"I'm okay." He looked worse than she felt. Disheveled and unshaven, with dark shadows under his eyes. His shirt was so wrinkled, she was betting he hadn't been home since she'd first disappeared. But to her, he looked perfect. "I know you were interrogating Nick."

His eyes hardened. "Yeah, we've got him. For all of it. Jacob's murder and what he did to you. Bastard."

She shivered. "I can't believe I didn't see it sooner. He was scary. Totally devoid of emotion. I really thought he was going to kill me."

"Monroe told me they got there just in time. Don't worry, he'll be going away for a long time. He won't be able to hurt you again."

She knew that, but hearing it made her feel better. "Thank you. What about Shannon?" The fiery redhead had been on her mind, ever since the confrontation in the parking lot. "What's happening with her?"

He shrugged. "She's been charged with hacking into a federal database, and of course, the murder of Sonia Del Ray."

"Do you think it really was an accident?" Kenzie asked.

"I believe her, but it's not up to me. A jury will listen to the evidence and decide her fate."

"I feel sorry for her," Kenzie said. "All that hate. Nick too. His vengeance consumed him."

"It's a dangerous emotion."

"How's Vargas taking it?"

He sighed. "Vargas is okay. He's back at work now, helping prepare Hammond's case for trial. Obviously, he won't be working on Shannon's."

"I hope he'll be okay," she whispered. "It must be a hell of a blow." She hadn't even been dating Nick and he'd played her like a fiddle. Imagine how Vargas felt.

"He will. I'll make sure of it."

She smiled. Reid was a good man. He cared about his team. It would take time, but Willie would mend. He might never be as trusting as he once was, but that wasn't necessarily a bad thing.

Reid's expression softened. "How are you feeling?"

"A little fragile. It's been a hell of a week."

He snorted. "You can say that again. I'm just glad it's over, and you're okay."

"Thanks to you. One thing I don't understand is how did you know to send Monroe to Nick's place?"

"It was the way you ended the call so abruptly. You only ever do that if you're following up on a lead." He tilted his head to the side. "Why didn't you tell me where you were?"

She glanced down at her feet. "I didn't want you to think I was there for romantic reasons."

When she looked back up, his eyes bore into hers. "I see. Were you?"

"No, of course not. What I really wanted was to talk to you, but you were so busy. When Nick invited me to his place for dinner, I thought it would do me good to get out. I'd been moping around the house for days."

"I'm sorry. I should have been there for you."

"Don't be silly. You had a job to do."

"I know, but still..." She wanted to go to him, to throw her arms around his neck and have him hold her, but the way he was standing, with his hands thrust into his pockets and a brooding scowl on his face, made her hold back.

"You *were* there for me. If you hadn't arrived at the warehouse when you did, Milo would have shot me."

He gave a little nod. "That's true."

"And when you realized something was wrong, you called Monroe. You saved me again."

He broke into a rare smile. "When you put it that way..."

She did go up to him then and slipped her arms around his neck. "You've saved me more times than I can count. One day, I'm going to save you back."

His hands snaked around her waist, and he held her against him. It felt so good, so right. "You have saved me. In more ways than you know."

She'd have to decipher that one later. At the moment, all she wanted to do was savor the moment.

He gazed down at her. "Did you mean what you said earlier? That when this is all over, we'd get together?"

"I did," she whispered.

A smile played at the corner of his mouth. "How does Saturday sound?"

Her heart surged. "It sounds great."

"Perfect. I'll see you then."

~ END ~

The story continues in *Fever Pitch,* the next Kenzie Gilmore Crime Thriller. Head to the next page for a sneak peak or order today by clicking the link or scanning the QR code below!

www.amazon.com/B0BP2T9MGZ

Stay up to date with Biba Pearce's new releases:

https://liquidmind.media/biba-pearce-sign-up-1/

You'll receive a **free** copy of *Hard Line: A Kenzie Gilmore Prequel.*

Did you enjoy *Deep Heat*? Leave a review to let us know your thoughts!

www.amazon.com/B0B2N6GGD8

FEVER PITCH: CHAPTER ONE

Saturday never happened.

Kenzie wanted it to. Desperately. She'd been so looking forward to their date, but Keith, her editor at the *Miami Herald*, had other ideas. Reid, and their tentative reconciliation, would have to wait.

"I need you up there before the weekend," the hard-nosed newspaperman had told her. "There's a massive buzz about this wedding. Most of Washington's political elite will be there, as well as President Sullivan himself. If you can get a comment..."

He didn't need to elaborate. She knew her job. It might seem like the celebrity wedding of the year—a beautiful supermodel with a shady past marrying the President's estranged son—but there were undercurrents of suspicion, malice and distrust. Emmanuelle Lenoir, the bride to be, happened to be the illegitimate daughter of Maria Lopez, the late Mexican cartel boss, something Maria herself had been at pains to hide, but like most big secrets, it couldn't stay hidden forever.

It had been Kenzie herself who broke the story. Indirectly. Her researcher, Raoul, had told their editor. She didn't blame him. He'd been new and eager to please, and Keith could be very intimidating if you got him on a bad day. Or even on a good day, for that matter.

A pang of guilt sliced through her as she stepped off the plane and took her first gulp of New York air. It was not something she felt good about, breaking a trust. Even if it was that of the infamous cartel boss. Kenzie had given her word, and that meant something.

Still, in this industry, if you didn't splash it over the front page, somebody else would, and MARIA LOPEZ'S SECRET LOVE TRYST had been a scoop she couldn't afford to lose. A scoop her editor would not allow her to lose.

The hard, white sun blazed down on the runway, making it shimmer like a mirage. Heels, boots, suitcases, voices. Rolling, clacking, talking all at once. She longed for the calm of her hotel room.

It had been an early start, the sun not yet up in Miami when she'd boarded the plane. Breakfast served at 30,000 feet in plastic containers, acrid coffee, synthetic milk. Normally, she didn't mind flying. It was a means to an end. New places, new faces, new stories. Plots to unearth and truths to be found.

But this flight lacked the familiar buzz of excitement. Perhaps because every mile was taking her further and further away from where she wanted to be. From who she wanted to be with.

She'd heard the disappointment in Reid's voice when she'd told him.

"Sure, if you have to go."

"I'm sorry, it'll only be for a week. We can get together when I get back."

"Okay."

"It's a celebrity wedding. Ridiculous really, the entertainment reporter should be going, not me."

A silence.

"Reid, I'm sorry about this."

"It's okay. Catch you when you get back."

And that was it. He'd sounded tired, like he was done waiting, done hoping.

That's all they seemed to do. Wait. And hope.

Kenzie walked into the terminal. She had to collect the suitcase she'd checked in. A celebrity wedding called for a designer wardrobe, so she'd packed her few items of clothing reserved for such occasions. An off-the-shoulder Oscar de la Renta cocktail dress. A Carolina Herrera poppy-print gown. Glittering shoes and leather purses. She had to look the part if she were to rub shoulders with fashionistas and charm the President and his entourage.

Kenzie Gilmore, award-winning investigative reporter. That's who she had to be this week. Everything else could wait. Would have to wait.

She collected her suitcase from the conveyor belt, squeezing in beside frazzled parents, one eye on their luggage, the other on their tired, irritable children; businessmen and women with bony elbows and caffeine-withdrawal scowls; and the occasional over-excited tourist.

New York.

The terminal was heaving. Summer was in full swing. Kenzie walked the route she'd walked so many times before. Diagonally across the concord to the nearest exit. A line of taxis catered to a longer line of travelers. Reluctantly, she joined it.

"Never changes," the man in front of her grumbled. "I've wasted hours of my life in this queue."

Had she? How many wasted hours had been spent at airports around the world? Mexico City. Rio de Janeiro. London. Rome. Paris. And further flung places on the globe. Manilla. Bangladesh. Johannesburg.

No, not wasted. Empty. Empty hours.

A means to an end.

The queue was moving steadily, but she still had some time to go. Taking out her phone, she rang Liesl. Liesl Bernstein was a reporter for the New York Times, originally from Florida. They'd studied journalism together after Kenzie's accident had seen her dreams of becoming a police detective crash down around her.

Liesl had pulled her out of that slump, infused her with a passion for the truth. For reporting the truth. For putting her thirst for justice into an article. Into a feature with award-winning potential.

Liesl was the real deal. One of those naturally curious people. Always questioning. Always observing. Nothing escaped her razor-sharp intuition. Like Keith, she was a born newsperson. She could sniff out a story from a hundred miles—and often did.

The call rang out. Liesl's voicemail came on.

Hello, you've reached Liesl Bernstein from the New York Times. Leave a message and I'll get back to you.

Liesl couldn't even leave a message without adding the New York Times. It was who she was. Not a friend, a sister, a wife. Only ever a reporter. Kenzie, a fellow student, now a peer, a respected colleague, was probably the closest thing she had to a friend.

It sounded familiar.

Finally, she was at the end of the queue. "Sheraton. Times Square," she told the driver, who took off even before she'd closed the door.

New York. Always in a rush.

The last time they'd spoken, Liesl had told her she'd tracked down the man who'd drugged, then brutally raped ballet student Gail Winslow back in 1998. Jeff Dooley, his name was. Except Jeff Dooley had turned out to be a married man from Queens. A leather worker who'd died from asbestos poisoning several years ago.

That's as far as they'd got. Kenzie planned to look into the case while she was here, if she had any free time. Gail deserved justice. Her rapist deserved to be punished for what he'd done to her and probably to a bunch of other young women. Men who roofied girls then took them to two-bit motels to rape them didn't stop at one. They didn't suddenly get an attack of conscience and repent.

Kenzie was confident there'd be other women out there with stories like Gail's. Lives that had been shattered because they'd accepted a drink from a handsome stranger. The star quarterback, that's what Gail had said he'd looked like. Blond, tall, good looking. A flirtatious smile, twinkling eyes. *Can I buy you a drink?*

The Sheraton in Times Square wasn't much to look at on the outside, but inside, it was contemporary and elegant. Above all, it was convenient. Right in the center of New York, it made getting around easy and Kenzie didn't want the hassle of trying to negotiate traffic if she could help it.

"Any messages?" she asked the stylishly dressed woman behind the check-in desk. Kenzie had left a voicemail for her friend yesterday with her arrival details. Liesl hadn't picked up then either, but that wasn't unusual. She did always get back to her though, which she hadn't done this time.

"Um, let me check." She clicked a mouse under the counter. Gone were the days of messages in pigeon-holes, unfortunately. It was all electronic now. Notes stored on a hotel database, readable by anyone who had access. More secure, or maybe less secure. "Yes, there is a message."

"Oh, great." She smiled. Of course Liesl hadn't forgotten. They'd arranged to have lunch, after all.

"It's a reservation. 1:45pm. Connolly's on W 45th Street."

"Thank you." Kenzie hadn't heard of it, but then Liesl would have chosen somewhere they could hear each other talk. At least it was only a few blocks away, easily within walking distance.

Kenzie deposited her suitcase and laptop bag in the hotel room, ran a brush through her travel-weary hair, smacked on some make-up and set off. It was warm, pleasantly so. Not the moist heat of Miami, but a dry heat that made her think of al fresco dining and outdoor bars. She wondered what kind of place Connolly's was.

To her surprise it was a traditionally Irish pub. It looked nice, but more suited to a cozy winter meal than a light lunch. Strange. She looked around but couldn't see Liesl.

"I have a reservation," she told the host who came to the door. A long, polished bar ran down the one side, the dining section on the other. It was stuffy inside, despite the front door being kept open. A television screen above the bar showed a soccer match that looked like it could be happening across the pond in Ireland.

"This way," he said, and headed off to a dark corner of the restaurant. Then Kenzie got it. This wasn't a catch up so much as a clandestine meeting about Jeff Dooley. It must be. Why else would her friend have reserved a table in such an establishment, and way out of sight of the doors and windows?

She felt a surge of excitement. Had Liesl found something else? Did she know who Jeff Dooley really was? Could she point Kenzie in the direction of Gail's rapist?

Kenzie checked her watch. 1:55pm. Liesl was ten minutes late. Understandable in New York traffic. She ordered a drink and browsed the *Herald's* latest news on her phone.

Congressman Leonard was up to his old tricks. A new initiative. Modernization of the tram system. An upgrade that would benefit thousands of commuters. There was even a comment by the mayor. She gave a snort. Funded no doubt with dirty money from Leonard's longtime supporter, Del Gatto.

Now Liesl was twenty minutes late. Kenzie frowned and took out her phone. She texted but it didn't go through. Calling made no difference. Liesl's phone was off.

Sighing, she leaned back and continued reading. She'd give it till quarter past, then go back to the hotel. Liesl knew where to find her. She'd just moved on to the next article when a loud screech followed by an ear-splitting crash had her jumping out of her seat.

"What the—?"

Kenzie ran to the door, followed closely by the host and the barman, who'd turned away from the game. Two cars had collided not fifty yards from the restaurant.

"I hope nobody's hurt," Kenzie said, moving down the sidewalk to get a better look. A crowd had gathered around the two cars. There was a shout, and a woman cried, "Oh, my God. Someone call an ambulance."

A horrible feeling crept over Kenzie, and she broke into a run.

She couldn't see who was injured because of the crowd. "Excuse me," she shouted, elbowing her way through.

God, no. Oh, please no.

Liesl was lying in the road, her body bent and crumpled like a crash test dummy.

"Liesl!"

Kenzie dropped to her knees beside her friend, and took her pulse, even though her head was telling her what her heart refused to believe. She could see it in the unnatural angle of her head, the way it was twisted to the side. Eyes closed, chest still. A tiny trickle of blood running out the corner of her mouth.

Kenzie pushed her fingers into Liesl's neck. *Please, find a pulse.* A tiny one. Anything.

But there was none.

Her friend was dead.

FEVER PITCH CHAPTER TWO

Kenzie felt the pavement press into her knees. The crowd swirled around her as if in a dream. Muted voices. Car horns. Sirens.

"Out of the way, miss."

She scrambled back and watched in horror as two medics tried to resuscitate Liesl, but she was non-responsive. Eventually, the one glanced at the other and shook his head.

Tears welled, and she swiped angrily at her eyes. What had just happened? *How* had this happened? She wobbled to her feet, looking around as if for the first time. The two cars meshed together, their fenders a twisted mess of metal. One vehicle was empty, the other had a woman inside, sobbing. A beat patrol officer who'd stopped to help was speaking to her. Kenzie slid closer so she could hear what was being said.

"Can you exit the vehicle, ma'am?"

The crying woman gingerly got out of her car. There was a gash on her forehead, and she clutched her left shoulder. The airbag had deployed, probably saving her life.

"I didn't see him," she sobbed. "The car came out of nowhere and crashed into me."

Him?

Kenzie looked around. Where was the driver of the second car?

Wrenching her brain out of its shocked stupor, she fished out her phone and took some photographs of the crash. The two vehicles. License plates. The sobbing woman. And of course, Liesl, who was now being lifted into a body bag. The sound of the zipper brought on a flood of nausea. Kenzie doubled over, retching, but nothing came out.

Oh, God. Liesl. How? Why? She couldn't process what had happened.

Sirens pierced her stupor. The NYPD had arrived.

Kenzie stood where she was and watched them swarm onto the scene. Brusque voices ordered everyone back, and a cordon went up. An officer began waving traffic on, guiding impatient motorists around the wrecked cars. The smell of exhaust fumes made her feel even more nauseous.

New York. Always in a rush.

She watched as an officer picked up Liesl's purse, which had fallen beside the body. No evidence bag. They weren't treating this as suspicious. Just a grim nod as he handed it to a female colleague. An unfortunate accident. A pedestrian caught in the wreckage.

Was that all it was?

Kenzie turned back to the second car, the one that had hit Liesl. Still empty. The driver was nowhere in sight. Had he been frightened and made a run for it? Had he been drinking? Was that why he'd disappeared? Or had it been deliberate?

She shook her head, trying not to overreact. Not everything was a conspiracy. Sometimes, things were as simple as they looked.

Kenzie took a few steps back. That's when she saw the phone. It lay in the gutter, several yards from Liesl in the body bag. Outside the police cordon.

Kenzie hesitated. It could be Liesl's. If she'd been holding it in her hand when she was hit, it could have skidded across the road in that direction. No one had noticed it yet.

Slowly, deliberately, she moved towards it. Bending, she sank down to pick it up. She'd just slipped it into her pocket when a cop came up to her. "Excuse me? I believe you were one of the first on the scene?"

She straightened up. "Er, yes. I was waiting to meet her in the pub. The victim is... was a friend of mine."

"You know this woman?"

A nod. "Her name is Liesl Bernstein."

He wrote it down. "And your name?"

She hesitated. "Kenzie Gilmore."

He glanced up. "Address?"

"I'm staying at the Sheraton."

His eyes narrowed. "You not from New York?"

"No. Miami."

"Then the victim—?"

"Oh, she's from New York. She worked for the *New York Times*." It defined her.

"A reporter?"

"Yeah." Kenzie bit her lip. A damn good one, too.

"Do you have a minute to give a statement?"

"I didn't see anything," she said. "I heard the crash, ran out of the pub, and saw a crowd of people. When I pushed through, I saw my friend lying on the ground. I could tell she was..." A lump formed in her throat. "I could tell she was dead the moment I saw her." A wave of sadness mixed with anger and bitterness swept over her. Why did this have to happen? Why Liesl?

"You didn't see the crash?" He sounded disappointed.

"No."

"Okay. I'm sorry for your loss." An automatic response, like he'd said it so many times it had lost all meaning.

"Thank you."

The cop moved away, on to the next bystander.

Kenzie watched as Liesl's body was lifted into an ambulance.

The purse was handed to the medic. The doors shut. Her friend was gone.

Kenzie walked back to the hotel in a stupor. Pedestrians jostled her, but she hardly noticed. Her mind swirled with unanswered questions. Why had Liesl's phone been dead for days? It was totally unlike the *New York Times* reporter to have her mobile device switched off. Rule number one: be contactable. What if a source called? What if something happened? A terror attack, a shooting, some other disaster. Their bread and butter.

She sighed. What a way to make a living.

How many times had she put her life at risk over the last few years? Too many to count. Luckily, she'd had someone looking out for her.

Reid.

A pang hit her in the chest, and she caught her breath. What was he doing now? Did he hate her for disappearing yet again? Had she ruined any chance she may have had with the gruff Miami detective? She quashed an overwhelming urge to talk to him, to tell him what had happened. She was overwrought, that's all. Emotional. He'd be at work now. Too busy to talk. She'd try him later. Maybe.

Liesl had no one. At least nobody Kenzie knew about.

She fingered the phone in her pocket. Cold. Silent. Useless.

Or maybe not.

As soon as she got back to the hotel, Kenzie took out the device. She pressed the power button, but nothing happened. It was dead. Broken? Or just out of battery?

She feared the worst. Why would Liesl have it in her hand?

Still, she plugged it into her charger and set it on the bed stand. A light flickered. She exhaled. Good. It wasn't damaged.

No. Not good. Liesl was dead. Kenzie stared at the phone for a full minute, her eyes burning. Then the tears came.

Liesl lived on the Upper West Side in a fancy apartment block with a concierge, underground parking, and an elevator with a one-hundred-

and-eighty-degree view of the city. Kenzie stood outside, looking up. The only problem was she didn't know the apartment number—which was why she'd brought the gift. She was hoping the concierge might help her.

Kenzie entered the marbled lobby, the wrapped present under her arm. She'd just gone through the revolving doors when a dark-haired man careened into her.

"Oh, I'm sorry." She gasped as his elbow poked her in the ribs.

He hurried on, not bothering to look up.

How rude.

Rubbing her side, she took a moment to compose herself. Recessed lighting gave the lobby a sophisticated air, as did the wide, marble-topped reception desk, the fancy flatscreen computer, and the burly concierge-slash-security guard standing behind it.

He looked up. "Can I help you?"

A smile. A batter of eyelids. "I hope so. I've got a birthday present for Liesl Bernstein."

He didn't smile back. "You can leave it here."

"I'd really like to give it to her." She tossed her blonde hair over her shoulder. "She's a friend."

The guard's gaze dropped to her chest. "Your name?"

"Kenzie Gilmore." There was no point in lying.

"I haven't seen you before."

"I live in Miami. I'm here for the week and thought I'd surprise her."

He took in her tanned arms, her strategically chosen T-shirt with *South Beach Miami* emblazoned on the front, then gave a nod. "Apartment 114, eleventh floor."

"Thank you."

Her smile vanished as she took the elevator to the eleventh floor. Liesl's phone had been locked, so she hadn't managed to get much off it. Only a missed call that had flashed up on the locked screen. Kenzie had jotted down the number but hadn't called it yet. The elevator pinged, and the doors sighed open.

She got out and looked up and down the plush corridor. The carpet under her feet made no noise as she hurried to Apartment 114. She wasn't even sure what she was doing here. Guilt, maybe?

It had been her idea to meet. It had been she who'd asked Liesl to look into the rapist. Was it her fault her friend was dead?

Gulping back the bitter taste in her mouth, she reached the door to Liesl's apartment. To her surprise, it was slightly ajar.

Her heart skipped a beat. Had Liesl left in such a hurry she'd forgotten to lock it? Gingerly, Kenzie pushed open the door and gasped. The apartment was a mess. Overturned chairs, cushions scattered on the floor, a deep slash in the base of the couch. Cabinet doors open and a vase lying on its side on the table, water dripping onto the carpet.

The place had been ransacked.

ALSO BY BIBA PEARCE

The Kenzie Gilmore Series

Afterburn

Dead Heat

Heatwave

Burnout

Deep Heat

Fever Pitch

Storm Surge (Coming Soon)

Dalton Savage Mystery Series

Savage Grounds

Scorched Earth

Cold Sky

Detective Rob Miller Mysteries

The Thames Path Killer

The West London Murders

The Bisley Wood Murders

The Box Hill Killer

Follow the link for your free **copy of *Hard Line: A Kenzie Gilmore Prequel.***

https://liquidmind.media/biba-pearce-sign-up-1/

ALSO BY WITHOUT WARRANT

More Thriller Series from Without Warrant Authors

Dana Gray Mysteries by C.J. Cross

Girl Left Behind

Girl on the Hill

Girl in the Grave

The Kenzie Gilmore Series by Biba Pearce

Afterburn

Dead Heat

Heatwave

Burnout

Deep Heat

Fever Pitch

Storm Surge (Coming Soon)

Willow Grace FBI Thrillers by Anya Mora

Shadow of Grace

Condition of Grace

Hunt for Grace

Time for Grace (Coming Soon)

Gia Santella Crime Thriller Series

by Kristi Belcamino

Vendetta

Vigilante

Vengeance

Black Widow

Day of the Dead

Border Line

Night Fall

Stone Cold

Cold as Death

Cold Blooded

Dark Shadows

Dark Vengeance

Dark Justice

Deadly Justice

Deadly Lies

Vigilante Crime Series by Kristi Belcamino

Blood & Roses

Blood & Fire

Blood & Bone

Blood & Tears

Queen of Spades Thrillers by Kristi Belcamino

Queen of Spades

The One-Eyed Jack

The Suicide King

The Ace of Clubs

The Joker

The Wild Card

High Stakes

Poker Face

ABOUT THE AUTHOR

Biba Pearce is a British crime writer and author of the Kenzie Gilmore series and the DCI Rob Miller series.

Biba grew up in post-apartheid Southern Africa. As a child, she lived on the wild eastern coast and explored the sub-tropical forests and surfed in shark-infested waters.

Now a full-time writer, Biba lives in leafy Surrey and when she isn't writing, can be found walking through the countryside or kayaking on the river Thames.

Visit her at bibapearce.com and join her mailing list at https://liquidmind.media/biba-pearce-sign-up-1/ to be notified about new releases, updates and special subscriber-only deals.

Printed in Great Britain
by Amazon

37510022R00155